THE

Dell Shannon is the nom de plume of the late Elizabeth Linington. Ms Linington wrote under a number of pseudonyms, but her series of novels featuring Lieutenant Luis Mendoza of the Los Angeles Homicide Department made Dell Shannon the most popular. Her extensive knowledge of police procedure and criminal laboratory techniques was based on research into the LA Police Department. Dell Shannon died in 1988.

THE DEATH-BRINGERS

by

Dell Shannon

GOLLANCZ CRIME

Gollancz Crime is an imprint of Victor Gollancz Ltd
14 Henrietta Street, London WC2E 8QJ

First published in Great Britain 1966
by Victor Gollancz Ltd

First Gollancz Crime edition 1991

A catalogue record for this book
is available from the British Library

ISBN 0-575-04966-9

Printed and bound in Great Britain
by Cox & Wyman Ltd, Reading

Then shall two be in the field; the one shall be taken, and the other left. Two women shall be grinding at the mill; the one shall be taken, and the other left.

Matthew 24:40–41

THE DEATH-BRINGERS

CHAPTER ONE

Alison Mendoza smiled out the front window of the house on Rayo Grande Avenue, as Máiri MacTaggart, that jewel of a housekeeper-nurse, hurried up the front walk, trowel still in hand. Mr. Warbeck, with a backward glance at her, continued on down the street. He was a funny little man, with his shock of untidy hair and overearnest manner.

"I believe," she said to Máiri, "you've acquired an admirer."

"Ah, get on," said Mrs. MacTaggart. "And me in shouting distance of sixty? What I——"

"No, really, but he does always stop to talk to you if you're out in the yard."

"Two, three times, is it? He admires the twins, is the truth. Daft over children the poor man is."

"You don't convince me—you didn't have them out there right now."

"Tosh," said Mrs. MacTaggart roundly. "The man's lonely, is all—retired and not knowing what to do with

1

himself. He talks to most people roundabout. What I—"

"Mmh," said Alison. Mr. Warbeck had become a tolerably familiar sight in this area for only a few months. This was a newly subdivided section, but Laurel Canyon was an old residential site and down the hill were older, shabbier homes; Mr. Warbeck, it was understood, rented a room in one of them. He seemed to walk a good deal, and all the kids and dogs for blocks around knew him. A nice little man, thought Alison vaguely; and if he was getting up the courage to lay siege to their Màiri, who was a widow, she didn't sound very receptive, which was a good thing.

"What I came in to tell you, if you'll stop joking a minute, he had his transistor radio on, and it was the news. There's been another one."

"Not another——"

"Another bank robbery is what I'm saying. Right downtown, the Security-First Bank on Spring Street. At noontime again, like all the rest, a couple of hours ago, and the villain got clean away."

"Oh, dear," said Alison inadequately.

"Clean away again, can you imagine it? But thanks to God he didn't shoot anybody this time."

"It doesn't seem possible . . . And I suppose that means," said Alison, "that we won't be seeing Luis until midnight again."

Lieutenant Luis Mendoza had never, as he expressed it, brought himself to resign from the honest job, despite the unexpected fortune his grandfather had left him; he was still, dapper as ever, holding down his desk at the Homicide Bureau at Central Headquarters downtown.

2

"Very likely," agreed Mrs. MacTaggart with a sigh. "All things considered. It does seem a great pity they can't be spaced out more sensible."

"Homicides, you mean?" said Alison gravely. "It does seem that way. But all this—it doesn't seem *possible* he can go on getting away with it. Maybe they'll get a useful lead this time——"

"The Invisible Man, the newspapers are calling him," said Mrs. MacTaggart. She looked serious. "And if they don't, then, maybe I'd best make a novena for it. The poor lieutenant, not in until one last night—ruining his health he'll be!"

It was the fourth bank robbery in twenty-seven days. All the jobs had apparently been pulled by the same man. He was a loner, and it just didn't seem possible that he could so utterly vanish moments after each job.

As if they didn't have enough on their hands already. As if September wasn't about the damnedest month of the year anyway, with the temperatures hitting a hundred degrees and over and the homicide rate naturally rising too. As if . . .

It was, in fact, turning out to be one hell of a month for the cops at Headquarters Homicide. Hackett, the senior sergeant, was still in the hospital, due to go home in a couple of weeks and spend another month convalescing before he came back on the job. Landers was on vacation, and so was Farrell. And Piggott, impossibly, was home in bed with the 'flu.

"The *'flu*," said Palliser bitterly. "How the hell could he catch 'flu in September, for God's sake?"

But that was the way the ball bounced, so they were

undermanned to start with. And there'd been that shooting over on San Pedro—that was three weeks old and looked like coming to a dead end; the corpse had been a near-Skid-Row drifter and anybody might have had some reason to cool him, good or bad—and the suicide that just possibly wasn't—though after a lot of probing into it Palliser was almost convinced that it was—and the teen-age gang rumble with two kids dead and several in the hospital, and yet another child-beating with the baby dead. And just this morning somebody, probably in some kind of car, had held up a Shell station on Figueroa and left a corpse behind him—the corpse of a nineteen-year-old kid who'd have been back at his classes at L. A. C. C. three days from now, if somebody hadn't wanted a little ready cash.

John Palliser didn't like to talk to bereaved parents. He was a young man for a sergeant, and a sympathetic young man who liked people. He didn't mind talking to the bad boys, and he could get as tough with them as need be, but he never knew what to say to people like Mr. and Mrs. Walsh.

"Why did it have to be Jimmy?" asked Mrs. Walsh. "Why my Jimmy?" And Palliser didn't know, so he couldn't tell her.

"He was a good boy," said Walsh numbly. "A good boy. Earning his own way through college. He wanted to be a lawyer. He'd've been a good lawyer. Never in any trouble, even if we don't live in too fancy a neighborhood." Walsh was a clerk in a Bekins' warehouse.

Palliser asked the questions that had to be asked. Jimmy had worked at the station two summers. The owner, Mr. Hammer, had liked him, treated him well, trusted him. "Why did it have to happen to Jimmy?" Walsh asked blankly. "Why did it happen at all? He said Mr. Hammer always told him—Jimmy and this other guy works there, the mechanic—anybody ever tries to hold up the station, play along, don't get brave, hand over the money. So Jimmy wouldn't have—— Why?"

There wasn't any immediate answer; possibly there never would be. The shooting had been done, as near as they could figure, about nine this morning, and you'd think that in those teeming city streets, in broad daylight, somebody would have seen something; but by noon it was apparent that nobody had, among immediately available possible witnesses. The shooting had been done not in the glass-enclosed station office but in the garage, set back farther from the sidewalk. The lab team was still going over every square inch of everything in there. The shooting had been discovered about ten o'clock when the mechanic, Mike Partridge, came on duty and found young Walsh's body. The owner, summoned down then, thought the heist man had got away with somewhere around forty dollars.

Palliser left Higgins and Dwyer still asking questions in the neighborhood and called the morgue from a drugstore phone. They hadn't, of course, got to an autopsy yet, but they had dug the bullet out. It was too much damaged for Ballistics to identify, thought the doctor, but he'd send it over anyway.

"Oh, great," said Palliser gloomily. He left his drugstore sandwich half eaten and went back to the Homicide office. As he came in, Sergeant Lake slammed down the phone and got up in a hurry.

"Lieutenant—another one! The same bastard—Secu-

5

rity-First at First and Spring—just now, the guard called in——"

"¡Bastante! ¿Qué es esto? For God's sake, it's less than a week since he hit that Bank of America——" Mendoza seized his hat and caught Palliser's arm. "All right, call the Feds and the lab, but we'll get damn all this time, too, I'll just bet. For *God's* sake. Come on, John."

"Well, I just——"

"Nobody else here, damn it," said Mendoza.

"It's hot as hell outside," said Palliser plaintively. "Where do you suppose he gets the energy? And how in hell does he do it—disappear like that?"

"By all we've got so far," said Mendoza, "he's found out how to dematerialize, is all I can figure." They got into the elevator.

Homicide, with quite enough on its plate, thank you, had not been concerned with the first bank job. That had been the Broadway-Washington branch of the Bank of America, and nobody had got hurt. The loner had just walked away and vanished with twelve hundred and fifty-three dollars of the bank's money, so that headache had belonged to Lieutenant Saul Goldberg of Robbery.

But exactly a week later, on August nineteenth, the loner had walked into the Security-First National Bank at Main and Commercial, showed a gun to the chief teller, collected a little under three thousand bucks in the inevitable paper bag, and started to walk out. The bank guard, belatedly catching on, had run after him and collared him at a side door, whereupon the loner had calmly fired three bullets into him and pulled his vanishing act again.

The guard died just as the ambulance got there, so

that laid it right in Homicide's lap, and the headache had been getting worse ever since. Of course the Feds were on it, too, but there was an old saying that you can't make bricks without straw, and while they had a rudimentary kind of description, it didn't give them any leads.

"It all happened so *fast*——" said the chief teller helplessly. And it was the same story five days ago, at the Bank of America at Ninth and Main. This time one of the male tellers had spotted what was going on and had quietly slipped out into the main part of the bank and waited for him—followed and tackled him before he got to the door. If the teller had hoped to be called a hero in the headlines he'd been sadly mistaken; what he was called in the headlines was dead.

They got all sorts of descriptions from various witnesses, which was par for the course; the general public, Mendoza thought, when asked to remember details, usually wound up proving the truth of that bit from Holy Writ: *They have eyes and see not.* But one thing the witnesses all agreed on was that the man was bald. Very bald.

But bald, curly-haired, white, black, or green, how the hell did he get away so quickly and completely? Somebody should have noticed him—which direction he went, at least—and unless he'd had the devil's own luck every time he'd never have found a parking space on the street near those banks, and even if he went off on foot, among the usual crowds somebody should have seen him . . . Although, of course, anonymity could hide in a crowd easily.

And very probably, thought Mendoza grimly, they

wouldn't get anything more suggestive on him from the new set of witnesses.

They didn't. They got just about what they'd got before. As far as it went, it was helpful, because it added up to the same boy—again allowing for the variations of the witnesses. They discounted the hysterical female at the bank last week, who claimed he was a big black man over six feet tall with a scar on his face, and the man who insisted the loner wore a beard. The descriptions they had from those who'd had the best looks at him roughly said the same thing. And there was nothing very useful there.

"Was he bald?" Mendoza asked the chief teller. Palliser was talking to the guard and the bank manager, and a handful of Feds had turned up and were questioning the other tellers, the few members of the general public who'd been here.

"Oh, yes, sir." The chief teller was a pretty youngish woman, brown-haired and brown-eyed; she had on a bottle-green linen sheath and a chunky five-strand necklace of green beads. She kept clutching at the beads nervously. "But it all happened so *fast*——"

"Just tell me what you remember for sure, how he looked."

"Well—well, he wasn't a *young* man, I don't think. I think his eyes were light . . . I couldn't say about his coloring, I mean, he was a white man, but I wouldn't like to say, I guess he was sort of medium—and he was bald as could be, I remember his bald head sort of shining . . . And he had on a dark-gray suit and a white shirt and a tie—a—a black tie, I think. Dark anyway. It was all so *fast*—I got the shakes when I saw that gun.

Mister, I really got the shakes. With those two fellows shot dead, I mean! It looked as big as a c-cannon——"

They knew about the gun, at least, and it would look something like a cannon to anybody not familiar with guns. The doctors had recovered bullets from both the guard and the teller, and Ballistics had examined their lands and grooves and looked in their records and come up with a make on the gun. It was a Smith and Wesson 1955 target revolver; it had a six-and-a-half-inch barrel, and it fired .45 ACP caliber slugs. It was a big gun. It was a heavy gun. In the hands it was now in it was a damn dangerous gun.

"What did he say?"

"He didn't s-say very much." Another similarity. What the hell good did it do them to find out it was the same boy? "He showed me the gun and just said something like—oh, 'You know what I want,' like that—and honestly, I was so scared and surprised—I mean, even reading in the papers about this guy, even knowing somebody like that's around, you just don't *expect*—I just started grabbing up money. I don't know to a penny what I had, but I usually have more on hand than the other—— Honestly, I just wanted it *over*——"

"He had a paper sack?"

"Yes, he did. It was, oh, a sort of medium-sized one, not really big. Now wait a minute," she said. "Wait a minute. That was kind of funny. See, I was stuffing bills into this bag, and all the time I was thinking—as well as I *could* think, you know—I mustn't let anybody see what's going on, Jean at the next cage, or Bill Harding over at Money Orders—they're nearest me, see—or somebody might try to get smart like that fellow last

9

week and wind up dead. So I was trying to be real quiet and easy about it, see. And I got the bag full, and there was still a little pile of bills left in my drawer, but he says, 'That's fine, Miss Thomas'—you see, there's my name plate right inside the window, he saw that—and before I could try to get any more bills in, he took back the bag and shoved it under his jacket and put the gun away, too, and off he went. I don't know, he didn't seem to walk fast, but he was just—gone."

"He saw the bag was full and took what was already in it. I see. Not a greedy fellow. You can't remember any of his features near enough to describe? Nose? Ears? Jaw?"

She shook her head. "I didn't really look at him but just at first, you know. After that I was concentrating on the money. Naturally. He had a sort of roundish face, I think."

"Which way did he go?" Mendoza looked around the bank. It was a large bank; this main-floor office was perhaps a hundred by a hundred and fifty feet, with marble counters around most of three sides. There were two doors giving onto Spring Street and one onto First. There was also a door out of the bank into the lobby of the building; it was, of course, an ordinary office building above the main floor.

That was the door she pointed at. And the lobby had a street door of its own, too, onto Spring.

"Mmh," said Mendoza thoughtfully. "You didn't happen to notice his hands?" No, she hadn't. They had a witness from the first job, a sharp-eyed private dick who'd been standing at the next window, had seen what was going on and had the sense to stay still. He said the loner had worn strips of flesh-colored adhesive tape on his finger tips. He could be right, though nobody else had noticed that. In this weather gloves would be conspicuous. . . . But, nothing. No lead. Here was the same dark-gray suit, the same dark tie they'd heard about from the other witnesses before. And she went on to give him more of the same. As far as she could tell, he wasn't either very big or very small—average. She couldn't guess his age; she wasn't very good at that. His voice—well, he hadn't said much—it was sort of average. Just an ordinary voice. No accent or anything. He wasn't very fat or very thin—average—"Of course we only see customers about from the waist up. I couldn't tell——"

¡Mil rayos! thought Mendoza irritably. And this was the one who'd seen him nearest to, this time. This time nobody had realized what was happening—had happened—until after the loner had got clear away and the chief teller had gone into hysterics.

"And *besides*," she said tearfully, "it's not *Miss* Thomas, it's *Mrs.* Thomas!"

People.

Mendoza thanked her and went over to the Feds. They hadn't got much of anything either.

"The Invisible Man," said one of them disgustedly. "Argh, maybe he is."

"Well, there's this and that," said Mendoza, lighting a cigarette. "All in the downtown area. Why? Probably the most crowded section of town. And he hits at the lunch hour—between twelve and one, a peak period when he'd be least likely to be noticed. But why pick banks in this area in the first place?"

"He hasn't got a car," said the Fed wearily, "and you

know how the bus situation is. He can't figure out where to catch a bus for anywhere else."

"Very funny," said Mendoza. "What it suggests to me is, he'll keep hitting banks in this area."

"So?" said the Fed. He was a big fellow with rough-hewn features; he reminded Mendoza a little of Hackett. "Do you see a lead there?"

"Stake out all the banks in the area bounded by, say, Washington and Sunset, Union and San Pedro?" Mendoza sighed. "Trained observers to describe him better, at least?"

"*Compadre*," said the Fed gently, "how many men you got? How many men you think *we* got? An army? Banks—there are thousands of them. Thousands."

"Nineteen, twenty in the downtown area," said Mendoza.

"Argh," said the Fed. "So four times he hits downtown. So next time he hits Federal Savings in Glendale or the California Bank in Culver City. Who can tell? *Compadre*, we got other things we're working on, you know, and just so many men."

"*Amigo*," said Mendoza, "so have we. So have we."

They would have to get a formal statement from Mrs. Thomas. They would be comparing what she said with what the other witnesses had said. They would—a waste of time so far—include Mrs. Thomas in the group being showed thousands of mug shots at Records, hoping for a possible ident.

At least this time the loner hadn't killed anybody. No telling when he might again.

A loner, for God's sake.

12

Hitting banks. Such very public places, with people all around.

And then disappearing. How?

Mendoza and Palliser went back to Headquarters. "This gas-station thing," said Palliser. "The hell of a thing. By all that shows, a nice young kid—ambitious and hard-working. I wonder if the lab came up with anything. Damn shame. Probably one of these damned hopheads, hunting easy money to support his habit."

Mendoza yawned and punched the elevator button again. He said, "Detective novels."

"What? What about them?"

"Mostly about the private homicides. *¿Cómo no?* Nice intimate killings. Largely very implausible. They do occur—but how many of that kind to the kind we mostly see—the impersonal, random, wanton kills?" He sounded dispirited.

They got out of the elevator and walked down to the door marked *Homicide Bureau*. Sergeant Lake looked up.

"You've got a new one, boys. Higgins came in just after I got the call. I sent him out on it."

"What now?" asked Mendoza resignedly.

"Over on Allen Street. Teen-age girl shot. Colored. Looks like something a little funny, what the squad-car man said. I don't know."

"All I need," said Mendoza. He picked up his hat again.

The city had tripled its population in the last ten years; the chief was clamoring for more money to hire more cops. The city was policing a territory ten times the size of New York City with a quarter as many cops, and the city had the top police force in the world; but it could only stretch so far and do so much. And of all the public services the city fathers granted money to, the cops were always last on the list.

Naturally.

CHAPTER TWO

When Mendoza and Palliser got to the house on Allen Street, the ambulance had just arrived; they wouldn't move the body until the lab team had seen it. Higgins, looking very hot and uncomfortable in the stuffy little living room, was talking to Mrs. Coffey.

It was an old frame house on a block of old frame houses. This was one of the oldest sections of L. A., and while you couldn't exactly call it a slum, you couldn't exactly say it wasn't, either. Whether or not a given block fell into the category of slum depended a lot on what kind of people lived there. Negro section or white section or Oriental, that held true.

Most of the houses on this block were kept up fairly neatly. A couple had been recently painted, but the strips of dry grass in front yards were faintly brown, in September, and a few other houses looked run-down, a pane of glass cracked in a front window, a curtain showing tears. L.A. had quite a population of Negro elite society, professional people who lived in some of the best residential areas of the county; but just as not all the white population belonged to elite society, neither did the people like the Coffeys.

"I don't know what happened, sir," Mrs. Coffey was saying now, agitatedly. She still had on a faded blue apron over her house dress, and she kept bunching it up between her hands, unaware of what she was doing. "I didn't hear anything like a shot. You're saying Carol was shot, and I guess you know, sir, but *I* didn't hear no shot. I was right out in the back yard. I don't understand— and you're saying she's dead, but it don't seem possible——"

She was a big woman and still handsome, with regular features, a medium brownish color—some white blood, thought Mendoza. There was a young boy in the doorway across the little room; the open door gave on a much smaller bedroom—glimpse of a narrow cot-bed neatly made, a cheap painted chest of drawers.

Higgins glanced at Mendoza wearily. "Mrs. Coffey, this is Lieutenant Mendoza, Sergeant Palliser. What——"

"How do you do," she said mechanically. "I've been out back. I never heard a thing. I just come in and found her laying there——"

"This was about twenty-five minutes ago," said Higgins to Mendoza. He went over to the two interns crouched over the body, and Mendoza followed him. "How long do you figure, boys?"

"Can't have been dead long when she was found. Call it half an hour ago, thirty-five minutes. Looks as if she got it right through the heart."

Mendoza looked down at the body. It was the body of a young Negro girl, eighteen, nineteen. She wasn't pretty

16

now—her mouth gaped, her blind eyes stared—but very likely she had been pretty; she had a slim, rounded figure. She lay on her back almost up against the rear wall of the living room, between the open door to another bedroom and the right end of the shabby chintz-covered sofa on that wall. She was wearing white shorts and a red halter-necked bra—a very nice figure indeed—and there was blood all over the halter and her warm brown skin and down on the shorts and on the worn beige rug.

"How could Carol be *shot?*" asked Mrs. Coffey. "I don't understand—who'd want to shoot *Carol?* Everybody likes Carol——"

"Were you here, son?" Higgins asked the boy.

The boy was sixteen or seventeen. He was darker than Mrs. Coffey or the dead girl and not as good-looking. He had on jeans and a clean white T shirt. He said, "I was in my room. In there." He nodded behind him to the little bedroom. "The door was shut. But I heard this noise. I didn't know it was a shot—it didn't sound loud like that, like you think a shot would be. Just a kind of pop, like. Naw, I didn't get up to look out the window or nothing. Little kids always fooling around with cap pistols. That's what—what it sounded like."

"Here's the lab boys," said Palliser, looking out the window.

"But everybody liked Carol——"

"You're the girl's brother?" asked Higgins.

"He's my son Verne," said the woman. "Yes, of course Carol's brother." There was a little crowd collecting from all over the neighborhood now outside. The squad-car men were out there. "You're telling me she's *dead.*"

She sounded nakedly incredulous; she was trying to see the dead girl beyond the interns' bent shoulders.

"I'm sorry, ma'am," said Higgins gently.

"In her own home—quiet neighborhood like this—— She was doing the dusting for me," said Mrs. Coffey. "We're having June and Frank for dinner, that's my married daughter and her husband. And I said to Carol if she'd straighten up a bit in here and dust things, while I went out back to cut some roses fresh——"

The lab team was in now. Mendoza said, "If we could go to another room, Mrs. Coffey? Maybe the kitchen? This is getting a little crowded in here, and you won't want to watch all this."

"Yes," she said dully. She turned and led them into the second bedroom off the living room, from there across a short dark hallway into a narrow kitchen. It was an old house, but the kitchen had plastic tile on the drainboards and looked very clean and neat. It was about the size of the living room and in one corner was an old-fashioned round oak table with four chairs around it. There was a plastic lace doily on the table, and sitting on it a cheap glass bud vase with a single perfect yellow rose in it. "Is this all right?" She glanced at the vase; her hands still bunched up the apron, nervously, unconsciously. She said, "I just picked that awhile ago. It's Carol's favorite one—she always cuts one of them to pin on her dress, going to a dance or something, you know. It's called Peace, that bush is." There was a little pile of fresh-cut roses lying on the drainboard on a sheet of newspaper.

"Mrs. Coffey——"

"I better call Sam," she said suddenly. "My husband.

18

Oh, my God, he'll be—— He's real proud of Carol. Real proud. Her going to college and all. This was going to be her second year. She went partly at night so's she could hold a job and earn the money, you see. She works at the Newberry's over on Central. Please, can I call my husband? I mean, ask somebody to—— I wouldn't know how to tell him. I just wouldn't know." Grief was taking the place of shock in her eyes now. "But she's only *nineteen*," she said.

Just like the kid the heist man had shot this morning.

"Of course, Mrs. Coffey," said Mendoza. "We'll want to talk to him too. It's just possible he might know of someone who had some reason to—— Where does he work?"

"He works at the General Hospital. He's what they call an orderly there. You know, he helps take the meals around and cleans up and like that. He'll be——" Mendoza nodded to Palliser, who slipped out to find a pay phone. Suddenly Mrs. Coffey drew a deep, deep breath and exhaled slowly. She turned to Mendoza almost as if by groping instinct; perhaps even in this confused moment she selected him as also one of a minority which had known prejudice, and she said, "Excuse me, sir, I want to ask you—I got to ask you— you take it easy with Sam, sir. With my husband. Questions and all. There's nothing like what you think, there's nobody had any reason at all, shoot our Carol. We all knew everything happened to her. She's a good girl, there's nothing like that, sir. Sam, he'll be just wild. Just wild. But I got to ask—— My husband, he's from Alabama, sir. I was born here, but he's from Alabama. A place called Kinston, he's from—little town. And—and

19

you see, sir, he don't know that—that policemen are different, different places. He don't believe it. Why, you got colored policemen here, but he still——" She stopped with a little gasp. "I mean, I don't want for you to think, if he acts scared of you or—or anything——"

"We won't upset him, Mrs. Coffey. We don't like to bother you at a time like this, but we do want to find out who did this, you know."

"Yes, sir," she said in a low voice. She had stopped bunching up her apron. She sat down in one of the chairs at the table. "I know."

"Did your daughter have a boy friend?"

"Not a real regular one. She's gone out with Dick Watkins, and Eddy Loman, and a couple times with the Kingsley boy—Glen Kingsley down the block. I guess she went with Dick mostly, but it wasn't like going steady. She d-didn't go out an awful lot. Carol's a serious girl. She's going—she wanted to be a teacher. That's what she was studying. She got pretty good grades, do you know? She got an A in English last year. Sam was pretty set up about that, him only having a couple years' schooling himself. Real proud of Carol——" For a moment her features crumpled and they waited for her to break down, but she controlled herself. "Not that Sam isn't a steady worker—he's always held a job, what job he could get. But college and all—it was something." She looked up at Mendoza a little blindly. "You go to college, sir?"

"No."

"Oh. A Mrs. Lyons my mother used to know, her boy went to college and then he joined the police here. I thought——"

"Yes," said Mendoza. Higgins looked a little grim. Neither of them had known Joe Lyons personally, but they remembered how he'd been killed, by a hopped-up j. d. he'd stopped for speeding. His name was on the Honor Roll at the Headquarters building.

There was a little silence; they gave her time. Presently she said, "There's talk, you know—a lot of talk. And down in the South, no question, it's bad—like where Sam comes from, he's all the time talking about it. But when our Carol was going to college, fixing to be a teacher, and no trouble about her getting in, why, half the ones in her class was colored—and colored getting in the police and all . . . I don't know, looks as if here anybody got any ambition and brains can get to be anything. . . . She got good grades, did I tell you that? She got an A in English——"

They sent the body down to the morgue. Palliser and Higgins started asking questions up and down the block. Depressingly, they heard from the neighbors just about what the girl's mother had said. A good girl, quiet and respectable and ambitious, helped her mother in the house. A nice family, always went to church regular, and both the elder Coffeys were death on liquor, real temperance—good Methodists they were, as the Reverend Williams would say too.

It got to be five o'clock, and the temperature was still something like ninety-seven, and Palliser gave up and went back to Headquarters to see if the lab had come up with anything on the gas-station holdup. Mendoza had been scheduled to join a meeting with the Feds to discuss the bank jobs.

Of course, Palliser reminded himself as he rode slowly up in the elevator, it was really only four o'clock by sun time. But since the population had shot up, what with the increased amount of water in use, and all the square mileage of new cement, the damn climate had changed —the nights didn't cool off the way they used to.

He had a date with Roberta tonight. He only hoped he'd get to keep it.

Mendoza was still with the Feds presumably. There wasn't any lab report waiting. He called the lab and was asked did he think they were miracle men. "Yes, I think you are miracle men," said Palliser. "Let's have what you've got."

"Tomorrow," said the lab man.

Palliser sighed and decided to call it a day. The night men were starting to straggle in. But before he left the office the phone rang and it was Dr. Bainbridge at the morgue asking for him. Palliser looked at his watch: five-forty. "Yes?"

"I think I've got something for you," said Bainbridge. "On this Walsh boy. Damn shame—well-set-up young feller. So damn young. Sign of age, I suppose, when the kids begin to look so very damned young."

"Yes. What is it?"

"I can't show you over the phone, damn it. I was just leaving. You stay put ten minutes and I'll come up."

"All right," said Palliser.

Dr. Bainbridge bustled his tubby little self into the Homicide office fifteen minutes later. He sat down in Mendoza's desk chair and said, "Maybe this'll say something to you. I don't know what the hell it is, but then I'm not a trained detective." He fished an envelope out

22

of his pocket and handed it over. Palliser upended it cautiously over the desk blotter, and a little something fell out. He turned it over curiously with one finger.

It was a small piece of metal. Very small. Between a quarter and an eighth of an inch long. But "long" was the wrong term, because it was curved slightly. It was straight for a little bit, and the inner surface rounded gently in a curve while the outer edge showed a definite point and then turned upward. Steel, steel alloy, darkened aluminum? Palliser fingered it. "Where'd you get this?"

"Out of the wounds," said Bainbridge, leaning back comfortably. "The boy was shot, but he was also beaten up. First. Banged over the head, to be non-technical. With something, not just fists. He was struck four or five times by our old friend the blunt instrument, and I think—from the angle of the shot—he was then shot as he lay prone and probably unconscious on the floor of the garage."

"Nice," said Palliser with a grimace. And why? Jimmy's father said that both Jimmy and the mechanic had been told not to show fight to a holdup man. So? Had the heist boy, just possibly, been somebody Jimmy knew and could identify? It was a thought.

"That," said Bainbridge, nodding at the little strip of metal, "was in the deepest head wound. I would assume it was broken off the blunt instrument. By the force of the blow."

"Yes," said Palliser, "but what the hell is it?"

"That," said Bainbridge, "I really couldn't tell you, Sergeant. You're supposed to be the detective."

"*¡Cara?*"

"You're going to say you won't be home," said Alison.

"Well, I wasn't," said Mendoza. "With a little provocation I might quote Omar Khayyam."

"That'd be a change. What part?"

" 'Myself when young did eagerly frequent Doctor and Saint, and heard great Argument about it and about, but evermore Came out by the same Door as in I went.' These bank jobs. I've been sitting around talking it over with the Feds. Very unproductively." Mendoza was at an unprotected public phone at a drugstore on Hill Street. A narrow aisle separated him from the lunch counter with its long mirror behind it; he could see the reflection of the slim dark man in the sharp-tailored gray Italian silk, the man with the narrow mustache and deep widow's peak; automatically he lifted a hand to straighten the discreet dark tie. The blonde waitress behind the counter smiled widely at him.

"When we heard about the new one we thought we wouldn't see you until after midnight again. Did you get any leads at all?"

"*Nada.*"

"But it seems impossible he should just *disappear*—— You should have got him the first or second time, by all——"

"*Presonar vino y vender vinagre.* I am," said Mendoza, "being ogled. By an emphatically blonde waitress. I can't see her legs, but she has a very fetching figure."

" 'Lover Boy Mendoza they used to call me.' *Mi hombre amoroso,* come home."

"I don't know," said Mendoza. "I got damn bored

24

with the Feds, and she's a very pretty blonde. The way she's eying me——"

"I'll bet," said Alison. "Teresa walked six steps today without falling down. I think she's getting the hang of it at last."

"Babies," said Mendoza, "are also boring."

"Then why," asked Alison, "did you want those negatives to have wallet-sized prints made?"

"A pure reflex," said Mendoza with dignity. "In our present culture, any man who has been so foolish as to— mmh—give hostages to fortune automatically carries photographs in his billfold."

"So he does," said Alison. "It's nothing to do with the fact that Terry looks like you and Johnny like me."

"Nothing at all," said Mendoza.

"Are you coming home at a decent hour?"

"Well, this blonde—— What have you got for dinner?"

"Chicken and avocado salad? Vichyssoise? Máiri's making scones, and there's unsalted butter and that imported jam."

"I'll pass up the blonde," said Mendoza. "After all, I can pick up a blonde any time."

"¡Amador!" said Alison, and her voice turned serious. "You're tired. It's a bad one—a tough one?"

"They're all being tough ones," said Mendoza. "One of these times."

"¡Máiri's going to make a novena for you."

"¡Maravilloso! These superstitious females."

"And she has an admirer. That funny little Mr. Warbeck."

25

"He's not going to take her away from us?" asked Mendoza anxiously.

"I doubt it. She's not interested."

"Good."

"Come home," said Alison firmly.

"Half an hour."

CHAPTER THREE

"At least," said the Fed, "we know our boy won't be working today." It was Saturday morning. The Fed's name was Dale, and he was a tall thin young man with a long nose and a humorous mouth. He sat down beside Mendoza's desk and brought out a long yellow teletype. "What do you think of this? The Washington boys just passed it along. This Alfred Siegal, five-ten, one-sixty, hair—oh, well, this is out-of-date anyway. Siegal has a pedigree—assault, armed robbery—and back in 1932 he pulled several singlehanded bank heists. As far as anybody knows he's never been mixed up with the big boys, no contact with the Syndicate at all. He's served time. The last anybody heard of him—on our side of the fence anyway—was back in 1949 when his latest probation ended. He was then forty-two. But add fifteen years, he might be bald by now, and God knows we haven't got very much else definite to go on."

"No. Anybody have any idea where Siegal might be?"

Dale shrugged. "Who knows?"

"Well, that's very helpful. Look." Mendoza sat up abruptly. "You missed our conference yesterday. What do you think's happening with the money?"

"Because none of it's been passed, or none we can trace? Hell——" Dale rubbed his jaw. The banks, of course, had records of the serial numbers of all the bills above singles. The loner had got away with more big bills than singles, but none of them had been passed so far anywhere in the country. And that was helpful in a negative kind of way.

Dale said, "He could be sitting on it until he figures we'll stop looking. Maybe he doesn't know we never do."

Mendoza shook his head. "What kind of people hold up banks? Much the same sort of people who steal, period. Not really very smart people—as Saul Goldberg could also say. Ninety-nine times out of a hundred they start right in enjoying themselves with the proceeds. throwing it around. And of all thieves, your bank robber is apt to be even more so—being more aggressive and more of a gambler by nature. I don't think he's sitting on it. I think he's selling it to a hot-money man."

"But, my God," said Dale, "the piddling amount he's got away with——"

"Call it that to the banks! I know, I know. He's taken exactly seven thousand, one hundred and eighty-two dollars in four hauls. Not a fortune, but a nice piece of change. He——"

"A hot-money agent wouldn't give him a third of that. Too much trouble for too little profit—channeling the actual bills out of the country, in a long series of elaborate deals, where eventually they turn up, completely untraceable, in Switzerland or North Africa. What the hot-money men largely deal in are the really big hauls, ransom money, that kind of thing."

"I know," said Mendoza again. "But let's try to read him from the very little we do know. I make him a very cautious fellow."

"Cautious?" said Dale. "Holding up banks all by himself?"

Mendoza grinned. "No, but look at the precautions he takes. He knows a lone man can't hope for a really big haul this way—getting into the vaults, for instance. But he does pick the chief tellers, who usually have more cash on hand than the other tellers. And by what they say he's very cool, plays it slow and easy. I think he might very well be a type to play it even safer by taking the loss and getting rid of the incriminating evidence. Anyway, we've got feelers out to all the stool pigeons. See what they come up with. We don't know, but of course there'll be at least one hot-money man here."

"Um, I don't know," said Dale. "You want to do anything about this Siegal?"

"What the hell could we do? No place to start looking for him, you said."

Sergeant Lake came in and handed Mendoza an envelope. He opened it; it was the formal autopsy report on Jimmy Walsh. Ballistics said the bullet was considerably damaged, no make on the gun. There was nothing else new from the autopsy. "Hell," said Mendoza, and reminded himself to be sure Palliser saw it. "Do you ever have spells like this when everything goes wrong?"

"We're human too," said Dale dryly.

"And who the hell wanted to shoot that nice little colored girl? It doesn't make sense."

Dwyer came in and nodded at Dale. "Think we might have something," he said.

"Don't tell me, a break at last!"

"Well, I won't say for sure." Dwyer had broadened out in the last couple of years and started to lose his sandy hair, which worried him; he'd developed the habit of fumbling with it, perhaps unconsciously checking to see how much was left, and one hand strayed to the top of his head now as he hoisted one hip to a corner of Mendoza's desk. "We've got eleven witnesses going through all those mug shots. Two of 'em picked out this same one about an hour ago. Well, two out of eleven— the others weren't sure. But the two who picked it were two of the chief tellers—Mrs. Thomas and the man, Clark. Which looks——"

"It does indeed. Who is he?"

Dwyer produced an envelope. "I pulled his pedigree for you. He's not a very nice boy. Daniel Fisher, first arrest at sixteen, back in 1930, car theft. Two, three, four more counts on that—probation—six months on the Honor Farm—probation—hell, you can tell the story for yourself. First arrest as an adult, break-in at a liquor store. Maybe he had a good lawyer—he got a suspended sentence, more probation. These judges. Then he got picked up for burglary—this was in 1936—and did a one-to-three. He's out about a year, probation just over, when he starts pulling heist jobs. He got picked up on that in 1941 and did a three-to-ten—additional count, resisting arrest. Matter of fact, he half killed a patrolman. He got out in 1947, and the year after that he was charged with knocking down an old lady and stealing her bag—in MacArthur Park, at night. She couldn't identify and he got off. Then in 1950 he got picked up for armed assault. It was a hung jury and the thing dragged on on the calendar and was finally dropped. He got picked up on the same charge six months later, did another three-to-ten, and got out in 1960. About a year later—he was still on probation— he was found with a gun on him—a .45 incidentally— and spent another six months in the clink. Since then apparently he's either gone straight—and I never did believe in miracles," said Dwyer, "or he's been too careful to get caught."

"Mmh, yes," said Mendoza. "Yes. He's always worked alone, he's not averse to using violence, and he's a thief. And once carried a .45. Men who carry guns at all usually have some preference. Is there an address there for him?"

"Old one—1961—but, sure. Over in the Atwater section."

"So let's go see if he's home," said Mendoza, and stood up. "Or at least ask questions about him if he's not there."

"According to all this," said Dwyer, "I'd say the chances are good. He's never moved around much. Same address in 1930 as when they picked him up in 1941, and he moved to this place in 1955. Went back there when he got out of jail last, I guess."

"I kind of think I buy Mr. Fisher," said Dale. "Does he match up otherwise to what we've got?"

31

"Well, we haven't got much, have we? He's five-ten, one hundred and eighty, medium coloring, blue eyes, no scars or deformities, and in 1961 he was going bald."

"I buy him," said Dale with decision, getting up. "Come on."

Mendoza took up his hat and started for the door. Dwyer stepped in front of him and said, "Uh-uh."

"What?"

"Art not being here, I figure I got to substitute for him. I'm the next senior sergeant, after all. Go get your gun."

"Oh, for God's sake," said Mendoza.

"Go get it or you can't play. This is not a little snotnose kid hopping cars we're going to see. And we need you around here, Lieutenant—you and your crystal ball. Not to mention that I kind of like that nice redheaded wife of yours."

"I suppose you've both got guns, and he's only one man."

"Maybe Art's right—you just don't like to spoil the set of your jacket," said Dwyer. "Go get the gun."

"Bullying me in my own office——"

"Sure, sure, so we get there and find this guy hopped up or something—he seems to've tried a lot of different kicks—and you get shot up, and everybody blames me."

"Now, Bert——"

"That butters no parsnips," said Dwyer firmly. "The gun."

"Oh, for *God's* sake," said Mendoza. He flung his hat down on the desk, took off his suit jacket, opened a drawer, took out the shoulder holster and strapped it on, checked the .38 Police Positive, and shoved it into the holster. He put on his jacket. "Satisfied?"

"Okay," said Dwyer mildly. "Let's go."

"Bullying me!" said Mendoza bitterly. "*Se lo digo*, it's no joke! Between you and Art——"

"We need that crystal ball of yours."

"And I have a hunch right now that this is all going to be very tame indeed," said Mendoza.

But his hunches weren't always right. Not by any means.

Palliser was not thinking about the bank robber. He was thinking about Jimmy Walsh. He wanted very much to find out who had killed Jimmy, the nice bright kid who'd wanted to be a lawyer. The little colored girl, Carol Coffey, that was something to think about, too, but he'd wait for the autopsy report, see if Ballistics could make anything of the slug; then he'd want to talk to some of her friends—she might have confided something suggestive to a girl friend. Everything seemed to be happening at once, the last couple of days, and nobody could be in two places at the same time. Higgins was out talking to Carol's boy friends, he thought.

And right now he had what looked like a very hot lead in the Walsh case.

"Let me get this straight," he said to the man sitting across the desk from him here in the communal sergeants' office. "You live on this street, Fig Court?" It sounded a rather improbable name, but the county had a lot of those.

"Yeah, that's right. Right off Figueroa. It ain't even a

whole block long, you know. Just our apartment, and two others same side o' the street, and a couple houses across the way." The man across the desk bore the elegant name of Rosario Jesus del Valle; he was a short, scrawny little man obviously dressed in his Sunday-best suit for this call on the cops, a cheap navy-blue suit, and a very clean white shirt, and a gaudy tie. He had a lot of curly black hair and earnest brown eyes; he was almost a handsome little man. He said, "I work for the railroad. The S. P. In the yards."

"Yes. And your apartment's in the rear of the building, so your side windows look down on that Shell station."

"That's it. See, I didn't hear about that poor young kid getting killed till I get home last night. That's a terrible thing, ain't it? Why, he filled up my car lotsa times just this summer. I just got a car last year, saved up for it, you know, and Margarita, she likes drive out around in the country, get outta the city, down to the beach, like that. She says it's not healthy for kids, all this city air. Crazy. I grew up in the city, it never hurt me none. But I love her, what do I do? I buy gas, drive to the country." He shook his head. "Gotta drive fifty miles any direction, get outta the city nowadays. And what's when you get there? Fields with cows in them. Fields with tomatoes in them—string beans, lettuce."

"Listen," said Palliser, "you said——"

"Oh, yeah, yeah, sorry, I was getting to it, sorry. So Margarita tells me about the kid, says isn't it terrible, and I right away think about what I seen yesterday morning, and I think, Jesus, he could've been the one did it. Because the paper said it was about nine A.M."

34

"That's what we figured," said Palliser.

"O.K. So I figure to myself, I better come in and tell you about it, see. Just in case it was the one. Jesus, a guy going around killing kids like that—nice kid he was, always polite. And besides, I happen to know that this Hammer who runs the station tells 'em all, don't get smart if a holdup happens, stand still for it. So why shoot the kid? I mean, maybe he's a nut."

"Maybe. What did you see?"

"So," said del Valle, "I say I better come in. That Margarita. She's *extranjera*, you get me, born down south of the border, and right off she gets the jitters, me mixed up with the cops. I got to take awhile, calm her down, explain you're right guys and all, and then I got to see the foreman and explain this is a legit excuse. You get me. So that's how come I don't get here until now." It was ten minutes to eleven.

"Sure," said Palliser impatiently. "So what did you see?"

"The baby was sick," said del Valle maddeningly. "Nothing serious, a little colic, but I guess we're both kind of foolish about her, see—she's a real doll, you know? Only six months, but a real charmer. She's got these eyelashes—— Well, anyways, it was my day off. I get a weekday and Sunday, see, and we usually sleep late the weekday on account of having to get up early Sunday for Mass. Father Rodriguez only has seven and nine o'clock Masses, but we was up early yesterday account of Elena. The baby."

"Yes, yes," said Palliser. "And so?"

"Well, Margarita says we got to take her to the doctor. Be sure it ain't something serious. So I'm in the bedroom

35

getting dressed, and I forgot to wind my watch the night before, and it's run down. So I yell to Margarita what time is it?—so's I could set my watch, see—and she yells back it's twelve after nine, so——"

Palliser sat forward in his desk chair.

"—I go over to the window so's I got good light to set the watch and I set it and I wind it and I put it on, and then—you know how you do things just sort of casual like—I look down outta the window." He paused. "No, I didn't hear no shot, but——"

"*Yes?*" said Palliser.

"Well, I see this guy come outta the garage there. He looked like he was in a hurry. I didn't see anybody but him—not the kid, not the mechanic Hammer has. Just this guy. He comes outta the garage, and he walks real fast across the blacktop past the station and gets into a car, and off it goes."

"Wait a minute. You said, 'off it goes.' Was he driving it?"

"No, no, there was a couple other guys in the car. He got in beside the driver, and there was another guy in the back seat."

"All right. Can you describe him?"

"I saw him, didn't I? Sure. I couldn't say at all what size he was, 'cause I was looking down at him, see? But he wasn't fat or thin, just average, and he had on dark pants and a green sports jacket. A light-green shirt, no tie. No hat, and he had kind of sandy hair."

"Good. What about the car? Did you get a good look at it?"

"Sure," said del Valle. "Look, I said I just got a car last year—in December. Cars I been lookin' at and studying

36

on a long while. I can tell you most any make and model, one look at it. On account I was trying decide what'd suit me best, see. Good mileage and all. What I ended up getting was that six-cylinder Plymouth. Good car. What d'you drive?"

"A Rambler," said Palliser. "What was the car?"

Del Valle nodded. "I thought about that one too—nice car," he said. "But I like the Plymouth O. K. Well, this car, it was one I'd looked at, so I knew it, see. It was an English Ford—the Anglia De Luxe—and it was light green. This year's. Yeah, solid color. And it had those things, you know, to carry skis like, on the roof."

Palliser felt a little excited. "I don't suppose you noticed the plate number, but that's very helpful, Mr. del Valle. There were three men in the car?"

"Yeah, I'm positive of that. Counting this fellow in the green jacket. And I did notice the plate number. Not all of it, naturally, because who does? But these new ones now, with three letters, sometimes they sort of spell words, and you do notice. If you get me. And this one, it started out HAH, like somebody laughing, which was sort of funny."

"Thanks very much," said Palliser fervently. "It was very good of you to come in—we appreciate it."

The Atwater section address turned out to be a very old and shabby four-family apartment. Fisher's apartment was Four, at the rear on the second floor.

They climbed uncarpeted stairs.

"I want to go and see Art this afternoon," said Mendoza. "He claims he's going stir-crazy, shut up with all those nurses calling him 'We.'"

37

They walked down a dingy dark narrow hallway where dust rose from an old, thin carpet. Dale said, "Art?" There was a door with a single tarnished numeral: 4. He knocked on it.

"My senior sergeant. He's still in the hospital. He got assaulted a couple of months ago. Won't be back to work until November, damn it."

"These thugs."

"Not exactly a thug."

Dale knocked again, loudly. The door opened suddenly.

"Yeah, what you want?"

This was undoubtedly Daniel Fisher himself. He had lost the rest of his hair. He was wearing a pair of polka-dot shorts and nothing else, and what hair he lacked on his head he had on his chest. He looked a little flabby but sufficiently formidable.

"Mr. Fisher?" said Dale. "F.B.I." He proffered his I.D. "We've got a few questions to ask you——"

"What the *hell*?" said Fisher hoarsely. He stepped back, to the middle of the room. His eyes moved nervously, wildly. He shouted suddenly, "Goddamn all you bastards, hounding a man—hounding——"

And quite suddenly there was a gun in his hand, and quite suddenly bullets started flying.

Dale ducked behind a nearby armchair, reaching for his own gun. Dwyer dodged over toward the left wall, and before Mendoza got his gun out Dwyer had jumped Fisher from the side and had him down. Dale piled onto the clawing tangle; they hauled Fisher up to his feet and took the gun away from him. Fortunately Dwyer had a pair of cuffs in his pocket.

"Whoosh, that was close," said Dwyer, inspecting the powder burns on the shoulder of his jacket. Fisher stood staring at them sullenly. "Well, they do say only the good die young."

CHAPTER FOUR

"All right, Fisher, let's have some answers," said Mendoza.

"I didn't do nothing. Why can't you guys let me alone? I ain't been in any trouble since I got out last."

"You're in trouble now, brother," said Dwyer dryly. "You didn't act just so smart, shooting at cops like that."

"What other cops have been hounding you?" asked Dale.

They'd brought him down to Headquarters and stood around him now in one of the interrogation rooms. Dressed, Fisher didn't look so formidable: just a shabby, paunchy, unshaven man on the wrong side of fifty.

"I didn't do nothing," he said sullenly.

"You pulled a gun on us." The gun had been sent down to Ballistics, but it wasn't the gun used in the bank jobs; it was a Ruger Black Hawk .44 Magnum. But a man who had one gun might have two, though if so it hadn't been in his apartment. They didn't bother to ask him about a gun permit—a waste of time. In

California you didn't need a permit to keep a gun on the premises, only if you were going to carry it in a car or on your person; and anyway, what pro hood ever had a permit?

"Yeah, well, I was nervous—you comin' in like that. I'm sorry," said Fisher. "You gonna give me the gun back?"

"Are you kidding?" asked Dwyer. "To a guy with a pedigree?"

"Where were you yesterday between twelve noon and one o'clock?" asked Dale.

"Betw——" Instant panic flared in Fisher's eyes. "Why? I dunno. I didn't do nothing. Honest."

"Where were you?" asked Mendoza patiently. "Think."

"I—— Listen, there's something all cockeyed here. I dunno why you guys—— Listen, we come through that door out there, it says Homicide! That's murder, ain't it? I never *killed* nobody! I didn't do nothing——"

"Matter of fact," said Dwyer thoughtfully to Mendoza, "you'd have to figure from about ten-thirty to eleven. He's got to get down there, and he hasn't got a car, and you know how the buses are."

"Mmh," said Mendoza. "So prove it to us, Fisher. Where were you between, say, ten-thirty and one o'clock yesterday?"

"Why? Was there a murder done then? I—— Oh. Oh, them bank jobs. Jeez, I never done nothing like that! You got me all wrong! Honest, I never——"

"Two witnesses identified you," said Mendoza.

The panic flared again, but also there was bafflement,

anger, in Fisher's eyes. "Two—— That ain't possible! They're plain cockeyed! I never done no such thing! I don't get—— Listen, you got my gun. They got a way to test, like on slugs, don't they? Match up—so you'll find out it wasn't my gun killed them guys. That's nuts! I never——"

"So where were you between ten-thirty and one o'clock?"

Fisher was silent, thinking. Judging from his expression, it was a painful process. Finally he said, "I was at my apartment. I didn't get up till late."

"Mmh-hm," said Dwyer. "Anybody with you?"

"No. No, I was alone."

"That's a pity," said Mendoza. "Make any phone calls? Any way to prove that's where you were?"

"Well, I'm telling you that's where I was."

"Brother, this one's a comedian," said Dwyer.

"What time did you leave the apartment—or did you?"

"Yeah. Yeah, I went out later on—got some cigarettes and——"

"See anybody around when you left? What time?"

"Oh, I guess about—about two o'clock. No, I didn't see nobody."

"Too bad," said Dale. "When'd you get home?"

"Well, I did see the landlady then. Around five o'clock, I guess."

"And she saw you."

"Well, sure."

"So you can't really prove where you were between ten-thirty and one, can you?"

42

"I just finished telling you I was home! That's all. You damn guys—a fellow makes a couple little mistakes and you're all down on him, don't——"

"Little mistakes," said Mendoza, "such as hitting an old lady over the head and robbing her."

"I never done that. Jeez, the way you guys——"

"I'm getting rather tired of you, Mr. Fisher," said Mendoza. "I suppose we could go on asking all over again—and hearing the same answers—but we're damn busy right now, so I think we'll just book you into jail. Bert——"

"Hey, hey, what for? I didn't do nothing——"

"A real comedian," said Dwyer, "this one. He pulls a gun and shoots at three cops, and he wonders why he's going to jail. Armed assault to start with, and then we'll have these witnesses take a look at you in the flesh and see what they say."

"Nobody can say I pulled them jobs—I never——"

"Oh, take him away, Bert," said Mendoza.

Dwyer obliged.

Mendoza went back to his office and sat down at his desk. Dale sat down opposite him and lit a cigarette. "And at that I don't know," said Mendoza. "Wait and see. But a lout like that—they never expect to be caught up with until they are, you know—would he have bothered to cache the operative gun somewhere else? And eyewitnesses—we've both known a lot of cases where they . . ." He let that trail off. Not so very long ago the state of California had executed an innocent man, and Mendoza would not soon forget what that had led to. . . .

43

"Yeah, I know," said Dale.

"I want to hear what Wolf says about him." Wolf was the sharp-eyed private dick who'd witnessed the first job. "He's trained to remember faces, notice details. I'd sooner take his word than that hysterical female's."

"Yeah. Well, I suppose we'll herd all of 'em down to take a look at him after lunch. Which I guess we've earned."

"I'll let you and Bert do that—visiting hours at the hospital are two to three. Come on, I'll buy you lunch."

Palliser had sent an urgent teletype up to the D. M. V. in Sacramento, asking about Anglia De Luxes with plates starting out HAH. The D. M. V., of course, didn't keep any record of what colors cars happened to be, nor was it interested in the various accoutrements on cars such as ski carriers, luggage carriers, and the like. Those two points of description would be useful in identifying the particular car from the list they would give him.

He devoutly hoped they had some electronic machines up there to get out such a list, because otherwise he wouldn't get it for a month. Maybe six months. The state of California, whose population had been shooting up astronomically of recent years, had the highest rate of car ownership anywhere in the world, and it was highest in L. A. County. L. A. County had a population of around seven and a half million people, to which population was registered approximately three million automobiles. Even taking into consideration the very large selection of automobiles on the market, domestic and foreign, there were probably a number of Anglia

De Luxes registered in the state and county. There wouldn't, of course, be too many which bore plate numbers starting out HAH. And there would be, he hoped, no more than two or three which were also light green and had ski carriers on the roof.

Mr. del Valle had done his good deed for the month.

Palliser went up to Federico's for lunch and ran into Mendoza and Dale. He told Mendoza about the Anglia De Luxe. "A nice hot lead," approved Mendoza. "But three men? So why shoot the kid?"

"Could be he knew one of them—the one that apparently did the job?"

"But then he'd have known the Walsh kid would be there. Why pick that station?"

"Oh, hell, I don't know," said Palliser gloomily. "And another thing, why pick such a funny time as nine in the morning? Anybody with any sense would know there wouldn't be much in the till so soon after opening time. There only happened to be the forty bucks there because a guy who owed Hammer for a windshield replacement had dropped in first thing to pay his bill. But I'd like to talk to those fellows."

"*Obvio*," said Mendoza.

"And would you have a guess as to what this is?" Palliser brought out the little curved piece of metal Dr. Bainbridge had given him.

Mendoza took it, looked at it, weighed it in his hand. "What *is* it? I've got the feeling I ought to know—it looks familiar in a way—but I'm damned if I——"

"Let's see it," said Dale. "Um. Would it be a part off a tool of some kind? Broken off? Where'd you get it—is it a clue to something?"

45

Palliser told them. "Piece broken off a wrench—a jack?" asked Dale thoughtfully. "I don't know."

Palliser took it back. "Maybe somebody at the lab will have an idea. And that's another thing, of course—why would the heist man beat the kid before shooting him? That looks as if it might have been something personal, doesn't it? I want to talk to his friends—see if there'd been any trouble over a girl, something like that. It could have been a private kill and the holdup staged to cover up."

"Anything's possible," said Mendoza. "We ought to get the autopsy report on the Coffey girl some time today. Let's hope the Ballistics boys can spot the gun."

"But even if they do—— Higgins saw two of the boy friends—didn't get much. I'm going to hunt up the one he missed this afternoon. God, this weather—— Tell Hackett I envy him. Nice air-conditioned hospital, nothing to do all day but sleep and eat and read . . . *Iced* coffee, please," said Palliser.

"That's Glen Kingsley back there, working on the green Dodge." The manager of Gus's Kar-Wash, Best in Town, looked at Palliser curiously. "He do something?"

"Not that I know of—I just want to talk to him."

"Well, don't take too long, you don't mind. We like to keep 'em moving. He's the one in the red berry."

Palliser walked down to the end of the lot, where a very black young man in white coveralls and a red beret was industriously polishing the hood of the Dodge. "Mr. Kingsley? I'm Sergeant Palliser—I'd like to ask you a few questions." He got out his badge.

46

Kingsley straightened up. Pain came into his eyes. "That'll be about Carol," he said. "Sure, sir. It's just an awful thing—just awful. You find out who did it yet?"

"Not yet. I understand she'd gone out with you sometimes?"

"Some," said Kingsley. He was very black, but his features were not those thought of as typically Negroid; he had a lean jaw, a high-bridged nose, very thick hair, a small fuzzy mustache. Palliser put him down as twenty-two or twenty-three.

"Were you serious about her?"

"Well, man, I was," said Kingsley. His mouth was still twisted with grief. "I might's well tell you right off—I know you got to ask around, ever'body knowed her—I wanted Carol to marry me. She was the nicest girl I knowed. Ever. Just—nice. Even if she was awful religious." He smiled a small smile.

"She turned you down?"

"Well, man, she did. She sure did."

"So I guess you'd feel a little resentful about that? Mad at her?"

Kingsley looked down at the wet rag he still held. He squeezed it absently and a small stream of dirty water dropped to the black asphalt of the lot. Nearby the automatic sprinklers on the car-wash line roared into life as another car entered the tunnel. "I wasn't mad at Carol," said Kingsley in a low voice. "Not like that, man. No. You couldn't get mad at Carol. She tried to be nice about it, she did. We—you could say we didn't go for the same things, 'n' I saw that O.K. I guess she was right, but —heart 'n' head ain't exactly the same thing."

47

"What do you mean?"

"Well, like I ain't much for the education bit. They tried tell me in school, get a better job and all, but all the book stuff I just don't make. I get along—I get jobs O. K. I coulda kept her O. K., but she got this college thing in her head. Wanted to be a teacher. Well, sure, she was a lot smarter 'n me, I knowed that. I mean, I guess I knowed from the first, her and I just didn't match up, but—but—I loved that girl," said Kingsley. He blinked down at the wet cloth. "Carol—I loved her, man. I just wish I had whoever—done that—right here in my two hands. I could—— An' I wouldn't give a cuss what you done to *me*. Anybody kill *Carol*—— She was a nice girl." He looked at Palliser earnestly. "Man, I c'n go pick up a floozy off the street any time I want. You don't get the ones like Carol so very offen, man. Like—like I tell you a f'rinstance. I don't talk so good, like by the book, y' know. I talk good 'nough for me, so what? But alla time Carol'd be with me, I could see—I ain't *dumb* even if I don't have the book stuff in my head—I could see she was just itchin' tell me, Don't say ain't—an'—an' like that, but she never. See? She was too—too kind, Carol was."

"I see," said Palliser. "Where were you yesterday afternoon about three o'clock?"

"When she was—was—? Oh, man, don't waste your time on me! Mister, I cried like a baby when I heard about it. Me, do a thing like—— I loved that girl."

"But where were you?"

"I was prob'ly down at Lee's pool hall 'bout then. Yesterday was my day off. Mister, but I cried like—— I loved her, mister."

Yes, thought Palliser. But *love is strong as death; jealousy cruel as the grave*.

"Do you own a gun?" he asked.

"Me? A gun? Hell, no, mister. What would I want with a gun?" asked Kingsley.

Mendoza had just got back from the hospital when Lieutenant Goldberg drifted into the office, sat down, sneezed, and looked at him sadly, groping for Kleenex in his breast pocket.

"How are the allergies?" asked Mendoza.

"The allergies are doing just fine," said Goldberg. "Me, that's another question. What did I ever do to you, Luis? I try to co-operate with Homicide, act like a right guy. Why do you have to butt in and foul up one of my arrests?"

"*¿Cóme se dice?* Scout's honor, I don't know what you——"

Goldberg sneezed, blew his nose, dropped the Kleenex into Mendoza's wastebasket, and said, "This pawn-broker. Down on Union Avenue. Yesterday. He gets hit over the head by a pseudo customer and robbed of about two hundred bucks in cash, four transistor radios, some miscellaneous jewelry, and a mink stole."

"Yes? What have I got to do with it?"

"So we go over the place. Just in case it's some ignorant lout who hasn't heard about fingerprints. As if," said Goldberg, "there were any such. But we have to go through the motions. Just in *case*."

"Yes."

"I really thought better of you," said Goldberg. "Of

course it's the same charge, and mine is even a little heavier, theft added. But it was sort of frustrating."

"¡Qué diablo!" said Mendoza. "I have a nasty foreboding—— What are you talking about, Saul?"

"Well, fortunately for us a lot of them are very damn dumb," said Goldberg. "Aren't they? There's a quotation—you ever hear it?—'The reason there are so many imbeciles among imprisoned criminals is that an imbecile is so foolish even a detective can detect him.' Somebody named Austin O'Malley."

"I never heard that one," said Mendoza, "no. Who was O'Malley?"

"Who knows?" Goldberg shrugged. "Anyway, the point is there were some prints. On the cash register. On —well, never mind the details. And so when I got the word from Records, I go out to pick up the guy, and what do I find? I find that our star sleuth, the great Mendoza himself, has had a running gun fight with him a couple of hours before and carted him off to the pokey."

"Oh, hell!" said Mendoza. "Hell *and* damnation. So that's why he didn't have an alibi. And *has* he got an alibi? And it wasn't me—I was an innocent bystander. Bert put the collar on him. Do you realize what you've done? The only lead we'd turned up——"

"I can claim him. A heavier charge, like I say. But what I'd like to know," said Goldberg, "is what the hell was Homicide's interest?"

"Two witnesses," said Mendoza. "identified him as our bank robber."

"Fisher?" said Goldberg. "This smalltime hood? Don't kid me, boy. That's wild."

"Well, there's his record—and he pulled a gun . . . You've really nailed him tight for this pawnbroker thing? Damn it. *Un momento*. When was that pulled?"

"About half-past twelve yesterday," said Goldberg, and sneezed. "Pawnbroker was just eating lunch in the back of his shop when the customer came in."

"*¡Diez millón demonios desde infierno!*" said Mendoza violently. "So we're right back where we started!"

"Pity, but these things happen," said Goldberg.

The autopsy report on Carol Coffey arrived at almost the same time as the ballistic report, and Palliser, who'd been about to leave the office, sat down to read both.

After digesting them, he began to realize dimly that he had a little problem on his hands.

The autopsy report said, to paraphrase the technical language, that Carol Coffey had died instantly from a single bullet in the heart. She would not have been capable of movement after the bullet struck; she had died and fallen instantly. That was the gist of it. Carol Coffey, the report added impersonally, if anyone was interested, had been constitutionally a very healthy teen-ager, and *virgo intacta*.

The ballistics report on the bullet which had killed her was also informative. The slug had been recovered virtually undamaged. It had been fired from a Colt Official Police .22 caliber revolver, a practice target gun.

The autopsy report said that it had not been a contact wound; there was no vestige of powder burns. So the shot had been fired from a distance of at least ten feet.

And Palliser had made a little sketch of the room at

the time, of the body's position. And he looked at it again now and realized that they had a little mystery on their hands.

Nice. In all this heat.

CHAPTER FIVE

"John," said Mendoza, "has a little problem."

"He certainly has," said Alison. "Going to have to explain his ancestry to everybody he meets. Whoever heard of anybody named Mendoza having green eyes?"

"I didn't mean our Johnny. Palliser," said Mendoza somnolently. He was lying on the sectional with the Sunday *Times* scattered on the floor beside him and El Señor curled up on his chest. El Señor was half Siamese and half Abyssinian and had turned out, surprisingly, with Siamese markings in reverse like a negative, his blond mask, paws, and tail making him look somewhat like a miniature lion. "He's getting fatter," he added, prodding behind El Señor's ears. "Crack a rib for me some day when he lands on me."

"Palliser?"

Mendoza didn't deign to answer that one. "Of course it's not John's own personal problem. Belongs to all of us. He told me all about it—reason I was on the phone so long. Little teaser of a thing. What you might call a problem in—mmh—space relations." Mendoza reached into his shirt pocket, which was under El Señor's forequarters, and El Señor, disturbed, said, "Yah!" "I made a little sketch. I've been ruminating on it, but damned if I can see the answer."

"You will," said Alison absently. Master John Luis, industriously crawling about the room, discovered Sheba curled up under the coffee table and squealed with pleasure. El Señor sat up and glared around at everybody. When he was taking his morning nap, he wanted peace and quiet. Miss Teresa Ann, taking off after her brother, added her squeals to his. She got a firm grip on Sheba's tail and Sheba hissed and fled.

Ostentatiously El Señor curled up the other way round and draped his blond-tipped tail across Mendoza's face. Mendoza pushed it away and El Señor muttered dark threats. "I thought I'd put it up to you," said Mendoza. "In a kind of way it's a domestic problem."

"I thought you said guided missiles or something." Alison put her book down. The twins had now discovered Bast on the credenza and were playing with her tail; Bast, as a settled older matron, put up with them more patiently than her offspring.

"What? Oh, well, what I probably meant was spatial relations," said Mendoza. Nefertite drifted in, licking her chops, from the direction of the kitchen, and pounced on Sheba who had just resettled herself in the green armchair. They both fell off to the floor and rolled over, feinting at each other.

The twins were entranced. El Señor muttered.

"Well, look," said Mendoza, and Mrs. MacTaggart came bustling in.

"You're not wanting to keep those magazines, *achara?*

The old ones of *Life* and the women's magazines and the fashions and so on?"

"No, I weeded them out the other day and put them in the garage."

"Then he can have them and welcome. It's Mr. Warbeck——"

"Again? He *is* courting you, Máiri. A respectable widower—I wonder if he's got any money?"

"You'll have your joke," said Mrs. MacTaggart indulgently. "It's for his children, he says. He's been telling me all about it—a kind little man he is. It seems he and his wife never had any, but he's all wrapped up, as they say, in this association—it's a volunteer organization of some kind, for needy children. He says it's surprising how many there are that aren't eligible for regular charity for some reason, yet the families can't afford things they'll be needing—special doctoring and so on, even with all the clinics. And orphans in homes, too. They make up special little treats for them, take a personal interest, you see. This association helps the ones like that. A kind man—he goes visiting them, takes them little presents and so on. Would you guess why he comes walking up the hill? There's a little orphan girl in a home downtown, she likes to press flowers—you know, the old-fashioned way—and he comes hunting wild flowers for her. There's poor orphans in the hospitals, too, he says, nobody to come and cheer them up a bit. He wants the old magazines to make scrapbooks for the children."

"Of course he can have them," said Alison. "What a nice little man."

"Indeed he is."

55

"Now don't go falling for him and deserting us!"

Mrs. MacTaggart gave her another indulgent smile, checked with one glance that the twins were behaving reasonably well, and went back to the kitchen.

"You know," said Alison, "that's real charity—real public service, isn't it? His own time and interest. I feel awfully guilty sometimes, *amado*. Just amusing myself—seeing friends—— That reminds me, we must have the Mawsons for dinner, we owe them. I really ought to——"

"So do a little work for a change," said Mendoza. He sat up, holding El Señor with one hand, but this was one disturbance too many for El Señor. To have his choice of Place for Nap suddenly move from under him just as he was finally settled down . . . He said bitterly, "Yow!" and kicked Mendoza hard on the chest as he left him in one spring. He stalked across the room, leaped up on the credenza, and cuffed his mother on the ear. Forgivingly, Bast started to wash him. The twins sat quiet as mice and watched.

"Sometimes they're almost as good as baby sitters," said Alison. "Except that El Señor will keep washing the twins."

"*¡Atención!*" said Mendoza.

"Your domestic problem," said Alison obediently. "Yes."

"Well, it's a funny little thing. This Coffey girl, shot on Friday afternoon. Leave out the fact that it looks odd because it's a nice upright Methodist family, there doesn't seem to be any reason for anybody to want her dead. It's the physical facts that pose a little mystery."

Mendoza lit a cigarette. "Come here and look at this. It's a sketch of the house plan. Palliser——"

"What an inconvenient one," said Alison, sitting beside him. "You have to go through the front bedroom to get to the hall——"

"One of those old places, probably added onto. Probably minus a bathroom to start, and they took the front end of the hall to make one. Never mind. Now, we know what the girl was doing when she was shot—she was dusting in the living room. The dustcloth was under her body, she dropped it as she fell. We know from the autopsy report that she was killed instantly—the only moving she did after the bullet hit her was to fall. So we know where she was standing when she was shot. She was found—by her mother, five or ten minutes later—lying just here." He put an X at the spot. "The living room is ten by fifteen, the long way across the front of the house. There are three doors and three windows in it. One of each on the front, both giving onto the front porch. You go directly into the living room from the porch, and the front door is almost at the end of the front living room wall and almost opposite the door in the rear wall leading to a bedroom."

"Well, what's the point?"

"There are two windows at the side of the living room, and on the inside short wall—just up from the front door—is another door leading to the bedroom occupied by Carol's brother, Verne Coffey. Now, she fell where she died, that we know. And she was lying on her back right here, in this space against the rear living room wall between the door to the bedroom behind the living room and the end of the sofa against the rear wall. So we can even guess what she was doing—or had just been doing—before she was shot. She wasn't dusting the sofa —it's upholstered. The only thing she could have been dusting is a framed picture hanging on the wall in that space, because there's no end table at that end of the sofa. What we don't know is what direction she was facing."

"Oh. She was shot from in front?"

"From directly in front—the way she was facing—and the slug took a very slight upward path. We don't know from how far away, but more than ten feet or so—no powder burns. When she was dusting the picture, she'd have been facing the wall, wouldn't she?"

"I should think so," said Alison.

The twins had discovered the Sunday paper and were making noisy little tunnels out of it, amid chortles of glee.

"But then—well, you see the difficulty. I haven't explained the full beauty of it yet. For one thing, as with most of these old frame houses, the house is well off the ground—those steep wooden steps up to the porch, you know. I'd say the living room and of course the other rooms are a good ten feet from the ground. So in order to get a direct shot through any of the windows, you'd have to be standing on a ladder or something like that. Now, the boys went up and down asking questions, of course. Other than about the family. And——"

"If," said Alison, "the picture is under glass, she could have stepped back and to one side or the other to get the light on the glass, see if it needed washing."

"That doesn't make any difference, *cara*. My first

58

thought was a sniper in a car. That would account at least partly for the height and the oblique upward path. But it was a hot afternoon and most of those old houses are like ovens—a number of people were out on their porches. It's a quiet side street, and we've got half a dozen witnesses that no car had passed for at least twenty minutes. The Coffey house is quite close to the houses on either side—those are narrow lots, you know—and the woman on the left side was out at that side of her house. In fact, she'd been talking to Mrs. Coffey across the hedge only a few minutes before. The people on the other side weren't home, but there were at least four people sitting on their porches across the street, who'd have seen anybody strange—or anybody at all, come to that—either in front of the Coffey house or at that side. Got that? So tell me what direction she was shot from?"

Alison studied the sketch. "That *is* a little funny," she said. "I don't see how it's possible at all. You've got all the directions covered by witnesses. If she was on her back—if she just fell backward when she was shot—that says she must have been standing sideways to that bedroom door, just *past* where the picture is, and——" She stopped.

"Yes," said Mendoza. "More or less facing the door to her brother's bedroom about six or seven feet away."

"But you said they're a nice upright family. What possible reason could the boy have?"

"¿Quién sabe? And even more to the point, how the hell could he have got rid of the gun? He says his door was closed, but it could have been open. He could have shot her from inside his room, which would make up the distance to ten feet. But what about the gun? If he im-

59

mediately passed it to some accomplice outside his bedroom window, that'd have been seen from across the
street. *Although*," said Mendoza suddenly, "there is
a tallish hedge around the Coffey yard, and just
maybe—— All right. She wasn't shot from the front
door or the porch window, because those people across
the street would have seen it. She wasn't shot from the
two side windows of the living room because Mrs. Rob-
inson was out there in her side yard, not twenty feet
away—and quite possibly also Mrs. Coffey, who was cutting roses and came around there from her back yard.
But on the other hand, Mrs. Coffey says she wasn't in
her side yard more than two or three minutes—they
didn't have a long gossip over the hedge, just 'Hello'
and 'Isn't it hot?' So there wouldn't have been time—
and it's the longest chance anyway—for somebody to
have come into the back yard and shot her through the
rear window of that bedroom which is exactly opposite
the doorway to the living room, where she might have
been standing looking into the bedroom."

"Then I don't see——"

"What it comes down to," said Mendoza, "unless all
the neighbors are in a conspiracy, which seems unlikely,
is that Carol could have been shot, inside the house, by
her brother from his bedroom—or she could have been
shot by her mother from that rear window. Only what
the hell happened to the gun?"

"But that seems fantastic. You said they're perfectly
nice, respectable people. What reason——"

"I'll say this. It seems just slightly less fantastic that it
was the brother. If Mrs. Coffey shot her daughter, the
stage has lost a second Sarah Bernhardt. But Verne——"

"Luis. They could have moved the body. Just not thinking, not realizing she was dead."

"They say not, and the ambulance boys said not."

"Oh."

"We'll take a long, hard look at Verne, anyway. You never do know. But how the hell could he have got rid of the gun? Search? Sure as hell we searched the place. We're not such innocents as to take stories at face value. The house was searched, and the yard was searched. No gun."

"Did you look under the house?" asked Alison.

Mendoza stared at her. "*Under* the house? There's no basement."

"Don't tell me I've found something you don't know. Of course, you haven't been a householder long. No, my darling, few California houses have basements, but they do have foundations. And there has to be a space between the foundation and the floor for pipes and things like that. And there'll either be a couple of trap doors in bedroom closets as access or a trap door outside, and in very old houses like that it's usually trap doors in bedroom closets."

"*¡Dios mio!*" Mendoza smote himself on the forehead. "Either I'm getting old or marriage is unsettling my mind. My God, I once found a corpse under a house too. And so we look, and there's no gun, that doesn't say there wasn't one on Friday. My God." He got up. He tripped over Master John who shot between his legs after Sheba; he clutched at the coffee table to save himself and shoved it hard against Miss Teresa's upended rump. Terry shrieked, Johnny grabbed Sheba's tail, Sheba spat, and Mendoza said, "I was out of my mind—voluntarily giving up the gay life of a bachelor!" He clutched his shin, which had come in violent contact with the table. "This place is a madhouse. I'm going down to the office."

He went down the hall to the bedroom after a tie and his jacket and disturbed El Señor who was napping on the bureau top. El Señor hissed at him.

"A madhouse," said Mendoza. "*¡Ésta no tiene remedio!*"

He found the office empty except for Sergeant Lake who was having Sunday duty this month. Lake told him that Higgins was out getting some additional statements on that gang rumble; the kids charged would be coming up for indictment some time this week. Dwyer had got a vague sort of lead from a stool pigeon on that San Pedro Street shooting and gone out to see what was in it. He didn't know where Palliser was.

"That thing," said Mendoza. "Ley—Lee—Leigh, with an i-g-h, wasn't it? Walter William Leigh. No pedigree with us, anyway. Drifted down to Skid Row the last few years—panhandling for half a buck for a gallon of cheap *vino*. Anybody could have cooled him."

"Yeah, but you remember there was some evidence that he'd been in the money a few days before. Looked a little funny."

"I'll tell you, Jimmy, I don't care one hell of a lot who shot Walter William. God knows he wasn't much loss. I would very much like to know who killed Carol Coffey. Is anybody here at all?"

"Galeano was in a minute ago. I suppose Palliser'll be in some time."

There was, of course, no vital urgency now about looking under the Coffey house. Though you never knew—people did stupid things; if Verne had shot his sister and then dropped the gun down a convenient trap door, he might just have left it there. Some time today they would look.

The lab report was in on the Walsh thing. The lab boys hadn't found anything extraneous in the garage: no nice fresh beach sand, or grains of flour, or quarry dust—or footprints in oil, or of course any strange fingerprints. Well, there were a lot of fingerprints in both the rest rooms, which opened off the garage, which didn't belong to the owner, the mechanic, or Jimmy Walsh; but that was only natural.

Mendoza sighed. Tomorrow somebody would have to appear in court when that child-beater came up to be indicted. Either Dwyer or himself—they'd both been on that. People—they sure as hell came all sorts. Beating a six-month-old baby because the baby cried. Beating the baby to death. The baby's father, saying sullenly, "I gotta get my sleep, ain't I? Working man like me, I work hard, I get tired. I just sort of slapped her, 's all. Didn't go to hurt her none."

People.

Omar Khayyam, he thought.

> Impotent pieces of the Game He plays,
> Upon the Chequer-board of Nights and Days;
> Hither and thither moves, and checks, and slays,
> And one by one back in the Closet lays.

At random? Sometimes, in his job, he couldn't help thinking so. But any cop had enough to think about without thinking about philosophies.

Palliser came in and said hello absently. "Jimmy said you were here." His long dark face with the heavy eyebrows and mobile mouth wore a look of abstraction. He said, "You going to the hospital today?"

"No, Alison's going with Angel—Angel'll leave Mark at our place. Look, I've just had a thought—or to be honest with you, it was Alison's idea—the———"

"I thought I'd go see Art," said Palliser. He felt in his pocket, brought out an envelope, looked at it, and said, "Oh, damn. I meant to take that little thing up to the lab, see what they can make of it. I got sidetracked. I wonder how much it means."

"What?"

"Well, I asked Walsh who were Jimmy's closest friends and if he'd been going with any girl and so on. Those poor damned people. An only son. Why the *hell* things like this have to happen———" Palliser was silent, fumbled in his pocket again, and found a pack of cigarettes. "So I went to see a couple of the boys, and I heard the same story from both of them. You know I said yesterday it could have been a private kill. And del Valle—when I checked back with him just now—said he thought the guy he'd seen leaving the garage was somewhere around thirty. He's a pretty good witness. Good on details."

"Yes? What was the story?"

"Both the boys—Eddy Beckwith and Howard Thompson—said that Jimmy had been pretty interested in a girl named Diane Rush. They were all in high school together, Jimmy'd known her since then. They said he was serious about her. Said Diane was kind of the flighty type and dated a lot of boys, and just lately she's

64

been going out with an older guy, a fellow about thirty she met on her job—she's a waitress at The Nest, which is a fairly fancy place. They said Jimmy had 'sort of' thought of Diane as being engaged to him and had raised quite a fuss about this. They also said that probably Jimmy's parents wouldn't know about that because they didn't approve of Diane and Jimmy wouldn't have told them."

"Mmh," said Mendoza. "Diane the flighty type. Evidently the older guy—*Dios*, it does depend where you sit how you use these terms, thirty, my God—was doing all right with Diane, and Jimmy on the short end of the stick. So why should the other fellow shoot Jimmy?"

"God knows," said Palliser. "I just wonder if it means anything, that's all. All they could tell me was the fellow's first name is Humphrey."

"Come on," said Mendoza. "Let's go look under a house."

CHAPTER SIX

Dwyer came in just as they were leaving, so they took him with them. "I don't know, but it doesn't look as if there's much in it," he said in the elevator. "I got the word from Tommy—you know that one." Mendoza nodded: a part-time Skid Row bum who on occasion turned pigeon. "He said this Walter Leigh had been acting a little funny about two, three weeks before he got it. Dropping hints that he was going to be in the money—and he'd been going to see certain people, like a bartender at some joint down there who, rumor says, can fix you up with anything from an abortion to a collection of feelthy pictures. I saw the bartender. I wouldn't doubt the rumor, by his looks, but there's nothing on him, and of course he never laid eyes on Leigh, according to him."

"Small loss," said Mendoza. "At the moment I'm more interested in Carol Coffey."

When they got to the Coffey house the boy Verne opened the door to them. He was not as easy and forthcoming with them as his mother; maybe he'd swallowed some of his father's uneasiness about cops. He said his mom and dad were at the funeral parlor—"you know, making arrangements."

"Yes," said Mendoza. "Now, we haven't got a search warrant, Verne, but we'd like to look around here a little. Do you think your parents would mind, or is that O.K.?."

Verne shrugged. "Who's to stop you? You're the cops."

"Well, we don't like to play rough unless we have to. John, suppose you and Bert have a look. I'd like to ask Verne a few more questions." He sat down on the sofa. He saw that all the chalk marks had been scrubbed out, where the body had lain, but there were other stains that would be harder to clean. "Sit down, Verne."

"I'm all right here. I was—was goin' over to see Benny pretty soon, anyways. We got a sort of date." The boy was nervous. Just because he didn't like cops?

"Has there been any trouble in the family lately, Verne?"

"I don't know what you mean. We never have n—any trouble. You mean like fights?"

"Just anything. Maybe Carol staying out too late and your dad being mad? Or you staying out too late? Or some new boy friend of Carol's your parents didn't like?"

Verne shook his head. He was a big boy for his age; he'd be as big a man as his father when he filled out. "There was never n—anything like that," he said. "You got any idea who did it yet? It was so sudden—and there wasn't n—any reason, anybody kill Carol."

"We don't know yet," said Mendoza, watching him. "Did you love your sister, Verne?"

"She was my sister," said the boy. He looked a little embarrassed; maybe in this upright Methodist home the emotions were considered a little embarrassing to discuss. "Sure, Carol was O.K. Sometimes—sometimes she was a little bossy, but I guess—sisters——"

"You ever have any quarrels with her?"

"Why? That d-doesn't matter now . . . I don't know nothing about this, why you're asking——"

"Did you?"

Verne swallowed and rubbed his hands along his jeans. "I—I guess so, sometimes. When we were littler. Nothing serious. Why? Listen, I really don't know nothing at all about it. It's just an awful thing to happen, and sure, I'm awful sorry and all, but how would *I* know anything? And I've got a date—sort of—to meet Benny. Can I go?"

Mendoza looked at him meditatively. Sam Coffey was undoubtedly scared of cops—any cops. Mrs. Coffey, who had lived here all her life, knew there were cops and cops; but maybe the boy had naturally taken his dad's word before hers. Maybe that was the only reason for his nervousness. He said, "Don't you think you ought to stay while we're here? You don't think your parents would mind your—mmh—leaving us in possession?"

"What's to mind? Mom seems to think you're all heroes—and what could they do, anyways? You're trying to find who did it—I guess."

"We're trying, Verne."

"Yeah. I was s'prised see you," said the boy suddenly.

68

"Why?"

"Oh—well—I dunno. I guess you just naturally figure, you guys aren't going to lay yourselves out over—somebody like Carol."

"Why not?"

"Oh—you know—because."

"Because why?"

"You know."

"Anybody who gets murdered in this county," said Mendoza, "we want to know who did it. That's damn foolish thinking, Verne. Did your sister have any trouble getting into college? Has anybody ever tried to keep you out of school? Pushed you around? Stopped your father from getting a job? Don't take any bets we won't be in there pitching until we find out all about this."

"Can I go?"

"You can go." The boy went without another word, slamming the front door after him. Mendoza looked after him thoughtfully. This was a very opposite response to the one they'd had from Mrs. Coffey. Just the husband's fault? Palliser said nervous, very nervous of cops—on Friday, too much upset and shocked to show it much, but it was there. And so the boy was surprised to see them back. Hadn't thought they'd bother much about Carol's murder. That was interesting.

He went into the boy's bedroom. Evidently Alison's little suggestion had paid off: neither Palliser nor Dwyer was there, but there were ghostly noises from under the house. The room was about eight by nine, very neat and clean; it held the cot-bed, the cheap chest of drawers, a small plastic-topped desk, and a straight chair. There was a small rag rug on the floor and a narrow door in the front corner of the room. It was open. Mendoza looked inside.

A small walk-in closet. It was sparsely filled with clothes. At the far end a shoe rack had been moved and a square trap door lifted up. Mendoza knelt down alongside it. "You finding anything?" he called down. He remembered the time he'd found the corpse under the pink stucco apartment house. A case with a lot more class than this, he thought.

"Give us time!" Dwyer's voice sounded muffled. "Lot of space down here." Mendoza caught the reflections from their flashlights.

He got up and went across to the front bedroom. Probably Mr. and Mrs. Coffey's room. It was also very neat and clean, and it also had a walk-in closet. And the closet also had a trap door in the floor.

He went from there into the hall, looked into a small bathroom with chipped plastic tile in bright pink, went into the spotless kitchen. The third bedroom—it was an odd house plan—opened off the kitchen, between that and Verne's bedroom, but had only the one door into the kitchen. Carol's room. Starched white curtains, a white bedspread on the twin-sized bed, a dressing table with a white organdy skirt. A rag rug on the floor. A walk-in closet, minus any trap door.

He came back to the living room just as Palliser stepped out of Verne's room. He looked hot, dirty, and disgusted. "What a hell of a place to chase us on a day like this! I'll bet it's ten degrees hotter down there. And no gun. Bert's still looking, but it's not there. For one thing, if the kid did drop it through that trap door, it'd have been somewhere right underneath—it wouldn't grow wings and move twenty feet back under the kitchen or——"

"*De veras*. Well, that doesn't tell us it wasn't there once. Bert might as well come up."

"*Cobwebs!*" said Palliser. He was still brushing at his suit. "Maybe I had a traumatic shock at three years old or something, but I've always had a horror of cobwebs. And the dust and dirt down there——"

"It's an old house," said Mendoza. He went into Verne's closet and shouted down to Dwyer to come up. The doorbell rang.

He heard Palliser's voice at the door and came out to find a pretty girl holding a large round Mexican-clay casserole on a tray before her and looking somewhat confused. The girl was nearly half-white and very pretty indeed, and she was looking confused, he thought, not solely because Palliser had opened the door instead of one of the Coffeys, but because she had on only shorts and a bra.

"Oh!" she said. "I just—where's Mrs. Coffey? I'm—— I met you on Friday. You were——"

"That's right, Miss Webb. Sergeant Palliser. We're just having another look around. Mr. and Mrs. Coffey are at the funeral parlor."

"Oh," she said. "Isn't anybody here? I mean——"

"Verne went off to see a friend of his," said Mendoza. "Someone called Benny. Would you know who that is?"

"I guess—most likely, Benny Lincoln. Over on the next block."

"Lieutenant Mendoza," said Palliser. "Miss Nancy Webb. She knew Carol very well."

"H-how do you do. Have you found who did it yet? I just can't get *over* it," said Nancy Webb. "It just seems impossible. Carol murdered! Please, do you mind if I come in and leave this? It's Beef Stroganov, and it's hot. I'd like to——"

"Certainly," said Mendoza. She seemed to know the house; she went straight back to the kitchen, looked in the right drawer for a hot pad, and set the casserole on it on the drainboard. The yellow rose had disappeared from the table. "You knew Carol well, Miss Webb?"

"I knew her all her *life!* Why, we started out Sunday School together when we were four." Tears stood in her eyes. "I never knew anybody nicer than Carol. Kinder. She was a really good person."

"You might describe yourself as her best friend?"

"Yes, I think I was."

"Well, I'd like to ask you . . ." Mendoza hesitated. He smiled at her. "Just take it that we have to ask all sorts of questions, Miss Webb. With our nasty suspicious minds. It doesn't really imply anything. But I think you know this household well—and you would know most of what Carol was thinking and feeling, what was happening to her."

"I guess so. Yes, we were back and forth a lot, double-dated sometimes. You see, our families have lived on this block a lot longer than some others, since Carol and I were just babies. Of course, since she was going to college we didn't see each other quite so much—I went to secretarial school, I'm a stenographer at Knott, Wiley

72

and Conger—they're lawyers. Over on Washington Boulevard. What d'you want to *ask?*" She looked at him curiously.

"Was there any sort of family trouble here lately?" he asked, purposefully vague. "Any really serious argument, or——"

"Oh," said Nancy Webb in a dropped voice. "Oh. You mean about Verne?"

"That's right," said Mendoza coolly.

"Well—I don't know that I'd best tell you about that. I mean, it's a private family thing—Carol only told me because it upset her—and besides, well, excuse me, but what business is it of yours? It's not as if it had anything to do with——" Her eyes widened incredulously on him, and he wondered why on earth this girl wasn't trying out for T.V. parts as Lola Rodriguez or Maria Alfonso and decided she was too honest and nice a girl. "But you're not *thinking*—— Why, that's impossible! Just——" She made a helpless gesture. "If you knew the Coffeys! It's——"

"But I don't, Miss Webb. We have to look everywhere, and naturally we look in a lot of wrong directions. We have to look at everything. To be sure when we find out the truth. You see? So I'd like to hear about Verne."

She looked at him carefully, in silence, for a while. Then she said unexpectedly, "I used to be crazy about *Dragnet.* It surely made out you're a real crack police force."

"Well, we are," said Mendoza. "Highest requirements for rookies of any force in the world."

"Honestly? A cousin of mine got turned down at Headquarters. Because he didn't have twenty-twenty vision. He joined the Santa Monica force instead." She was silent again and then said, "Look, it was silly. It wasn't anything much. I mean, we go to church, too, and —and so on, but Mother and Daddy aren't as strict as the Coffeys are about some things. Not as if they *drink*, but a glass of wine on Christmas and birthdays—like that, you know. But Mr. and Mrs. Coffey are really death on it. And—what it was, you see—about two weeks ago Verne didn't come home at the usual time for dinner, so Carol went looking for him. And—well, look, Lieutenant, kids like that, it sounds exciting to them. Goodness, you know as well as I do, in *some* neighborhoods down here, by the time kids are twelve or fourteen they've done *everything*—the real slums. But kids like Verne, that've been pretty well brought up——"

"So what was he up to?"

"Well, he and Benny Lincoln and Marvin Cross had got a half gallon of cheap wine from an old fellow over on Main, and they were sitting behind a billboard on that vacant lot down the block. I don't know if they were really—you know—high, maybe so. Probably the first time Verne, anyway, had ever tasted it. But Carol— brought up the way she was—she was just horrified. I mean, I don't want you to think I approve of people getting drunk, because I don't. Naturally. But I'm not a *fanatic* about it. It was the kind of trick kids that age do."

"So what happened?"

"Well, I don't really know. Carol just told me that and that she 'gave him an earful,' that's how she said it, and

74

made him come home. I expect she told the Coffeys, or anyway, if Verne was tight, they'd have seen it."

"Yes. Was he punished in any way?"

"I don't know. Really. And really, Lieutenant, to think that *that* could have anything to do—— Please, don't think that. They're really awfully nice people, after all," she said earnestly.

"Well, we like to think we're smart enough to tell good from bad," said Mendoza. "Thanks very much, Miss Webb."

"Because it must have been a—a nut of some kind. Who *did* it. Just wandering around. Because nobody could have any *reason* to kill Carol——"

"We'll find out," said Mendoza.

They waited for the Coffeys to come home. They asked questions and met unexpected resistance from both of them. Unexpected because Mrs. Coffey had been very co-operative before, and because Sam Coffey was very leery of the boys in blue and before had been inclined to fawn a little on them, sycophantic.

"I don't think that's any of your business, Lieutenant," said Mrs. Coffey. She looked very tired and she'd been crying. "It's nothing to do with what happened to Carol, and it's a—a private family matter, how we raise our children. How we believe in raising children."

"I realize that may be how it looks to you, Mrs. Coffey," said Mendoza gently. "But we have to look at everything that had happened to her lately, how she'd been feeling and thinking. And——"

"That didn't happen to Carol, it happened to Verne," said Coffey. "It happened to him good!"

He was a big man, a broad man, deep brown; his son looked more like him than like the mother. He had a deep bass voice and a Deep South accent.

"Did you punish him, Mr. Coffey?" asked Mendoza.

"That makes no never mind to you, Officer," said Coffey. "He's my boy—I raise him way I think right. Wine is a mocker and strong drink is raging. I just try raise my children in the right way."

"Yes, sir," said Dwyer. "Did you punish him?"

Coffey looked very confused for a moment; Mendoza thought that *sir* had stopped him dead in his tracks. "That don't matter now," he said. "Boy do somethin' wrong, he got to expect punishment. Why you askin' about that? It ain't nothing to do with Carol. My little Carol laying there dead." Tears sprang to his eyes, coursed down his cheeks; he did not lift a hand to brush them away. "My little girl, never did nobody no harm all her life, just sweet and kind—an' some basser come along an' shoot her—— It don't make no sense! Nothin' don't make no sense!" A deep wrenching sob shook his big frame.

"Sam," said the woman quietly. "Sam, it's just God's will."

"An' God's will don't make no sense either! Oh, the Lord forgive me, I don't mean be a blasphemer—I know that, Amy—but—but——" He stood silent, with bowed head.

Mendoza turned to her. "Verne was punished, Mrs. Coffey?"

76

She didn't answer and then said woodenly, "It's a private family thing, sir. I'm sorry, but I don't see what——"

Coffey raised his head. "The boy got what he deserved," he said dully. "Have to raise children right. They stray off the way you show 'em, you got to chastise them. My wife, she said I was too hard, but you got to be strict with children, they start going wrong. I whupped the boy good, I did."

"Sam——"

"I see," said Mendoza.

"You see, you see!" shouted Coffey. "What you see, white man? I told 'em—I tell my children—we got to set an example! Let the white man see we ain't needfully lazy drunken niggers—don't I know how you all think——"

"Sam!" said the woman.

And the savagery died from the big man's eyes, and fear came there, and he said in a mumbling voice, "Oh, now, I'm sorry, sir. Nevah meant offend you, sir. I guess the shock kinda unhinged my mind——"

Mendoza opened his mouth and shut it. There was nothing he could say to this man: this man, with provocation enough, who had built an Enemy in his mind and perhaps would never wholly believe that some of the Enemy were men of good will, regardless of color. This man who, resenting authority, automatically assumed that authority was venal and would seek vengeance for words—mere words.

Sticks and stones, he thought. Words could be dangerous things. In the wrong mouths.

77

He said evenly, "Thanks very much, Mr. Coffey. That's all right now."

They went out.

"What do you think?" he asked Dwyer. They got into the big black Ferrari. The Ferrari had attracted all the little boys in the neighborhood, who were lined up, staring.

"I think it's possible," said Dwyer. "Not that I exactly approve of seventeen-year-olds getting drunk on cheap wine, or anything else—but it's an age where they're naturally experimenting with the grown-up things. And me, I'm all for morality and going to church and so on, but a set of parents who weren't quite so strict about it would have understood better, handled it more sensibly. When will they learn that that kind of thing usually just turns the kids in the opposite direction?"

"You find your boy with a half gallon of cheap *vino* and just lecture him?" asked Palliser.

"Steve's only ten," said Dwyer. "Hell, no, I'd take him down to the emergency hospital and show him some of the results. But I can see that kid Verne feeling resentful of his sister. Who told on him. After all, Papa's still the boss—until the kid gets a little older, anyway—so I can see the resentment centering on stool-pigeon Carol. Who found him and hauled him home tight." He ruminated. "The gun could have been dropped down there and then hidden somewhere else after we left on Friday."

"Or given back to whoever he borrowed it from," said Palliser.

"All right, let's find it," said Mendoza mildly.

"See all his friends." Dwyer sighed. "Ask around. God,

in this heat. Why do all the tough ones come in hot weather?"

"Law of nature," said Palliser.

"Let's just hope our bank robber doesn't pull another one this week," said Mendoza.

"And I hope to God," said Palliser, "the D.M.V. gets that list out by tomorrow or Tuesday—— A nineteen-year-old kid——"

"Two nineteen-year-old kids," said Mendoza, and they were silent.

CHAPTER SEVEN

The Fisher thing, negative as it looked, was helpful in a way. They had not attempted before to use an artist and/or the Identikit, in trying for a possible sketch of the loner, because all the witnesses they had were too vague on details. Now, when two of them had, if hesitantly, picked out Fisher's picture, they knew at least that the loner must look a little like him.

Wolf, their private-eye witness, hadn't been in on the parade of witnesses who were taken to look at Fisher—that had been before Goldberg had pitched his little bombshell. Seeing Fisher in person, Mrs. Thomas had said no, Clark had said not sure, and nobody else had had much to say at all, but then nobody had had a really good look at the loner.

Wolf had been off on a job; Mendoza got hold of him first thing Monday morning and haled him up to his office. Mendoza had a little idea about all this. Maybe not one that would pay off, but sometimes you never knew what would pay off.

He had Fisher's mug shots, full-face and profile, on his desk; he passed them over to Wolf. "How much does he look like our X?"

Wolf smiled. He was a lean, rangy fellow, very dark, with a good deep voice. "This is the guy the two tellers picked out? Bad luck, Lieutenant. Well . . ." He discarded the full-face shot and looked at the profile. "It's not him, of course. Not the same profile. I only saw him in profile, you know, and the boy you want has a nice straight nose and not so much jaw as this bird here. But it is something like him."

"Yes. Well, I'd like to try to get out a sketch," said Mendoza. "If possible. We know now he looks something like Fisher, and with you adding what details you can, we might get a fairly good one. Frankly, I'd rather rely on what you remember than the rest of them—trained observer." Wolf was an operative with a big firm which had a good reputation, and he was an experienced man. "I realize it's a gamble. Pity you didn't see him full face. But we might get *something*."

"I don't know—do my best for you, but—— For reproduction in the papers, you mean?"

"No, we probably couldn't come close enough for that. How many thousand men of that general type are walking around? No, my idea was to pass the sketches to every bank guard—in the general downtown area to start with. A good many of them are retired cops, and most of them are pretty good men, in an unobtrusive sort of way. If one of them spots somebody resembling the sketch, he can walk, not run, to the nearest phone, we send over the nearest squad car, and—well, it'd give us a hell of a lot better chance, even if we wound up accosting a few innocent citizens first."

"I see that. Well, do my best."

"Such as it is?" Mendoza smiled. "I'm putting a lot of

81

faith in your experience, Mr. Wolf. Your trained eye. You gave us a couple of things nobody else noticed at all, and I just hope the trained eye wasn't taking a few minutes off and all the other witnesses aren't right after all."

Wolf looked interested. "Where did I stray off the rails?"

"Everybody else says a suit. On every job. We've got a whole range of colors to choose from, black to light brown, but you know eyewitness accounts as well as I do. All the tellers and one guard say a gray suit. But you said he had on a gray corduroy jacket and gray slacks."

"That's right," said Wolf. "I'll swear to that. The jacket was the first thing I noticed about him. Because it *was* corduroy—on a day as hot as that. What else did I notice nobody else did?"

"You said he put the paper bag full of bills into his *outside* pocket. Where the tellers said anything at all about that, they said the inside pocket."

"Sure of that, too," said Wolf comfortably. "I was only about three feet away, you know, at the next window to his right. Nobody else but me knew what was happening. He was alone at the chief teller's window and he held the gun close to him, in front. The girl at my window was typing up my money order, with her back turned. I spotted the gun, and so I looked him over carefully. With just this in mind. And when the teller handed over the bag, he took it with his right hand and all in a hurry shoved it way down in the outside jacket pocket. Another reason I know it was a sports jacket—the ordinary suit jacket wouldn't take a parcel that large, but you know the big patch pockets they put on sports jackets."

82

"I'll take your word," said Mendoza. "But I hope you're as good as I think you are." Wolf laughed. "So, we'll get an artist up here, and he might like to try using an Identikit, too—and you feed him whatever you have."

"O.K. by me," said Wolf. "I only hope we can come up with something reasonably good."

Mendoza saw him settled down with the police artist, in one of the interrogation rooms; they'd probably have a long, long session. And come up with anything bearing the remotest resemblance to their boy? God only knew.

Palliser and Higgins had both left reports on his desk. They had both gone calling again on Carol Coffey's boy friends. Dick Watkins had said he and Carol had got along fine, had discussed marriage, "but not seriously," because they were both interested in getting an education first. He was a second-year law student at L.A.C.C. Eddy Loman had said he'd only dated her a few times; she was a nice girl but damn strait-laced, and he hadn't felt this way or that way about her—just another girl. And why anybody'd want to shoot her, he couldn't imagine.

But Glen Kingsley, who had told Palliser he was probably at Lee's pool hall about the time Carol was shot, couldn't be placed there. Maybe he was, maybe not, said the proprietor; he'd had quite a crowd in that afternoon and he just couldn't say.

But how in hell could Kingsley—even if he'd wanted to—have shot Carol? With neighbors covering the front and both sides of the house, and Mrs. Coffey out in back? Mendoza sighed. He'd never believed there were such things as Locked Room Mysteries in real life, and he didn't feel like getting credulous at his age. He thought he'd buy Verne for it. Verne, resentful of what he might regard as Carol's holier-than-thou attitude, acquiring a gun somewhere and shooting her. And where was the somewhere?

And on the other hand, the boy wasn't stupid by any means, so why do it in such a damn-fool way? With his mother not thirty feet away, neighbors all around to say nobody had approached the house?

Where could he have got a gun? Palliser now was out with Dwyer questioning all Verne's friends. He might have said something; one of them might have helped him get a gun. How? Crooked pawnbrokers—they tried to keep a check on them, but in a city this size . . . And then again, it looked as if money was tight in that household. Where would Verne have got the cash to buy a gun?

And also, if Verne really thought that the cops wouldn't bother much about a little colored girl shot, he just might have done it that way.

The D.M.V. (and he could almost hear the names those clerks in Sacramento were calling Palliser) had made a start on that list of Anglia De Luxes with plates starting out HAH. At Palliser's suggestion they were starting out with Los Angeles County. The list wasn't very long yet, but it was growing. And what the hell of a list to check once they had it. Short cut, set Jimmy to phoning all the owners—we're taking a poll of preferred colors for automobiles?

Had this Walsh thing been a private kill? Mendoza thought he'd go out and see some of the people in it, find out what it smelled like.

84

He put the reports tidily away, brushed ash and tobacco off the desk, emptied the ash tray, lined up the desk box with the blotter. There was a small folded envelope on the blotter; he frowned at it and picked it up.

Palliser's little metal clue out of the Walsh boy's head wound. He'd left it here, all absent-minded; it ought to be up at the lab. Well, it was damned hot weather and they were being run off their legs; a little absent-mindedness could be forgiven.

Mendoza put it in his pocket and went out to see Mr. and Mrs. Walsh.

When he dropped back to the office at twelve-thirty he found Wolf just emerging from seclusion with the artist. They both looked tired and irritated. "Well, we got sketches," said the artist. "Your guess is as good as mine how accurate they are."

"Let's see." Mendoza studied them interestedly.

The first sketch showed the head and shoulders of a man who looked to be in the middle fifties. He had a roundish face with a suggestion of jowls, and a good straight nose, not too prominent, and a straight mouth a little small for the rest of the face. The man was smiling slightly. There were four sketches; the first showed the man wearing a soft felt hat pulled down over his eyes. The second showed him hatless, and he looked like another man, with a dome of a bald head above a high forehead. The third showed him in profile—"That's a good likeness, I'm sure of that," said Wolf—with the hat on, and the fourth showed him in profile hatless. He had small ears, the lobe joined to the cheek.

The artist said gloomily, "Of course we can't guess at

the shape of his head. You see some funny ones, and it makes a hell of a lot of difference."

"The profile is good," insisted Wolf. "It's O.K."

"If you say so," said the artist, shrugging. "So what do we do with them, Lieutenant?"

"I want copies run off—make it a couple of hundred to start with. Oh, hell, I suppose the Feds'll be offended if they don't get some—make that two hundred and fifty. Then we pass them out to all the bank guards in the downtown area and also the vice-presidents and stock advisers—you know, the fellows who are sitting around waiting to arrange loans and so on—they generally have a good open view of the whole bank. And we wait for somebody to spot X. On his next call."

"O.K.," said the artist. "I'll set it up. Probably get them out for you"—he looked at his watch—"by four-thirty, five."

"Good. You two have had quite a morning," said Mendoza, surveying them. "Suppose," he said to the artist, "you set this up and meet us in the lot in ten minutes. I'll buy you lunch, and I might even run to a drink beforehand."

"You've got a deal," said Wolf and the artist simultaneously.

Back in July, Art Hackett had got himself assaulted. He'd been sent off a cliff in his car, and everybody had been surprised he hadn't been killed. He had a broken pelvis, a lot of things broken, and a severe skull fracture, and for a while there it had looked as if Art Hackett wasn't going to make it.

But he was a big man and a tough man, and he had a

good deal to live for, including a wife named Angel and a son named Mark and another baby due in December. And he had made it. Just a question of time now, said the doctors; and at this stage of the game Hackett was getting very damned sick and tired of that phrase.

He was sitting up in the hospital bed when Mendoza came in that afternoon, looking even bigger than he was in white nylon pajamas, a big broad sandy man dispiritedly leafing through the new *Reader's Digest*. "How do I feel?" he echoed bitterly. "I feel fine, Luis. I want to go home. They won't let me out. I tell you, I'm going nuts. I'm tired of reading, and there's nothing on T.V. I can get around on crutches, and at least at home I'd have a different view out the window. *And* Angel's cooking. Damn it, I know I'm spoiled, but the *meals* here—if you can call them that! I walked down the hall this morning and weighed myself—I'm down to a hundred and ninety."

"Well, congratulations," said Mendoza. "You can forget about dieting for a while."

"Damn right," said Hackett with a sigh. "When I get home . . . And they say I can't go back on the job until November fifteenth. Hell, as soon as I can get rid of these crutches I'll be O.K. And get some decent food in me." He moved restlessly. "I understand you're being kept busy. These bank jobs—hell of a thing."

"And other things. You're jittering to get back to the rat race, Arturo?"

"Oh, I know," said Hackett. "When you're on the job, it gets you down sometimes. John's upset as hell about this Walsh kid, and I know how he feels. But it is the job, and if you're a cop——"

87

"So all right, do some armchair detecting," said Mendoza. He sat down beside the bed, gave Hackett a cigarette, and told him about Carol Coffey, produced a sketch of the house and yard. Hackett frowned at it.

"Now that is the hell of a funny little thing, isn't it? I'm with you. I can't see any answer but the boy, but if you can't tie him up with the gun, you'll never get him. And you said he's a well-brought-up boy, respectable family—would he know where and how to get a gun?"

"Mmh," said Mendoza. "Neighborhoods—overlap, down there. He's probably going to school with a few j.d.'s, even if they aren't pals of his."

"Yes, but even so—— Is that enough motive? Don't answer that," said Hackett wryly. "I know the stock answer—what motive is enough, it depends who has it. You'd better be lucky in tying Verne up to the gun."

"And if so," said Mendoza, "what a hell of a shock to the parents . . . The job. Why the hell are we doing this dirty thankless job, boy? Dealing with the dregs of things? The muck at the bottom of the human pool? I sometimes wonder."

Hackett smiled. "You remember what Lockhart said? That good cops are like good sheep dogs, they just come equipped with the urge."

Mendoza laughed. "He's right about a lot of things . . . They've got a new grandson." He smiled, thinking of Lockhart; if it hadn't been for Lockhart, a while back, Alison wouldn't be waiting for him in the house on Rayo Grande Avenue, or a lively pair of twins.

"Good," said Hackett absently.

Mendoza reached into his pocket for his cigarettes and brought out instead the envelope with Palliser's mysterious little metal bit. On impulse he dumped it out into his palm and looked at it. What the hell was it? Something almost on the tip of his tongue . . .

"Art?"

"Hum?" Hackett was still studying the sketch of the Coffey house.

"What is this?"

Hackett looked up and Mendoza laid the little thing in his hand. Hackett looked at it casually and said, "Bit off the trigger guard of a gun. Revolver most likely."

"¡*Válgame Dios! ¡Naturalmente—ya lo creo! ¡Vaya con el mozo! ¿Sabe una cosa?*—you know what? You're a very, very smart cop, my Arturo, and all the rest of us have been blind! *Adiós*—I've got work to do!" He snatched up his hat and fled.

Hackett stared after him.

It was no trouble for the Ballistics man to identify the gun. "If you'd brought this thing to us in the first place, anybody up here could have told you——"

"We acknowledge our sins," said Mendoza.

Palliser was still muttering, "But I should have *seen* it —am I going blind? Of *course* it's part of a trigger guard——"

The Ballistics man was studying it interestedly. "Just have to look in our books," he said. "Shouldn't be too difficult—you don't often get a guard that isn't completely round. That little point on the outside edge—if you'll just give me a few minutes . . ." He went away.

Four minutes later he came back and said, "It's that J. C. Higgins Hi-Standard .22 nine-shot revolver. Comes in either a four-inch or six-inch barrel."

"Oh, *hell!*" said Palliser. "That's the brand Sears, Roebuck sells, isn't it? My God, anybody at all—— Between Maine and California! For God's sake——"

"This just isn't our week," said Mendoza ruefully.

The Ballistics man smiled at them gently. "I'd advise you," he said, "to take this up to the lab. The Higgins people have just brought out a new model of this particular revolver, and it utilizes a different alloy than the old model. It's only been on the market about two months. If this is from one of the new models——"

"*¡Dios se lo pague!*" said Mendoza. "Come on, John!"

The city is alive; the city is exciting, and it is as addictive as the big H. You can get hooked by this city without loving it, without hating it. But the city itself is a bringer of death, and never twenty-four hours pass without death by violence in the city.

Sometimes it strikes with intention—a violent man points a gun, circles a neck with his two hands, raises the blunt instrument. More often it strikes at random; death is wanton. A child runs after the ball into the street—a shriek of brakes, driver not held, involuntary manslaughter. Brakes fail on a hill, the blaring warning horn, the scattering crowd—death choosing at seeming random, driver not held, involuntary . . . The sleeping pill swallowed, just one more cigarette before turning out the light, and the sirens screaming in the night and the flames towering to the sky, vying with neon. My dad's got a real gun, I know where he keeps it, naw, it's not loaded, but we can play like—— Bam, you're dead! You are. Did I turn off the wall heater? Sure, must have, good night, honey. And death comes quietly, so quietly, in the dark night.

The city is a place of death, because it is a place where many, many people come together, all kinds of people doing all kinds of things.

And there is the in-between death. At random, wanton death, but born out of violence.

The shopkeeper hit just a little too hard, so somebody can get at the cash register.

The throat squeezed just a little too long, so the mugger can grab the handbag.

The noisy child beaten. I didn't mean to *hurt* her.

The argument with the wife, the husband—— I guess I was a little tight, Officer, I didn't know what I was doing.

The city can be beautiful, and sordid, and rapacious, but it is death-ridden. Death visits the country, too, but more often the city, because there are more potential victims in the city.

Any city.

Cops are always potential victims. They all know this. But the incidence of cops running into violence, while it is higher than that of the average citizen, is not all that high; and they get used to living with it.

Bert Dwyer, this hot Tuesday, was not thinking about violence. He was thinking, as he walked along Grand Avenue from the lot where he'd left his car, that he'd be lucky if he got home in time for dinner—or at all, for dinner. Thursday was his wife's birthday, and after he'd made this call he was going to steal a little time off to buy her a present. She'd be thirty-six, but she didn't look it, and even after twelve years and two kids they were still in love, so it was going to be a present where she'd say, "Bert! You shouldn't have—we can't afford——"

He was nearing the corner of Seventh Street. The bank was on that corner—the Security-First Bank. All he had to do was hand over the sketches, explain, ask them to keep an eye out.

Much good this would do, he thought. Well, maybe.

The bank was a bank on the main floor and mezzanine, an office building the rest of the way.

Dwyer pushed open the first street door he came to. It let him into the lobby of the office building. There were stairs going up at the end of the lobby and two elevators in the left-hand wall. There were double doors to the right, leading into the bank.

He came in and saw the man. The man standing beyond the elevators, at the foot of the stairs. He saw what the man was doing.

His eyes widened in astonishment and understanding. Involuntarily his right hand went up under his jacket after his gun. He said, "Hold it right there, mister!" and he brought out the gun.

He had time to fire twice before the .45 slugs hit him.

He lived for one minute. To the bank guard who was first to reach him he gasped something that sounded like, "Two——" and then he died.

CHAPTER EIGHT

The squad-car men found his I.D. in his wallet and called in.

Lake got hold of Mendoza and Palliser at Federico's. Higgins walked into the office three minutes later, to hear the news; he got to the bank before anybody else from Homicide. Detective Bob Schenke was on night duty and it was Detective Nick Galeano's day off, but they both showed up after Lake called them.

Mendoza and Palliser got there just as the ambulance arrived. In the narrow lobby there was a little crowd, with Higgins and two uniformed men holding them back away from the body.

Dwyer lay a few steps inside the door, on his right side, feet toward the door. His gun had fallen from one outstretched hand. The interns came in and Higgins said in a taut voice, "Just a minute, boys. I make it four or five slugs in him, Luis. There are two shells gone out of his gun. They hit up there by the stairs, I think. A couple of chips out of the marble stair well there."

"Yes." Mendoza came up and looked down at Dwyer. "God damn this bastard," he said softly.

"Amen," said Higgins heavily. He stared at Dwyer's outflung hand almost touching the gun. "Oh, God, Bert." There were tears in his eyes. "We were at the academy together. Fifteen years back, do you know? God——"

Somewhere in the crowd a woman was exclaiming hysterically, "There were seven shots—I counted them. I stepped on the alarm as soon as he went out the door, and then there were seven shots—loud shots——"

"God," said Palliser. "Half the blood in his body——"

There was a lot of blood under Dwyer and around him, soaking his clothes. Forty-five-caliber bullets make big holes in a human body.

"Fifteen years——" said Higgins numbly. "This son of a bitch bastard, we got to get——"

"Yes, George," said Mendoza. He had to step in the blood to bend close over Dwyer's body; gently he probed in pockets and found the big envelope of the artist's sketches Dwyer had been carrying and his parking-lot ticket. Both were bloodstained. He said remotely, "His wife will want the car."

The interns took over then.

"Excuse me, sir, I'm Tripp—Donald Tripp. I—I was here when he died. Who is he? You——" The bank guard, in uniform. A uniform bloodstained where he had knelt over Dwyer.

"He was a cop," said Mendoza in the same remote voice. "A very damned good cop, Mr. Tripp, and he leaves a big hole, Mr. Tripp."

"Oh, my God!" said Tripp. The woman was still talking about the seven shots. "Oh, God, that's terrible. I

94

saw it all, inside, I mean, and I was running for the phone and Mrs. Von Papen started to scream, and then I heard the shots and I came——"

"Did you see anyone else here?"

"No, sir, no, there was just this man lying here, and all the blood—but I saw he was alive. I went to him—and he said just one word, he said *Two*. I don't know what it meant—and then he died, and I——"

"We'll want a statement later on, Mr. Tripp. There was a holdup here, yes. Did——"

"The same—the same one, sir, yes, the same man— but it was very odd, what made me notice him—and I thought, with the gun and all and the people he's shot, better let him get out quietly and then—— And *this* has to happen! Oh, my God——"

"Bert walked right in on his getaway," said Higgins savagely. "He must have spotted him somehow, and—— *Two*. What the hell——"

"There's time for speculation," said Mendoza. "Right now let's get that marble stair well dusted for prints— very unlikely, but it seems to be where X was standing when Bert spotted him. Spotted him for some reason. Let's for the love of God clear this crowd away—hang onto anybody who says they saw him." He picked up Dwyer's gun and put it in his pocket. He said, "After we've sorted out the story, George, you can trail me in Bert's car. His wife."

"I could——"

"You know it's my job," said Mendoza.

That was when Schenke got there, and a minute later Galeano. They helped herd the crowd back into the bank; they asked if anybody besides the teller and the bank guard had had any kind of look at the loner, and three women and a man said yes, so they asked them please to wait. Then they came back and stood around the interns, reasonlessly, because it didn't seem exactly right to leave Bert Dwyer there alone with strangers, while they got on with the job—even the job of trying to locate his killer. The interns handed Mendoza his wallet, which was covered with blood, and his watch. Then they got him onto the stretcher and covered him up and took him away, and all there was left was a lot of blood all over the marble floor.

They went up to where a couple of slugs had chipped pieces out of the marble stair well. A man was coming down the stairs and Higgins said, "Please don't touch the banisters, sir. Police." The man looked very surprised but came on down without touching the sides of the enclosed stair. When he saw all the blood on the floor, he turned green and bolted into the bank.

"Nothing to say Bert nicked him."

"No. I think it could be he fired before Bert did, and Bert was falling as he fired," said Mendoza.

"The Prints boys are on the way," said Schenke. "My God, I can't believe this—this Goddamned—— He must have just walked into it blind! If he'd been a minute later, probably this bastard would have made his get-away——"

"Or ten minutes earlier and Bert might have been out of the bank when our boy showed up. No profit in thinking if, Bob," said Mendoza.

"He said *Two*," said Galeano. "What did he mean? If I know Bert he was trying to tell us something——"

"He *told* us, all right," said Higgins angrily. "He told

us how the vanishing act is done! It's a pair, not a loner. One man walks in and gets the money, comes out, and immediately hands it over to a second man who walks out with it, while the first guy probably goes upstairs in the same building and hangs around until all the excitement's over. Doesn't it say that to you, Luis? Bert saw two men here, and I'd take a bet he saw the loot being handed over, and that's what——"

"That's what it might sound like," agreed Mendoza. "But let's not jump to any conclusions."

"Well, that's sure to God how I make it! So we're going to have a look in Records for any pair that's ever pulled a heist job, and we're going——"

"We're certainly going to do that," said Mendoza.

They did what had to be done. They asked the questions and wrote down the answers. They got names and addresses for all the witnesses. The boys from Prints came and dusted the teller's cage where the heist man had stood, and all around the end of the lobby out there, and the door the man had used, and came up with a lot of confused prints, all too smudged for identification.

They heard only one new and rather odd thing, from the bank guard. "It was the reason I noticed him first, see? I don't suppose I would have noticed if I hadn't happened to be facing that direction, because he was very—very unobtrusive about it. I saw him come in, you see—he came in by the same door he went out, the door into the lobby of the building. He came in very—oh, quietly, and as soon as he got in he turned around and pulled down the shades on both the doors there. Just the way I do when we're closing at night, you know? Naturally I noticed that, and I thought it was very funny, and

97

I started toward him, but by the time I got across to that side he was nearly at the chief teller's window—Mrs. Von Papen's window—and I think, Oh, boy! He's *that* guy, and I think about those people he's shot, and I think I'd just better watch until he gets away. If you take me. God," said Tripp, "if I'd known what was going to happen—I don't wear a gun, but my God, looking back, if I'd alerted a couple of husky guys—we could've jumped him from behind——"

"He pulled down the shades? Why the hell?" wondered Galeano.

"Look at the position of those doors," said Higgins harshly. "Right in the middle of that side wall, and all glass. Anybody watching him—as at least the teller would be—could see which way he turned when he went out. And we're pretty sure he turned toward the stairs, not the street door as he'd be expected to. He didn't want anybody wondering about that, about why. We know why—he turned the other way to meet his partner and hand over the loot. And——"

"And just then Bert walked in on it. Of all the lousy Goddamned luck," said Schenke.

That was certainly what it looked like. And by three o'clock there wasn't anything more to do at the bank. There had been reporters, but Mendoza hadn't given them anything yet. He didn't want Dwyer's wife getting it over the radio first.

"Oh, Christ, I don't *want* to see her," said Higgins. "I don't want to do this, Luis. Don't tell me, nobody does— you don't. It's just a hell of a thing. We all know it can happen to any of us any time, but when it comes like this —just the bad luck to walk in on that, not expecting it, not——" They walked up Grand Avenue, and the people passing in both directions passed uncaringly; they did not know that violent death had walked here three hours ago.

"He came to Homicide ten years ago. From Vice. He was a detective second-grade then. The boy had just been born," said Mendoza. "I remember. Have you ever met his wife?"

"No," said Higgins. "I don't want to meet her now. Her name's Mary. Christ, I don't. There's a girl too. Seven or eight, I think. What do you say to them? There's never anything to say."

"Never, that makes sense. But somebody has to say it."

Dwyer had lived up on Silver Lake Boulevard in Hollywood. It was an old single house on a mixed block of apartments and houses. There was a boy's bike in the driveway, and a black Scotty yipped at them from behind the driveway gate.

She knew, of course, when she saw Higgins get out of Dwyer's car in front. She didn't know how bad, but she knew. But somebody eventually had to say the quick, brutal words. *I'm sorry, he's dead.* Such very final words. And she didn't go to pieces right then—there were the children to think of; there was so much to think of.

. . . That she wasn't thinking of right now but would have to sometime. Such as the payments on the house, and on the car, and the grocery bills, and—— There would be a pension, of course, but not a very big one, because even on this force, which paid its cops good salaries, they weren't as high salaries as could be earned in easier, softer, pleasanter jobs.

What in hell's name, wondered Mendoza again, made a man want to be a cop? Ever?

And she did go halfway to pieces, and Mendoza managed to get the names out of her and called her mother up in Spokane and her sister in Portland; they would fly down at once, but that wouldn't get them here until tomorrow at least. He called the house on Rayo Grande Avenue and talked to Alison.

"You'll ask Máiri to come over at once, *amada?*"

"Yes—yes, of course, Luis. She'll look after them until—Luis, I——"

"Now. Don't make it tougher, *cara*. It wasn't me this time, that's all."

"No. But—Art was bad enough. I know Sergeant Dwyer isn't quite so—close to home, for you, but——"

"I worked with him for ten years," said Mendoza.

"Yes. Will you be home?"

"I don't know, *cara*. I'll call if not."

"Yes. Take care."

"Of what? I wish to God we knew."

"You'll get him. You'll get him now."

"We'll be looking hot and heavy. Send Máiri."

"Yes, love."

They waited until Mrs. MacTaggart came. Both the children were at a nearby playground, for which they could only thank God. But even Higgins felt they'd be all right with Mrs. MacTaggart. He got into the Ferrari with a little sigh. He said, "She's pretty. Even when she's all broken up like now. God, what a thing to happen . . ."

Palliser, Schenke, and Galeano had gone straight to

Records and were pawing through all the different kinds of holdups for years back, looking for a pair who habitually worked together, looking for any pros who liked to work in pairs. They hadn't called in with anything yet, said Sergeant Lake. He was looking pale and grim. He asked questions; Mendoza told him what they'd pieced together.

"God, of all the rotten damned luck, just walking in that particular minute——" The phone rang; Lake picked it up. "Homicide, Headquarters . . . Oh, sure, just a minute." He looked at Mendoza. "Art."

Mendoza went into his office and picked up the phone. "Art."

"Luis, I just heard it on the radio. My God, how did it —— What happened?"

Mendoza told him, tiredly. "Christ!" said Hackett. "He had to walk in just *then*—— Oh, God. His wife?" Mendoza told him about that. "Well, that's—— What do I say? God. God, I wish they'd let me out of here. I couldn't do any of the leg work, but I could at least help out typing reports, looking—— Oh, hell. And I suppose they won't even let me go to the funeral——"

"Don't fuss about that, Art," said Mendoza. "Bert won't be there either—just the corpse. . . . Well, it looks like a pair. From what he got out to the guard. I don't know, we'll dig at that awhile anyway. See what shows. I expect Bainbridge has got the slugs out and sent them up to Ballistics by now. Small doubt it'll be the same gun. But that's a long way from collaring him. Or them."

"Angel called. She heard it too. She was—upset."

"Yes, wives will be. It makes the headlines when it

101

happens, but it doesn't really happen all that often. Most of us die peacefully in our beds."

"We were at the academy together," said Hackett. "George Higgins and Bert and me. We always said, funny we should all three end up at the same place. God, I wish there was something I could do——"

"Lie still and get well, *hermano*. There'll still be work to do two months from now."

"But Bert——" Hackett was silent and then said, "I forgot to ask Angel to bring me some stationery. I've got to write a letter at least."

"Yes," said Mendoza. "Just concentrate on getting well. I'll try to drop in sometime tomorrow." He put the phone down. Letters, he thought. The chief would write a letter of condolence to Mary Dwyer, saying nice things about Bert. The mayor would write a letter. Quite possibly the governor would write a letter. Almost every man in the Homicide Bureau would find time to pay a little duty call, awkwardly, say what a right guy Bert had been. And they'd take up a collection from the whole force for Mary Dwyer. And the name would go on the Honor Roll downstairs. Albert Dwyer, another cop killed on duty.

By one of the violent men. One of the death-bringers.

So there was a big hole left in the personnel of Homicide. George Higgins would move up to first-grade sergeant, and Landers, next in line, to second-grade, and presently they'd get a replacement, a new and probably green detective third-grade out of Forgery or Robbery or somewhere. Mendoza wondered who it would be.

Sergeant Lake came in with a longish yellow teletype. "More on that D.M.V. list," he said.

"What?" said Mendoza blankly. "What—— Oh. That."

The D.M.V. list had completely slipped his mind. *Of all the lousy Goddamned luck,* they had all said. But death was random—violent death. There was no sense in it, no sense at all. That intelligent, reasoning men could divine. Jimmy Walsh beaten and shot and dead on a dirty garage floor. Carol Coffey senselessly and impossibly dead, dusting the living room for her mother. Nineteen years old.

Bert Dwyer dead on the marble floor, his blood around him, thirty-seven, the wife and two kids—— Mendoza remembered suddenly that Bert had been a transfer to Homicide after Sergeant Conchetta had been killed by that hood.

He looked at the new addition to the D.M.V. list of Anglia De Luxes. It seemed, suddenly, vastly, unimportant.

Palliser had got to Homicide by way of Auto Theft, which bureau didn't often run into violent death, and although he'd been on the force for eleven years, this was the first time he'd had the experience of having a colleague killed on the job. He had liked Dwyer and respected him as a good cop, and the sight of Dwyer there on the floor with the blood all around had shaken Palliser more than he would admit.

In a queerly sharp sort of way he suddenly understood the job better. For the first time in those eleven years he saw that, whatever else you could say about police work, it was life stripped down to the raw essentials. There were no fuzzy edges to police work. Very simply, it was

Good versus Bad, whatever fancy titles you might dream up: it was order against anarchy, reason against violence, sanity against mindless impulse; the drawn lines were stark; there were no fuzzy edges.

And there was (did he remember Mendoza saying that sometime?) no discharge in that war. You had to declare, one side or the other.

He worked with Schenke and Galeano and the Records men, hunting out names and past crimes, until past six o'clock. They turned up a few possibles. One from away back, 1946. And then there wasn't anything more immediate they could do. Except start looking for the men to match the names they'd turned up.

Schenke and Galeano went out to look up a pair of brothers who'd pulled a bank stick-up in 1952 and were just out of the pen, and Palliser dropped into a drugstore for a hasty meal of sorts and went back to Homicide to leave a report for Mendoza.

Sergeant Thoms said Mendoza had gone out for dinner, would probably be back, and there was a uniformed man asking to see Sergeant Palliser.

"Oh?"

"David Laskin. Squad-car man."

"Oh?" said Palliser blankly.

"I've got him waiting in the sergeants' room. Figured you'd be back."

"Oh," said Palliser. He went into the sergeants' room. The patrolman stood up, a big, good-looking young man, fingering his cap.

"Sergeant Palliser? You put a request in to Traffic, anybody on the beat that takes in Allen Street, as to whether we've ever had anything on this colored kid Verne Coffey . . ."

"Oh," said Palliser, adjusting his mind. "Yes, sure. Sit down. You got anything?"

"Sorry, sir, but nobody recognized the name. He's never even been picked up for a street scuffle or anything like that."

"Oh," said Palliser. It had just been a thought. And right now Verne Coffey seemed vastly unimportant.

CHAPTER NINE

Mendoza got home at half-past ten. He slid the Ferrari
into the garage beside Alison's Facel-Vega and went in
the back door. It hadn't cooled off much even after dark,
and the temperature was nearly ninety. The house was
still and mostly dark. He switched on the kitchen light
and stood there for a moment, lax.

Alison came hurrying from the front of the house. A
transparent green nylon peignoir swirled about her; the
light was soft on her shining red hair. Coming toward
him, she said, "You're tired to death, *amante* . . ."

He kissed her. "Twins asleep?" At thirteen months,
blessedly, the twins had learned to sleep at night—sometimes.

"Thank God, yes. You've had a day. Luis—I'm so
sorry. But it just makes the rest of us—well," and she
sighed. "Angel was upset too."

"So Art said. I need a drink," said Mendoza.
Unprecedentedly he stripped off his jacket and hung it
carelessly over a chair, followed it with his tie. He
opened a cupboard and got out the bottle of rye; inevita-
bly El Señor heard the clink of glass on bottle neck and

arrived in a hopeful rush for his share. Mendoza regarded him resignedly and poured half an ounce of rye into a saucer for him; El Señor settled down to it happily, purring. For once neither of the Mendozas commented on their alcoholic cat.

"But I *never* can understand," said Alison, "why everyone just—just submits to it so tamely. Bank robbers. Especially a man alone, like this. Why, there must have been quite a few men in the bank, every time he's come in—just stand around and let him get away with the money, instead of ganging up on him! And the people behind the counters—heavens, all they'd have to do would be to duck down—no bullet would get through those——"

Mendoza drank rye. "You can never be quite sure what a man with a gun is going to do, *novia*," he said dryly. "And you can never be quite sure where a bullet's going to go. He's shot two people before today, and everybody knows it. Nobody wants to get to be a hero the hard way."

"Well, I see that in a way, but—— I'd better go to see Mrs. Dwyer," said Alison unhappily. "And I thought afterward, how you said it happened, he just walked in on it all unexpected. Two minutes later, and he might still be alive. Why? It's senseless."

"A lot of things seem to be. No business of a cop's to philosophize," said Mendoza, "but it looks as if the time's marked out for each of us. This much and no more. For some reason or no reason."

" 'To everything there is a season, and a time to every purpose under the heavens'? I'd like to think there *is* a reason."

"But that goes on, 'A time to be born, and a time to die.'" Mendoza finished the rye. El Señor finished his and thumped down to the floor from the drainboard to find another cat to cuff. "I don't know the answer, *chica.* But he may have helped to break the case. It looks as if he was trying to tell us it's a pair, not a loner. . . . Come on, let's get to bed."

But in the middle of undressing he suddenly stopped with his shirt in one hand and said, *"Only——"*

"Only?" Alison was hanging up her robe.

"Only—what? It's a very little thing," said Mendoza, "I grant you. But Bert was a cop, and he talked like a cop. If it was that—that he saw two men, one passing over the haul and maybe also the gun—wouldn't he have said, or tried to say, 'a pair,' instead of 'two men'?"

"I don't see that at all," said Alison. "For one thing, he was dying—he must have known he was badly hurt at least. He'd say the natural thing, two men."

"Es posible. A lead, anyway . . . We'll get this bastard if it takes ten years."

He was tired, but he didn't sleep very well.

He'd known Bert Dwyer a long time.

Piggott came in on Wednesday morning. "I wasn't coming back until tomorrow," he said, "but I figure you need all the help you got. I'm all right." He looked a little pale and wan, but then he'd known Dwyer for some time too. "God, what a way to get it! Are there any new leads at all?"

Sergeant Lake was telling him about that when Tom Landers walked in. He'd been up visiting his sister in Oakland, heard it on the radio at eleven last night, and got the midnight plane down. "You've still got five days of vacation," said Lake.

"Vacation hell," said Landers, looking grim. His tall, lank figure looked taut, and the boyish face that was the bane of his existence, making him look ten years younger than he was, didn't look so boyish now, mouth a thin line and brows drawn. "It was Bert Dwyer got me to try for rank. I was on the point of quitting the force, but he talked to me—— I want the son of a bitch who killed him! Who's seen Mary? Is she all right? And have we got any leads on it at all?"

If that *two* meant what it sounded like, they had some leads. Palliser, Schenke, and Galeano had turned up fifteen possibles—men with records of heist jobs who worked in pairs, and a few pairs who usually worked together. There were other names of men like that in Records who could be eliminated on account of age or looks—though of course they didn't know what their present X's partner might look like.

If a pair was working it that way, and it would be a very damned clever way, the vanishing act was explained. Nobody on the street had seen the man who'd actually pulled the job come out, because he didn't leave the building; the man who left the building with the loot and very probably the gun was the second man. So even if the building was searched, or even if later on somebody from the bank spotted the first man, say, leaving the building, and raised a hue and cry, he'd be clean: no money, no gun—mistaken identification. If it was like that, this was a very cute pair indeed.

Item, first, this pair of brothers. Walter and James Senk. Long records of burglary, heist jobs. They had both started out as usual with grand theft auto and graduated to bigger things, both doing time before they pulled the bank job in 1952. They'd knocked over a bank in South Pasadena and been collared a block away by two squad-car men. They'd both drawn three-to-tens and got out in 1961.

Item, one Lester Cullinane, a pro from away back; he had a record of burglary, armed assault, forgery, grand theft auto. On nearly all his jobs he had worked with a pal: somebody to stand lookout, or help carry away the loot, or just for company.

Item, one Leandro Lucasta, another old pro with a monotonous record of heist jobs; he had hit liquor stores, supermarkets, bars, and might conceivably have decided to try banks. Nine out of ten jobs he had pulled had been in the company of his brother Joe or one Mario del Rojas. They had all served time.

Item—well, there were about fifteen men they wanted to haul in for questioning. For Wolf to look at in profile. Men with records like that, who by age and description could be their boy, or one of them. For one thing, the man was not a young man but at least in his middle fifties, and it wasn't very often that a man that age suddenly went on the bent; the chances were that he had a record.

And this was urgent—it was very damned urgent now, with Bert Dwyer lying in a mortuary—but at the same time they had these other cases on hand, and they couldn't just forget about them. Somebody had to go on giving some attention to the Walsh case and the Coffey case. There was unfinished business there too.

Mendoza kept Palliser and Piggott for that and told

them so. "I'm sorry, I know you want to get after this boy, but we can't just ignore all other business. And maybe a fresh mind on this Coffey thing—— Matt, will you go and see this Verne's pals again? Get a little tough, see what you can get."

"Sure. I see that, Lieutenant. But I'd like to look over somebody's notes on the case. I'm not familiar——"

"You can have mine," said Palliser sourly. "And I wish you joy of it. I can't see how anybody else could have killed her, but I don't think we'll ever get enough evidence to prove it." He handed over his notebook.

Piggott was a plodder, but tenacious; he usually got there in the end. "I'll get with it, then," he said, and went out.

"That D.M.V. list," said Palliser. "I see it's grown some more. It doesn't seem to mean much to me. With Bert—— That kid, God, yes, we've got to get whoever— but——"

Mendoza leaned his forehead on his palm a moment. "I know, John. It'd be nice to believe, all firm and comfortable, in some very orthodox creed. The benevolent old gentleman in the nightshirt, sitting up there arranging everything just the way it ought to be. Whether it seems that way to us at the time or not."

"I don't think any cop ever could, all the way. The things we see every day, every week."

"'A time to weep, and a time to laugh,'" said Mendoza. "And that at least is true. Everything passes. . . . I liked Conchetta. He was a damn good man. When I caught up to that bastard who gunned him, I brought him in half dead. And you know, John, I was thinking last night, I don't remember Conchetta

111

much any more. The way he looked, the way he talked and laughed."

"That's not—that's all the more reason—— Oh, hell," said Palliser. "All right. I know somebody's got to stay on these other things. What do you think about Walsh?"

Mendoza sat up. "I don't think it was a private kill. I saw the parents. I saw a couple of his friends. He shows up as a nice ordinary bright kid. Sure, he was involved with this girl, but he was only nineteen, evidently he had some respect for his parents' opinion, and he'd probably have gotten over her. Nothing shows up of any kind of personal motive—nobody was jealous of him, anything like that."

"But he wouldn't have put up a fight to the heist man —he'd been told not to. So——"

"So," said Mendoza, "how many cases have we had where somebody played along with the heist man, handed over the money, and got it anyway? Because he might identify X afterward, or because X was hopped up —or just because X felt like it?"

"But the way he was beaten up—— Well, I know. I called the Higgins outfit yesterday morning, I told you that? Got hold of their sales manager. Seemed like a very nice guy, and he understands it's urgent. One thing might be a break for us. This new model of their nine-shot .22 hasn't been distributed all over the country yet —just to the western states. But——"

"No, you didn't tell me that. That could be a break," said Mendoza. They knew now, from the lab, that the piece of trigger guard had come off one of the new-model Hi-Standard revolvers.

"Well, with Bert—— And is it? By western states he

meant everywhere west of Kansas," said Palliser gloomily. "How many is that? Colorado, Wyoming, Montana, New Mexico, Arizona, Nevada—er——"

"Idaho, Oregon, Washington——"

"Oh, Utah," said Palliser. "Yes, and us. For God's sake, how many stores sell guns in that territory? And I don't know how all the state laws read—it could be that some place like Montana, you can just walk in and buy a gun over the counter without even signing your name."

"I shouldn't think so," said Mendoza doubtfully. "I think they've all got laws of some kind, about showing I.D., even if they don't require a permit. But look, better check that first, because obviously it's no good asking for any information if that's so in any of those states."

"And if so, that'll be just the place our boy got the gun."

"Don't be so pessimistic."

"Pessimistic!" said Palliser. "So we check, how many of those guns have been sold in that area, even in just two months? So I go gallivanting all over on a tour of the West, chase them all down—oh, well, not that necessarily, we can get other forces to check—to find one with a broken trigger guard. Two hundred, three hundred, more? Oh, that was another thing. The sales manager did say—one ray of comfort—that nobody could have that repaired without buying a whole new unit, so eventually we'd know about that too. Maybe."

"Which is nice," said Mendoza. "What about this D.M.V. list? Maybe a short cut—if the gun belonged to the fellow del Valle saw. Easiest way, put Jimmy on the phone. Ostensibly a poll-taker or maybe a salesman for a car-painting outfit. The owners wouldn't be suspicious of that, tell us what color the Anglia was right away. You're going to have to narrow it down some way."

"All right," said Palliser dispiritedly.

Higgins and Galeano brought in the Senk brothers about eleven o'clock. Landers had just come back from an abortive hunt for Cullinane, so he stood in on the questioning too.

Walter Senk was fifty-seven, almost totally bald. He was five-eleven, a hundred and seventy, light-eyed, and he had a lot of tattoo marks all over him, but of course their bank robber had been pretty well covered up. James Senk, who could be the silent partner, was fifty-five, five-ten, a hundred and fifty-eight, light-eyed, and also bald, minus the tattoo marks. Both of them had been married and divorced and were at present sharing a room in an old rooming house on Flower Street, where they'd been picked up.

They didn't like being picked up and said so. "You got nothing on us," said Walter. "What's the beef now?"

"Maybe nothing," said Higgins. "Where were you both between noon and one o'clock yesterday?"

"What the hell?" said Walter. "Noon and—— Why? I don't hafta talk to you, bloodhounds. I don't hafta——"

"Talk," said Higgins gently. Higgins was almost as big and broad as Art Hackett, which was saying something, and he was smiling at the Senk brothers, but it wasn't a very nice smile. "You'll talk, brother, or I'll make you."

Walter Senk looked up at him, half surprised and half sarcastic. "You'll make—— A guy on *this* force? One o' you real gents? I'm laughing."

"So stop laughing," said Landers. "There was a cop

killed yesterday, Walter. Maybe we're not playing real gents today."

"Listen," said James nervously. "Walt, maybe——"

"The *bank* jobs?" said Walter blankly. "Oh, Jesus, you ain't tryin' to tie us up to *that?* Oh, Jesus. There's a laugh. You can't—besides, that's a loner. You know that."

"Well, just maybe it isn't," said Galeano. "Let's hear where you both were between noon and one o'clock yesterday."

"Oh, Jesus," said Walter. "You're not gonna pin that one on us, bloodhounds. We learned our lesson, dint we, Jim?" He smirked at his brother.

"Yeah, I'll just bet," said Galeano. "Both holding nice regular jobs. Where?"

"Well, I—we come into a little money," said Walter. "Not much, just so we don't hafta work. If you——"

"A little money," said Higgins, "from jobs we haven't dropped on you for. Yet. Where were you?"

"Look, Walt, all we gotta do is tell them. They can check easy. Mac's a right guy, he'll say we was there."

"Where?" asked Galeano.

"Oh, for Christ's sake," said Walter disgustedly. "It's a crime to eat lunch? We was in Mac's bar and grill on Third. All the dee-tails you want, I had a corned beef on rye and a couple beers an' Jim had a Swiss cheese on rye and three beers."

"This Mac know you by name? Serve you personally?"

"Yeah, yeah, it's legit, he'll say. Jesus, tryin' pin somethin' like that on us——"

Higgins nodded at Galeano, who went out to check the alibi. "So we'll just wait and see what Mac says."

Neither he nor Landers showed disappointment. That had come too easy and quick to be anything but the truth. But then, this kind of thing didn't break first time round.

Galeano came back forty minutes later. He said Mac had backed them up; and he'd checked downstairs: Mac —who was Robert Bruce MacDonald, incidentally—had no record, had a good reputation with Traffic.

They let the Senks go. The Senks went hurriedly.

Bob Schenke brought Leandro Lucasta in at one o'clock. He brought him in with some difficulty, because Leandro Lucasta was noisy drunk and fighting mad, and he'd given Schenke what would develop into a beautiful shiner. Schenke had picked him up at home, in the middle of a fight with his wife.

They wouldn't be able to question Leandro until he'd sobered up. They plied him with black coffee, finally gave up and stashed him in a cell at the new jail a couple of blocks away for safekeeping.

There were, so far on the list, seventy-eight Anglia De Luxes registered to owners residing in L. A. County which bore plate numbers starting out HAH. Rosario del Valle had said this year's model, but there wasn't all that difference between the 1963 and 1964 models, and Palliser had asked for coverage on both. Sergeant Lake was doggedly looking up phone numbers, dialing. "Mr. Baron? We are making a survey of——"

These days, what with all the polls and statistical surveys, the public wasn't surprised at anything and remained surprisingly polite and co-operative.

Sergeant Lake had made twenty-three calls and hadn't yet found a light-green Anglia De Luxe.

Higgins brought in Jan Czimchyk at four forty-five. Czimchyk had a long record—armed assault, robbery, burglary, Peeping Tom, rape, name it and he had it— and on most of the assault and robbery counts he had had a pal along. He was four months out of San Quentin. He was fifty-nine years old and he'd spent thirty-three of those years behind bars. He was five-nine, dark complexioned, blue eyes, a hundred and fifty pounds, and bald. Higgins had found him, via his parole officer, in a cheap room on Alpine Street.

"I never done nothing," he said sullenly.

Higgins asked him, "Where were you between noon and one o'clock yesterday?"

"I dunno why you got to pick on me. I done nothing. I do something, they put me back there—parole man says. I done nothing. I get job—dishwasher, drugstore on Broadway—I go straight O.K."

Until parole was up. They knew about that. "Where were you?" asked Galeano. "Between noon and one o'clock?"

"Please, I go straight O.K. You got me wrong. I done nothing bad. I dunno——"

"Then tell us where you were," said Higgins. These punks. These—— Unconsciously his right hand balled to a fist. God, these punks. In the fifteen years since he'd taken the oath he'd never laid hands on a suspect unless he'd been attacked, but it sometimes needed one hell of a lot of self-control. This one was just stupid, not like the arrogant can't-touch-me-I'm-under-eighteen juveniles, or some others, but right now, with Bert Dwyer at—— "Where were you? Just give us a straight answer, for God's sake."

117

"When? Where I was when, please?"

"Between noon and one o'clock yesterday, you stupid bastard!" shouted Higgins.

"Noon—this is twelve, O.K.? Yes. I done nothing bad —swear on my mother. One o'clock? I am at work— washing the dishes—drugstore on Broadway—they say, O.K."

"So we'll check it," said Higgins tiredly.

So they checked it. And four waitresses and two other dishwashers said that Czimchyk had been on the job between noon and one o'clock on Tuesday. Visible. Indisputably there.

Routine, it was called. It broke a lot of cases—in the end. But it took a lot of time, and it was damn boring.

Only the boys at Headquarters Homicide didn't find it so boring right now. The next man they brought in might be the man who had shot Bert Dwyer, and that man they wanted bad.

CHAPTER TEN

On Thursday morning the coroner held an inquest on Bert Dwyer. They would hold his funeral on Friday.

Carol Coffey's funeral had been on Wednesday.

Galeano brought in Lester Cullinane at ten o'clock Thursday morning. Mendoza was still at the inquest over at the Hall of Justice, and nobody else was there but Schenke, so they took turns questioning him.

And that turned out very unsatisfactorily, because Cullinane couldn't offer any alibi at all. With much prodding, he said he'd had the hell of a hang-over on Tuesday morning and hadn't got up or gone out until after two o'clock. He lived in a funny old rooming house near the Plaza; the men in the rooms nearest his couldn't say whether he'd been there or not. Nobody at the place could say. Nobody had heard Cullinane either staying in or going out.

That wasn't so good. It didn't say Cullinane was their boy; it just said he could have been. They hadn't one solitary thing otherwise to say he was. They couldn't hold him indefinitely without making a charge; they didn't have anything to charge him on, and if he went on saying, 'Don't know nothing about it,' they never would.

They let him go, but they'd keep him in mind. They would take a look at his pals, and requestion him, if somebody else more promising didn't turn up.

Mendoza came back to the office in time to see the last of Cullinane as he scuttled out and heard about that. "Pity," he said absently. "But I've got a few odd little thoughts in my mind, boys. That's a beautiful eye, Bob."

Schenke touched it tenderly and said, "All for nothing, too. When Lucasta sobered up, he gave me a straight story. He was at a wedding—his niece's wedding. About the time our boy hit that bank, Leandro was sitting in a pew at St. Michael and All Angels, solemn as could be." He looked at Mendoza. "What kind of little ideas, Lieutenant?" Sometimes Mendoza's little ideas turned out to be interesting.

"Well, I don't know," said Mendoza absently. He went on into his own office and they both followed. "Listening to that teller this morning, I kept thinking of what the other tellers said, and a couple of points struck me. First"—he sat down and lit a cigarette—"on all the jobs, he hasn't used the standard technique of handing over the little note saying, This is a stick-up. Of course, he's always gone to the chief tellers, who aren't as likely to have a line waiting in front of the cage, with somebody behind X to overhear him. But it's a point—he's just announced himself in a few brief words."

"Well?" said Galeano. "What's the point?"

"And then all of them said something to the effect that he spoke in a very polite and cultured voice. No, cultured isn't the word I want—grammatical. No

120

profanity, no threats—and twice he used the tellers' names, seeing their name plates propped in the windows. That does strike me as just a little offbeat."

"I see what you mean," said Schenke, "but does it say anything in particular?"

"It might," said Mendoza meditatively, "say something very damn discouraging. It might say that he's a man of middle class and some education, who's just recently taken to a life of crime. It might say he's an amateur."

"Oh, my God," said Galeano. "If that's a hunch, I hope to Christ it's a dud one! I don't see it, anyway. What that says to *me*, he's got some education, sure, maybe before now he's pulled the kind of jobs your better-class crooks do—con games and——"

"Offhand, do you recall any con man who ever went on to armed violence?"

"Well——"

"Heist men don't usually bother to say please. That's the point. I just wonder why this one does, that's all."

"And then shoot people without turning a hair . . ." Schenke felt of his eye again. "Higgins and Landers are out looking for that Scott guy. Oh, and Scarne called . . ." Scarne, somewhat against his will, was back in Washington, taking a course at the F. B. I. academy. "He's wild. He can't get back until next week."

"We started this one handicapped all right," said Mendoza.

And then Higgins came in with Bill Scott, another one out of Records, so they all sat in on the questioning.

Palliser, cursing the heat, cursing deadly routine,

cursing bad luck, was just entering the San Fernando Valley via the Golden State Freeway, bound, of all places on a hot day, for Chatsworth.

Sergeant Lake had turned up a green Anglia De Luxe, 1964 model. It was registered to a Richard S. Wembley who lived in Chatsworth. Chatsworth was way out at the end of the valley; the valley was always about ten degrees hotter than L. A. even at the Glendale end, and the farther west you went the hotter it got. Palliser estimated that it was about a hundred and ten degrees in Chatsworth.

He found Richard Wembley's address with the help of a county guide. It was an old house on about an acre of ground, and a sign in front read *Sunaire Kennels, Yorkshire Terriers.*

The green Anglia De Luxe was parked in the drive. It didn't have ski carriers on its roof. Palliser went up and rang the bell, mopping his forehead.

Mr. Wembley was at least sixty, tall and thin and white-haired. He was surprised and curious to find a police sergeant on his doorstep, but by using the just-routine bit, Palliser got answers out of him.

Last Friday morning Mr. Wembley had been en route up to Santa Barbara, with four of his Yorkshire terriers, to attend the Santa Barbara dog show over the weekend. He had driven up in the Anglia. He never drove the Anglia in downtown L. A.—he never had occasion to go there.

Routine.

Palliser thanked him, got back into his Rambler, and found that the few minutes of sitting in full sun had turned the steering wheel so hot he could hardly touch it.

He started back to L. A.

You just had to keep looking everywhere. Eventually, maybe, you'd hit the jackpot.

Bill Scott went on for quite a while saying sullenly they hadn't nothing on him and so what if he couldn't prove he was just home that Tuesday noon? Unfortunately he lived alone, in another cheap room, and there wasn't any way to prove it. He wasn't the world's biggest brain, and it was some time before it penetrated his mind why they were asking about that particular time. When it did, he started talking.

"Them *bank* jobs? Jeez, is it about that? Oh, my God, fellas, I'd never pull nothing like that, you oughta know me better! I'd never knock off nobody, I'm not as dumb as that! Jeez, they get you for life for that! Jeez, you got my record, fellas—I hardly ever even *hurt* nobody, did I? Did I, now? You oughta———"

"Well, there was that woman you hit over the head," said Mendoza. "Back in 1950, wasn't it?"

"Oh, my God, that was sorta an accident like. I never go to hurt nobody. Listen, jeez, you ain't gonna say *I* did them jobs? I'm clean, honest to God, I never——— Listen, for God's sake, *I* don't want no trouble with Benny, but he'll just hafta see——— Look, fellas, I was in a crap game. At Benny Guttieriez'—this pool hall down on Main. It was the hell of a hot game. I was really riding high, see——— Jeez, I ended up with half a century! Look, if Benny won't say, you ask some of the other guys was in

123

the game—there was Jim Lopez, an' a guy named Moreno, an' Ray Foss, an'——

He added addresses where he knew them, and Higgins and Landers went out to check. Probably he'd been there. And they'd pass on Benny's name to the Vice office, which was a necessity most men on the force considered ridiculous, but there it was; it was the law. It did seem pretty ridiculous that it should be legal to place bets inside the fence around a race track and illegal to start a friendly crap game or even a hand of poker anywhere else—except down in Gardena where you could legally play poker and nothing else. Probably nothing very drastic would happen to Benny.

But it would take some time to check out that alibi. Mendoza sighed and asked Sergeant Lake to send out for some sandwiches and coffee and added, "And then there's another thing. That bank guard."

"Yeah? . . . Ham all right? Egg salad? Chicken salad?"

"Chicken salad. You might have them send up ham for Scott . . . The bank guard," said Mendoza, wandering around the anteroom to his office, "is a former cop. Retired as sergeant from the state force in Pennsylvania. That's a pretty good outfit. He's a trained observer—like Mr. Wolf—and as he says, he spotted our boy when he came in, because of his pulling down those curtains and making straight for the chief teller's cage. So, having decided to play it safe—for which I can't blame him—and not interfere while our boy was at work, he kept his eyes on him, to notice everything he possibly could. And he tells us just what Wolf told us. He says a corduroy sports jacket with big patch pockets, and he says that the man not only shoved the bag of money into an outside pocket, he is also pretty sure he put the gun in the other outside pocket."

"Oh, he does?" said Sergeant Lake. "That strikes me as very funny, Lieutenant. I've never seen a couple of thousand bucks cash close to, but even if most of it was in fairly big bills, seems to me that much in a paper bag would make a pocket bulge out some."

"It would indeed," said Mendoza dreamily. "He got twenty fifty-dollar bills, fifty-seven tens, nine one-hundred-dollar bills, and about twelve singles. It was a sizable parcel. I wonder why an outside pocket." And then he said suddenly, "But I'm a fool. Of course. If we're right about how this caper is pulled, that explains itself. He's going straight out to the lobby of the building to meet his partner and hand over the haul and the gun—he wants both of them handy, because they can't waste a second. Yes, of course, I see that——"

They had gone back and checked the plans of all the banks. It looked as if their reading was right, because in each case X had left by the door into the building lobby, and on one other occasion he had evidently pulled down the shades there, too, though nobody had noticed that until afterward. In that bank the teller would have had a clear view of him past those doors; in the others the tellers couldn't have seen which way he turned. So that, of course, made it look as if they'd figured out his M. O. in detail.

Scott's alibi checked out; he had been in that crap game. But Higgins and Landers didn't track down all the witnesses until nearly five o'clock that afternoon.

Then they let Scott go.

At three-thirty Piggott came in, looking pleased with himself. He had in tow a tall, thin, shambling colored kid about seventeen. He met Palliser just going into the Homicide office and said, "It just takes a little brains, you know."

Palliser glanced at the kid, who was looking scared to death. "Don't tell me you turned up some evidence?"

"I sure did. Want the lieutenant to hear it."

"My God," said Palliser, "maybe I ought to get religion." Piggott just grinned at him; Piggott was a staunch Free Methodist and got a little puritanical sometimes, but then (a lot of L.A.P.D. men thought ruefully) so did the chief, who happened to be a devout Catholic.

Mendoza was reading reports. He looked up as they came in and looked as surprised as Palliser. "Something? ¡No me diga—don't tell me!"

"Something," said Piggott. "Sit down, Lee." The colored kid didn't move or look up. "Go ahead, sit down. We just want to talk to you. Just hear over again what you told me before."

The boy's eyes moved sidewise, warily. He was poorly dressed, in shabby torn jeans and a dirty T shirt; he wasn't a bad-looking kid, but his expression was wooden and his eyes were panicky. He sidled nervously over to a chair and sat down as if he expected it to explode under him.

"This is Lee Roxhite," said Piggott. "He ties up the gun to your Verne Coffey. *A* gun, anyway."

"The hell!" said Palliser.

"How very gratifying," said Mendoza. "How? And how did you reach in and put the finger on him inside a few hours?"

"Well, I used my head," said Piggott. He looked complacent; he had reason to. "You said this Verne was from a good home, wouldn't know himself how to get hold of a gun. But there were bound to be some tough guys in the same school he goes to—school opened last Monday, you know—and could be he'd contact one of them. So I went to the school and saw the principal, and he picked out some names from their records, kids who've been in a little trouble and so on, that Verne might know. I've been talking to 'em ever since. No dice until I turned up Lee here. Now, look, Lee, we just want you to tell the truth. Understand? What you told me before?"

The boy said in a hoarse voice, "I—I say ennathing you want me to, suh. That right. Suah. You doan do nothin' if I say what you want? Do nothin' to me?"

"Nobody's going to do anything to you, Lee," said Piggott patiently. "Now, you know Verne Coffey? He's in your English class, isn't he?"

"Man, that teacher mean. She doan like me. I can't help, I don't dig that bit."

"Verne Coffey. You know him, don't you?"

Lee blinked nervously. "Yes, suh."

"Has he ever talked to you? Asked you something?" Piggott looked at Mendoza. "This is how I heard it first, see."

"Yes, suh."

"Did he ask you about a gun? How to get hold of a gun?"

Lee blinked again. His eyes shot to all three of them in turn. "Y-yes, suh."

"You've been in a little trouble, haven't you, Lee? For

127

carrying a switchblade. Yes. And your dad's done a little time for burglary. You belong to that Knights gang down on Fowler Street? Yeah. So Verne might sure enough think you'd know where to lay hands on a gun."

"Man, I ain't—I ain't got no—I didn't——"

"Did Verne Coffey ask you where he could get a gun?"

"Yes, suh," said Lee docilely.

"Did you tell him or get one for him?"

Silence. "I—I——"

"Did you?"

"You gonna do somethin' to me?"

"Well, that depends. You just tell us what——"

"I tell you ennathing you want, you don't hafta beat nothin' out of me, suh, I tell you—just whatever you want me say——"

"Well, that's fine, Lee. Did you?"

"I'm right sorry, suh, did I do what?"

"Did Verne ask you where he might get a gun?"

"Yes, suh," said Lee meekly.

"And what did you tell him?"

Silence. "I—I—I dunno what you want me to say, suh."

"Did——"

"Just a minute, Matt," said Mendoza. He got up and came to stand in front of Lee Roxhite. "What else did Verne ask you, Lee? Did he ask you where he could get a switchblade too?"

"Y-yes, suh."

"I see. Did he tell you he was planning to kill his sister Carol?"

"Yes, suh."

"Mmh. Did he tell you," asked Mendoza, "he'd met some Martians off a flying saucer and was going back to Mars with them?"

"Yes, suh. I tell you whatever——" And then Lee blinked and half grinned. "Hey, man, what you mean, flying saucers?"

Mendoza grinned back at him. "So, whatever you think we want to hear, you tell." He looked at Piggott, whose mouth was open. "You should remember rules of evidence better than that, Matt. All leading questions!" He looked back to the boy. "You've got some funny ideas about us, Lee. We don't beat up people these days. Not colored people or white people—or even Martians. All we want to hear is the truth. Now let's start over, Lee. You were scared to death when the police officer started asking questions, and you thought if you just told him what he wanted to hear, he'd be satisfied and let you go. Then you got in a little too deep. Right? You haven't been telling the truth, have you?"

Lee swallowed. "No, suh."

"What is the truth? Do you know Verne Coffey?"

"No, suh. Nevah spoke a word to him."

"All right, Lee. Matt, suppose you drive him home. And, Lee! Another time, don't get funny ideas."

Without a word Piggott ushered the kid out.

"Maybe not too bright, but maybe just scared," said Mendoza. "Maybe another dad like Sam Coffey—of course, man with a record—all the boys in blue are bullies, kowtow to them."

"I will be damned," said Palliser. "But I thought it was too good to be true."

"Has that information on retail gun dealers come in from the Higgins people yet?"

"Can't expect it until at least tomorrow. Their home office is in Hamden, Connecticut."

"Nor I can't get that poor woman out of my mind," said Mrs. MacTaggart. "Mrs. Dwyer. Like a lost soul she is. A nice woman." She picked up Master John's plastic rattle from under the coffee table and Miss Teresa's cuddly soft stuffed poodle from the credenza. "The mother wants her to come back and live with her, but she was saying she'd take time to decide."

"I think that's wise," said Alison. "You shouldn't make decisions like that in a hurry."

"Indeed not," said Mrs. MacTaggart. She wrinkled her short nose. "The mother is all right, in a manner of speaking, but an awful autocratic body and spoils the children terrible." She went out with the toys.

"Luis——"

"¿*Amada?*" Mendoza was stretched out on the sectional with Bast the Abyssinian purring on his chest. He stroked her whiskers and the purr increased in volume.

"I'm superstitious," said Alison. "We're too lucky."

"Mmh?"

"We've got too much. Some awful thing's bound to happen to us. We've got *too* much. I mean—each other, and the twins, and Máiri to look after them, and Bertha coming in so faithful to take care of the house, and—— It can't last. Something *awful*——"

130

Mendoza laughed. "*Todo lo cual no es verdad.* Don't be silly, *querida.* Superstitious!"

"Well, I am. But maybe it does go by luck. Some people born lucky—under the right stars—and some unlucky. Under Saturn or whatever. I just feel—— That poor woman. I just suddenly felt——"

"Yes, *cara,*" he said gently. Mrs. MacTaggart came in again, detached Master John from Sheba's twitching tail, and bore him off. Miss Teresa squealed excitedly as El Señor stalked in and pounced on his sister. Sheba rolled over and began kicking him furiously with both hind feet. Nefertite sat placidly on the credenza, front paws well tucked under her, and watched the mock battle detachedly.

"I left some catnip out," said Alison in explanation, also watching. "Are you getting anywhere on it?"

"Routine," said Mendoza with a sigh. He squeezed Bast's ears gently. She redoubled her purring.

Mrs. MacTaggart came in and collected Miss Teresa from under the coffee table. "Nah!" said Miss Teresa rebelliously.

"Talking before we know it they'll be. Yes, love, time for beddies it is."

"But you've got some leads?" said Alison.

"For what they're worth."

Alison sighed. The rear door chimes sounded. "Now who on earth——"

"You forgot to pay the milkman," said Mendoza lazily.

"And he comes at eight o'clock at night? *¡Necio!*" said Alison.

Mrs. MacTaggart came and stood in the doorway. "It's

Mr. Warbeck," she announced perplexedly. "Of all things, at the back door like as if he wasn't good as anybody. I've mentioned your job to him, and he's saying he wants to ask your advice, that just maybe he's knowing something about this bank robber. Though I don't see——"

Mendoza sat up.

CHAPTER ELEVEN

"I'm very sorry to intrude like this, Mrs. Mendoza—Mr.
—oh, no, Mrs. MacTaggart said it was——"

"Lieutenant. Now just how do you happen to know
something about this bank robber, Mr. Warbeck?"

"Well, I don't know that I *do,* actually. But I feel very
badly about this, sir, if I *have* any information for the
police, of course I should have gone immediately and
told them, but you see I didn't know anyone had been
killed. I didn't even know about the robbery, and then I
thought—— Oh, dear, I'd better explain . . ." Mr.
Warbeck looked alarmed and upset. He was a medium-
sized man about fifty, sallow-skinned, with a rather
untidy head of thick dark hair and weak blue eyes
behind gold-rimmed glasses.

"Why don't you take Mr. Warbeck to your den and
talk comfortably?" said Alison. "Can't we offer you a
drink, Mr. Warbeck?"

"Oh, no, thank you, no, I am a teetotaler." He trotted
after Mendoza to the seldom-used den down the hall and
sat down obediently when invited. "I must explain, Mr.

—Lieutenant?—I seldom trouble to read the papers, and just lately I have been so worried about Marion Holderby's teeth, I really haven't—but I should tell you properly. You could tell me if it's anything at all the police should hear, and I'm afraid I wouldn't even know —er—*which* police to go to. I know there are different— ah—stations——"

"Central precinct. Headquarters. My office," said Mendoza. He smiled at Mr. Warbeck. "Suppose you tell me all about it, and we'll see."

"Oh, really? Oh, how very fortunate. What a coincidence! Well, it was like this, you see. I am a member—in fact, I am the treasurer—of this little philanthropic group. We call ourselves the Good Samaritans. It would surprise you, Lieutenant, even with the charitable civic groups, the city relief and all such services, how many poor children are not able to have needed medical care and so on, and the children are our chief interest. For one thing, we feel that many boys and girls from poor sections can be—er—set on the upward path, children who might otherwise be led into antisocial behavior, by the little things we do for them. Such as Marion Holderby's teeth——"

"Mr. Warbeck, if you'd just——" But Mr. Warbeck was well launched.

"They need straightening, you see, very badly. And while Mr. Holderby is gainfully employed—he drives a refuse truck—he is quite indifferent to the situation and refuses to supply the money. His wife is a downtrodden little woman and of course she has no money of her own. I am happy to say," said Mr. Warbeck happily, "that we have found the money—Mr. Holderby was concerned only for the money, you see, as long as someone else pays the bill he will not object—and she is to go to the clinic next week for her initial examination. It is the children like this, you see, we try to help——"

"That's very laudable," said Mendoza, "but——"

"Oh, dear, I do apologize. I'm afraid I get carried away. So many people *are* indifferent, or think the Health and Welfare Departments provide all the necessary services. But there are many who—— My wife and I never had any children of our own, but we were always active in charitable groups working for children, as both of us were so fond—— That was back in Auburn, of course. Auburn, New York. I was for a good many years the head floorwalker at Websters', an independent department store there. But then the owner died and it was taken over by a chain, and naturally they had their own personnel to bring in, one couldn't expect—— Most fortunately I have a small private income left me by my father, enough for my needs, and Emily being gone then—and I have so much bronchial trouble, the doctor advised a warmer climate, so I——"

"Mr. Warbeck——"

"I do beg your pardon, that's really irrelevant, of course. But you see, since I have been here I've been very interested in our little group. I had to explain this to explain to you how I came to see this man at all. You see, we maintain a very small office—one room, actually—on the eighth floor of that office building at Seventh and Grand Avenue, Lieutenant. A *very* small office—just a mailing address and a place for Miss Corsa, our very able secretary, to make up her mimeographs and so on. We send out appeals for donations quite often, but the response, I'm afraid, is not very good." Mr. Warbeck took off his glasses and began to polish them with his handkerchief. "I am generally there for a little while at least two or three days a week, and occasionally—if I am making up our accounts or drafting a new appeal—I am there all day. And as it happened, I was there most of last Tuesday afternoon. First I was calling clinics all over town, trying to discover what the lowest figure might be for Marion Holderby's braces, you see, and then I drafted an appeal for Miss Corsa to mimeograph and mail out, and then I was looking over our current account——"

Mendoza opened his mouth to ask a pertinent question but was overridden.

"And perhaps I have too narrow interests," said Mr. Warbeck apologetically. "But somehow, since retiring and coming out here, I don't seem to take much interest in the news any more. So much trouble, so much trouble! Occasionally I see Mrs. Tranter's paper—I rent a room from Mrs. Tranter, down on Oakdawn Avenue—but more often not. I—er—had heard about these bank robberies, but none of the details. Which is why I feel so badly about this, Lieutenant. If I *had* heard, if I *had* known, I would have realized sooner that what I had seen might be important——"

"What did you see?" asked Mendoza in a voice rather louder than usual.

Mr. Warbeck put his glasses back on. "Well, at first I wasn't sure that it is at all important, because it was *in* the building—on our floor, the eighth floor, you see. It didn't seem likely that this bank robber would stay *in* the building after holding up the bank. But the more carefully I thought about it, the more it seemed that it must have been almost immediately after that, and immediately after he'd shot that police officer—a terrible thing!—and I said to myself, Eugene, you had better take some advice on this at least, perhaps it *is* important. And then I remembered that Mrs. MacTaggart had mentioned that you are a police officer, and I came straightaway." He sighed. "I don't, of course, know a great deal about policemen or police work. My—my older brother was a little wild, there was trouble with the police over him, before he left home—my poor mother was so embarrassed—but of course that was back in Auburn, years ago. You see, at the *time*—on Tuesday, I mean—I never heard about any of the excitement. I didn't leave the building until after five o'clock, and by then it was all over. I didn't hear about it, in fact, until this afternoon, from Mrs. Roberts, who is also a member of our little group, when she called to tell me about little Jamie's adoption. A sweet child. I'm so happy we have found parents for him at last. And she did not mention the—er—time it had happened. But I had thought it a trifle queer at the time, and so when I came home tonight I looked at the newspapers—Mrs. Tranter always keeps them at least a week—and that was when I began to think it might be important." He looked at Mendoza anxiously.

"*What?*" asked Mendoza.

"The man I saw. You see—I went back in my mind, to be sure of all the details, and I am sure it cannot have been more than ten minutes after—after all the shooting down in the lobby. A terrible thing," said Mr. Warbeck. "I left Mrs. Tranter's house at a little after ten. I walked down the hill to Hollywood Boulevard and got the bus there, at the corner of Fairfax Avenue. I knew the schedule, of course, as I frequently take it, so I didn't have to wait long. And I must say, for so large a city, the public transportation is extremely poor. However! It generally takes the bus between thirty and forty minutes, at that time of day, to reach the corner of Spring Street and Seventh Avenue where I get off. And it seldom takes me more than ten minutes to walk the two blocks down to Grand and get up to our office. So I must have reached the office at very nearly eleven-twenty or a few minutes before. Yes. And I had been there for over an hour. In fact, I had only just glanced at my watch a minute or two before I got up, and it was then twenty-five minutes to one."

"Yes?" said Mendoza impatiently. Possibly it was Mr. Warbeck's fussy and maddening manner, but he had the growing feeling that something important was about to emerge. "Yes?"

"And you see, Miss Corsa had said she would be there at twelve forty-five, and I was rather anxious to speak to her about that Mrs. Riley, who—well, well, I mustn't be irrelevant! Anyway, I knew my watch had been running slow, and when I heard steps in the corridor—it's not carpeted, you see, and I hadn't bothered to latch the door, being there alone—I got up and went to the door to see if it was her. And I saw this man."

"Yes?" By piecing together what various witnesses said, and the surgeon, they had placed the bank heist as occurring between twelve twenty-five and twelve-thirty and the shooting about two minutes later. "How slow is your watch, do you know?"

138

"Oh, perhaps four or five minutes, I think. I saw this man——"

All right, they guessed that the actual heist man stayed in the building. If it was really twelve-forty when Warbeck's watch said twelve thirty-five, that gave him about eight minutes to reach the eighth floor. Reasonable?

"—And he looked so—queer—that I really did notice him, if you know what I mean," said Mr. Warbeck. "There's a skylight, too, the corridor is fairly well lighted. He was coming along from the direction of the elevators, but very slowly. Our office is on the left-hand side of the corridor as you come from the elevators—which are self-service elevators, of course—and so I was looking out the door to my own right. This man was all bent over, with one hand sort of holding himself under his jacket, as if—as if he were hurt, or in pain——"

Bert winged him, by God! ¡Claro es! thought Mendoza triumphantly. They had found the two empty shells from Dwyer's gun, but neither of the slugs—they had taken it for granted that both had ricocheted off the marble and gone out the rear door of the lobby, which was open, into the parking lot. They'd hunted around for them, but since at that time it didn't look as if X had been hampered in getting away, it hadn't seemed too important. Now . . . !

"In fact, when I first saw him, he was leaning on the wall. I thought perhaps he'd been taken sick suddenly, or even had a heart attack—and then he came on past me, but walking as if he *was* in pain, bent over, as I say, and one hand—— Well, you can see why, Lieutenant,

139

when I did hear there had been shots fired and a man killed, I thought at once——"

"Yes. Did you see where he went?"

"Oh, I spoke to him. Yes." Mr. Warbeck adjusted his glasses. "As he came past, I asked if I could help him, if he was taken ill. He didn't answer, just sort of shook his head and—er—shuffled on past. Well, it was queer, and I watched him. He went into the public lavatory at the end of the corridor."

"Did you see any blood on him?"

"No, that I did not, Lieutenant—if I had I would most certainly have realized there was something wrong *then* and reported it."

"Can you describe him? His clothes and so on?"

"Oh, yes, sir, I can do that. Spending so many years as a floorwalker, one gets into the habit of noticing things, you know. I think he was taller than I am, even if he was bent over like that, I would guess he was five foot ten or a bit more. Quite thin, I would say. Of course I didn't see his face too clearly, and just for a moment, but it was —er—more full than thin. He had on a gray suit, a white shirt, and some kind of tie, I think. I couldn't see that because his hand was over it, inside his jacket like this." And Mr. Warbeck demonstrated. "Do you really think it could have been the bank robber, Lieutenant?"

"It sounds like one very damn hot lead, and I wish to God we'd had it before," said Mendoza. "Was——"

"Oh, *dear*," said Mr. Warbeck. "I am so sorry. If I had only heard about it at the *time*, of course, I'd have told someone."

"Yes. Was his right or left hand inside his jacket? In

other words, what part of him might have been injured?"

"Oh, dear, that's rather difficult to——" Mr. Warbeck shut his eyes, evidently trying to think back and visualize. "I *think* it was his right hand. As if he were holding his left shoulder, or a spot just below, you know. But I'm not absolutely sure."

"He had on a suit? Not a sports jacket and slacks of the same color?"

"Well, I *think* it was a suit," said Mr. Warbeck. "I do feel so horribly guilty that I didn't realize before it was —— But as I've explained——"

"Yes, yes," said Mendoza, getting up. Owing to Mr. Warbeck's ramblings, it was past nine o'clock. "I want a detailed formal statement on this *pronto,* Mr. Warbeck. Come on, I'll give you a ride down to Headquarters. And then I think we'll rout out the cleaners responsible for that office building——" He took Mr. Warbeck's arm.

"Dear me," said Mr. Warbeck, looking flustered. "You really think this is important?"

"Very damned important!" Mendoza hustled him to the living room where he'd left his jacket and shrugged into it.

Alison was attempting to read with El Señor and Sheba sharing her lap. She eyed Mendoza. "You look as though you'd just found the pot of gold at the end of the rainbow. Don't tell me——"

"Maybe we have," said Mendoza. "Expect me when you see me, *querida!*" He hustled Mr. Warbeck out to the garage.

141

Thoms was there, of course; Schenke was there, and Galeano was there of inertia—a bachelor, he hadn't much to go home to and had hung around, keeping Schenke company.

"By God," he said, hearing Mr. Warbeck, "I thought it was damn funny Bert would have missed the bastard entirely. He wasn't an extra-money marksman, but he wasn't that bad a shot either." They all, of course, had to keep up to a certain standard on the range.

And they all were feeling a little excited at this break. They got a formal signed statement from Eugene Howard Warbeck, who twittered excitedly and obviously felt very important himself, and sent him home in a squad car. And then they got hold of the manager of the office building, with some difficulty. He wasn't at home; he was enjoying a session of poker with some pals, but his wife reluctantly parted with the phone number.

The manager, one Frederick Reising, snarled at Mendoza. "Now who the hell are you and what do you want? The first time I've held any cards in weeks—three jackpots I've took, I'm really hot—and why anybody has to come bothering——"

"Congratulations, Mr. Reising," said Mendoza, grinning into the phone; a poker ace himself, he meant it. "Lieutenant Mendoza, Headquarters. I——"

"Oh," said Reising. "Oh-oh! Oh, my God. Listen——"

"Nothing to do with your poker game, Mr. Reising. Homicide, not Vice. No raid."

"Actually I'm at a poker palace in Gardena," said Reising casually.

Mendoza laughed. "At a Madison exchange? Quite a

142

trick! Don't worry about the poker—I like a few hands myself occasionally. Look, what we want . . ." He explained.

"Oh, hell," said Reising. "Hell and damnation. Listen, Lieutenant, I'm hot—really hot. I don't want to miss this. Is it O.K. if I just call my wife, tell her to give you the keys? Is that all right? I'll answer all the questions you want tomorrow, though I don't see what *I* can give you, but—— The cleaning people will be there now. It's the Ace-High Service——"

Mendoza took pity on him—he'd had winning streaks himself—and said that would be O.K. "You're a right guy," said Reising fervently.

They collected the keys from a sleepy Mrs. Reising at midnight, out on Cumberland Street in Hollywood, and drove on down to the tall dark office building at Seventh and Grand.

As they came into the lobby, in the reflected glow from street lights and advertising neon, they all involuntarily looked at the place where Bert Dwyer had fallen. The blood had all been cleaned up now, of course, but they could see it.

"But he got the son of a bitch," said Schenke in grim satisfaction. "He winged him."

Mendoza was spotting a flash around, looking for light switches. As they had come up, they had seen that there were a few lights in the building, on upper floors. The cleaners. Reising had said only the upper floors, not the bank, which had its own cleaners. The Ace-High Service came every weekday evening to clean the rest of the building.

"And what a forlorn hope," said Mendoza now. "If

143

anybody had noticed anything on Tuesday night, we'd have heard before."

"You think so?" said Galeano. "I don't suppose anybody on that kind of job is just so awfully damned brilliant. Look at a mess of bloodstained paper towels and figure some female had maybe been caught short by her period or something——"

"In a men's rest room?" asked Mendoza.

"Well——"

It was an eerie place at night, a big office building. It seemed to have echoes, secrecies not apparent during the busy daytimes when it was crowded with people. They rode up in an elevator; they found the cleaning women, who were surprised and disturbed to see them. The cleaning women didn't seem to be mentally deficient, just tired, hard-working women who didn't have the education or training to be anything but cleaning women. Eventually they found the two who would be responsible for the eighth-floor public rest rooms. A Miss Rubio and a Mrs. Marx.

"When you cleaned that men's rest room on Tuesday night," said Mendoza, "did you find anything—different? Unusual? Such as bloodstained towels?"

Miss Rubio looked at Mrs. Marx. "Why, no, sir, we didn't, did we, Rita? Just the usual mess. People are like pigs in public lavatories, honest, the things we find! I wouldn't like to tell you, sir. You're *police?* Well, I know there was that awful shooting here that day, but——"

"No bloodstains? Anywhere?" asked Galeano.

"Why, no, there wasn't. Naturally, if there had been, we'd have *said* something—told somebody, like Mr. Reising. No, there wasn't. Why do you think there was?"

"So he was cute," said Schenke. "They're very cute boys, this pair. He took the bloodstained stuff away with him to dispose of outside. Elsewhere. But with a bullet in him—even if it wasn't so bad, and he got away—he'd have needed a doctor. A crooked doctor. Or if he couldn't find one, maybe he's a lot worse off by now. I *said* Bert couldn't have fired twice without hitting *something*——"

In a house on Emma Street, an old frame house, the tall brown woman said, "Pork chops. Your favorite. What's the matter, you sickenin' for something?"

"No'm," said the brown boy. "I'm all right." And that had been six hours ago.

"Well, you sure don't act all right. Moonin' around like you was only half here. You miss your dad, I guess." Her voice had softened. "I know, honey. The good Lord knows, so do I. So do I. But we got to believe it's just God's will. You're not in any trouble at school?"

"How would I be? No, I'm O.K. Stop fussing."

"Well," she sighed, "you bein' kind of off your food, like. You feel all right?"

"I'm all right!" he said angrily. He began to eat. The pork chops had given him indigestion. He still didn't feel too good, even after all this time later.

He didn't want to go home. He ought to, but she'd fuss some more.

He stood across the street from the Coffey house and stared at it. He was thinking about what had happened there last Friday.

CHAPTER TWELVE

Half the men from Central division were at the funeral.
The sheriff's county boys were co-operative at such
times, coming in to patrol the area for a couple of hours
so the men could get away. All the Homicide men were
there, and Goldberg, and Pat Callaghan from Narcotics,
and Fletcher of Traffic, and men from other offices.

Mendoza, sitting between Alison and Angel Hackett,
wished he could believe all that the minister was saying.
He hoped maybe Mary Dwyer did; he didn't know. And
the minister, oddly, chose to read from Ecclesiastes.

" 'To every thing there is a season, and a time to every
purpose under the heaven: a time to be born, and a time
to die; a time to plant, and a time to pluck up that which
is planted . . . a time to embrace, and a time to refrain
from embracing . . . a time to love, and a time to hate;
a time of war, and a time of peace. What profit hath he
that worketh in that wherein he laboreth? I have seen
the travail, which God hath given to the sons of
men . . . That which hath been is now; and that which
is to be hath already been; and God requireth that which

is past . . . I said in mine heart, God shall judge the righteous and the wicked: for there is a time there for every purpose and for every work.' . . . Let us pray."

And presently they all drove up the hill to the grave, and listened to the minister again, and saw the coffin lowered. And then it was over, and it was time to remember life again. Mary Dwyer went quickly away in the limousine.

Alison and Angel had come together. "We're going to lunch somewhere and then to see Art. I don't suppose you know whether you'll be late?"

Mendoza shook his head. "I'll call, *cara*." He added to Angel, "You'd better look more cheerful than that for Art."

"Cheerful!" said Angel broodingly. "I know better than anyone how that woman feels. When they called about Art, that time——"

"Well, he was lucky—and lightning never strikes twice in the same place," said Mendoza. He kissed Alison and went on down the hill toward the Ferrari.

The Homicide boys all went back to the office and made up hasty plans, glanced over their lists, and started grimly to work again.

There were eight men on their list of possibles from Records whom they hadn't located yet. "I added a couple more this morning," said Galeano. They were still looking at Records; there were a lot of pedigrees to go through down there.

"So I see," said Mendoza. "That one rings a bell—Eric Blaine. An offbeat one, I seem to—— Is this a current address, I wonder. It's an old one." He stared at the name for a moment. "I'll go check on him. The rest of you——"

Palliser was sending out teletypes. Thousands and thousands of teletypes, he felt; it wasn't really that many, but there were quite a few. The information had come in, special delivery, from the Higgins head office where that new-model Hi-Standard revolver was made. It listed every retail outlet which had been supplied with the new models. They might have a couple of small breaks, by what the rest of the information said. Sears, Roebuck wasn't, of course, the only retail firm which sold these guns; hardware stores, gunshops, a few other places sold them, too, but the largest supply of the new models had gone to Sears. Palliser knew that in California at least all handguns sold by Sears had to be ordered through the catalogue and all orders had to be accompanied by a voucher signed by an officer of the law, that the purchaser was and was not this, that, and the other. He doubted, therefore, that the gun had been purchased in California. Practically all of the guns sold by Sears, however, were purchased through their catalogue; and one small break here was that while the new model had first been distributed from the manufacturer two months ago, owing to the fact that a new Sears catalogue had not been printed until a month ago, to all intents and purposes the gun had only been on the market for four weeks, as far as the Sears outlet went.

But he sent teletypes everywhere—to all the retail Sears stores in the unfortunately large area concerned, to all Sears central warehouses, to a great many sheriffs and chiefs of police, asking urgent co-operation. Covering that area, that took him most of the afternoon, and even after all those other people sprang into action, there was going to be a deadly lot of routine to get through and it might get them nowhere in the end. In that area how many of those guns might have been sold? He couldn't guess. A .22 handgun was popular with a lot of men. Try to have somebody, in all those places, get a look at the actual guns which had been sold, to locate one with a broken trigger guard? God. It looked hopeless; but given the leads, you had to go through the motions.

About four o'clock, as he was taking a break over a cup of coffee, Piggott wandered in and sat down. "Ah, air conditioning," he said. He looked hot and untidy. He said, "What kind of service was that for Bert? The minister had robes on." He made it sound sinister.

"I don't know. Episcopalian, I think. Or Presbyterian."

"Oh," said Piggott darkly. "Robes."

"Well, why not?"

"Trappings of luxury," said Piggott. "I sometimes wonder what Luther and the rest of them would think, come back and see how far away from original Protestant principles——" He shook his head. "It *was* a Protestant service, wasn't it?" He looked suddenly alarmed. Palliser reassured him and said in any case he didn't think Piggott's immortal soul would have been endangered if it hadn't been. Piggott looked sinister again but said, "It's too hot to argue . . . I can't make head or tail of this Coffey thing. But one thing did occur to me—when I was looking over all the statements and so on. I hadn't seen the house, you know. And I thought, what about the screens? I mean——"

"Oh, didn't I put that in? All the screens——"

"Yeah, yeah, I know now. Coffey had taken all the screens off to paint the frames. Funny time to do it, hot weather and all the flies. I mean, just like the lieutenant said at first, it could have been a sniper in a car. Only if the bullet came through an open window, there'd still have been a hole in the screen. Only there weren't any screens. So it could still have come through a window."

Palliser shook his head. "I don't see it, Matt. They're all pretty high off the ground, that old house. And while the slug took a slight upward course, it was a very slight one. To get a straight shot through any of the windows, you'd either have to be on the front porch or standing on a ladder. And we know nobody approached the house from in front, so——"

"Well," said Piggott, "I read a story once. A funny kind of story—it was in a collection of stories I happened to pick up at the library. It was about this Catholic priest who's a kind of detective, supposed to be, and there was a lot of highfalutin talk and so on, but the point is, it was kind of the same situation we've got here, man killed and a lot of witnesses all swore nobody had gone near him. And you know who it turned out to be? The mailman. Everybody'd seen him go up to the door, but he was just such a familiar figure nobody mentioned him."

Palliser, who did not read detective novels and had never heard of Father Brown, looked skeptical. "That seems very thin to me. *Somebody* would have mentioned him—he couldn't have counted on it. Are you supposing the mailman shot Carol Coffey and none of those neighbors saw it?"

"Well, somebody familiar in the neighborhood, you know—so familiar they'd all look right through him. A neighborhood kid? A—somebody like that Webb girl?"

"And what reason would a neighborhood kid or——"

"*I* don't know," said Piggott. "All *I* know is that the only other answer is Verne, and I don't think we'll ever tie him up to a gun. The right gun. We can bring him in and grill him a little and maybe in time he'd break down, but maybe he wouldn't too. My only suggestion is to get him to take a lie-detector test."

"Yes, I thought of that too. Tell us right off, yes or no, and when they can see we've proved they're lying, a lot of times they do break down and tell all."

"I'm going to ask the lieutenant."

"More to the point," said Palliser tiredly, "ask the Coffeys. We can't force anybody to take a lie-detector test if they don't want to, and of course it's not admissible evidence. Verne's a minor. Even if he agreed to take one, Sam Coffey could say no, and we'd be stymied. Of course," he added thoughtfully, "Sam Coffey might not know that."

Piggott looked as if he'd like to swear, if he had been a swearing man. "And you know as well as me we'd have to tell him. Tell people all their rights under the law. You know, I'm all for law and order, but I think sometimes we play too nice. All the—what d'you call 'em?— Queensberry Rules. I mean, sometimes, what with all the rules about evidence and prisoners' rights and all, it looks like *we* haven't got many rights working for us."

"How well I know what you mean," said Palliser. The outside phone rang and he picked it up. "Headquarters Homicide, Sergeant Palliser."

"Oh, hello, John," said Hackett. "Luis out?"

"Like everybody else. Piggott and I are sitting here

151

deciding that all the citizens have got rights except cops hunting the bad boys. Rules of evidence and so on."

"You just discovering that?" said Hackett. "Add in those softhearted judges who rap us over the knuckles for charging the juveniles who are just being normal mischievous kids."

"Oh, yes," said Palliser. "How are you feeling?"

"I'm all right, but I tell you, some night I'm going to break out of here. Find out where my clothes are hidden and get *out*. Home. I've never been so sick of a place in my life. And when I did get one nurse who didn't have a face to stop a clock—in fact, a very cute little blonde— what the hell do they do but transfer her to Maternity! I——"

"Oh-oh," said Palliser. "I guess you are coming along all right, if you're taking notice of females again."

"Purely reflex action," said Hackett. "I'm a respectable married man. But I didn't call about that. I was lying here just now—Angel and Alison just left—and that Coffey thing came into my head, and all of a sudden I wondered about the screens. Weren't there any? On the windows, you know. Because that would be one way to tell whether she *was* shot inside the house——"

"Yes, it would have been," said Palliser, and told him about the screens.

"Oh," said Hackett. "Well, it was just a thought."

"Yes. You need cigarettes or anything?"

"I need," said Hackett, "some clothes and a military pass out of this damned place. Well, see you."

"See you." Palliser put down the phone.

Sergeant Lake came in and said he'd found another

light-green Anglia De Luxe. He added apologetically, "In Pomona."

"For God's sake!" said Palliser. "Doesn't anybody down at the beach buy Anglias? Pomona! *Twenty* degrees hotter out there!"

Mendoza had spent a somewhat irritating afternoon tracing the Blaines back, address by address, sixteen years. The man he was hunting, Eric Blaine, interested him just faintly as a new possible because he had been a funny one, an unpredictable one, and just might have taken to bank robbing as a new kick. True, he didn't have a record of violence—but that might be his partner.

Eric Blaine and his older brother Charles had lived with their widowed mother. There was money—not millions, but a substantial amount of money. The boys hadn't had to work. Boys they remained until well into their thirties, enjoying themselves, but all strictly legal— oh, they'd both been picked up on D.-and-D. counts now and then, but that was all. Until Eric got the idea it might be fun to pull a holdup. Just for kicks, he said airily later on. It could be suspected that Mama held the purse strings a little too tight. At any rate, Eric had done a heist job on a liquor store in Hollywood and got himself a criminal record at the age of thirty-eight, which was unusual. He'd left his prints all over the place, and as he'd obligingly also left his thumbprint for the D. M. V. on his driver's license—— When he got out, ten years back, Mama had been dead and he and his brother had had a high time running through all the money. During that period they'd made a few headlines —wild parties complete with call girls, the attempted theft of a private plane (" 'Always wanted to know how it felt to bail out,' says ex-con seriously"), and one rather unsavory episode involving the suicide of a twenty-year-old girl. Charles was sued by somebody for alienation of affections; for a while they both ran around with the coterie surrounding an ex-Syndicate hood who'd retired to Beverly Hills. Then, when the money was gone, they'd both dropped out of sight.

Mendoza didn't really think Eric—or Charles for that matter—was the particular X they wanted now; but you never knew. Eric certainly had the boldness this X needed to have, and maybe with encroaching years he had developed the caution.

They were now pretty certain that Bert had winged one of the pair. A waste of time to circulate flyers to all doctors; an honest doctor would already have reported treating a gunshot wound, and a crooked one never would. But because most doctors were honest, the chances were that the wounded man hadn't risked one at all. That he'd tried to take care of the wound himself, or some pal had. And if that were so, the chances were also good that the wound was a lot worse by now, infected—maybe the slug still in him (pray to God!). So they'd haul in every possible on their list and then take a long hard look at all the pals they'd ever run with, and then they'd take another look through Records for more possibles.

This one they'd never stop hunting for.

The Blaines had moved around a lot, Beverly Hills to Hollywood to Venice to Santa Monica to, finally,

Bellflower. They had left forwarding addresses—apparently they'd stayed together—but because a number of different post-office branches were involved and phone calls were never satisfactory on a thing like that, Mendoza did a little traveling around in traffic, cursing the heat. The Ferrari wasn't air-conditioned because as a very cautious driver he felt it was dangerous to drive with all the windows up, not to hear the sirens maybe, or catch their direction. There were always a lot of sirens going in L. A. While he drove, he ruminated on that once-overheard remark of a stout matron touring Olvera Street on a hot day, to the effect that Mexicans didn't feel the heat.

It was a convenient theory.

God, it was hot.

He came to the end of his hunt, surprisingly, down on Bellflower Boulevard, at about four o'clock. Of all things he would have expected the unpredictable Blaine brothers to be doing, running a tavern was the last choice. And he wondered how in hell they had managed to get a liquor license. Well, Charles hadn't any record, of course, and it wasn't too uncommon a name—he could have claimed he was a different Charles Blaine, and with Eric well in the background—— He could also, of course, have bought the license under the counter before the new, stricter law was in effect.

Anyway, there he was behind the bar of a very classy-looking tavern, smartly advertised in neon as the Five O'clock Club. It had synthetic-stone panels on its front, a stained-glass window in its front door, and inside it was paneled in synthetic oak and liberally furnished in Ye Olde English, with red-leather banquettes and captain's

chairs and little round tables. There was another bar-
man and two very attractive cocktail waitresses—at least
attractive in this dim light.

There were only three customers in the place at this
time of day. Doubtless they got a brisk trade starting
about an hour from now. A man sat alone at the bar,
slumped over a half-empty glass, and a man and a woman
bent heads together over a table, holding hands, full
glasses forgotten.

Mendoza strolled over to the bar, hat in hand, and
ordered straight rye. He recognized Charles Blaine from
his resemblance—his quite remarkable resemblance—to
Eric's mug shots. Both were biggish men, not so tall as
broad, with round faces and solid jaws; both were fair.
Charles had lost most of his hair; Mendoza wondered if
Eric had too. That ran in families, didn't it? He
smoothed his own thick black hair absently, sipped the
rye, and wondered how to get at Charles. Was Eric in on
this deal, or had they at last parted company? No sign of
Eric.

Come out all open and ask? He drank rye. He decided
that no finesse was necessary, and just then the man
sitting on the bar stool five feet away said, "Hey, Charlie,
how 'bout 'nother shot? I'm good for it, you know that."

"Sure thing, Joe." Blaine came up with the bottle.

"How's old Eric doin' these days? Still livin' it up with
the dames? Boy, he sure does make a hit with the dames,
don't he?"

"He's got a touch of 'flu right now, in bed upstairs,"
said Blaine casually.

Upstairs, thought Mendoza. They lived here, over the

tavern? A touch of 'flu, he thought, and suddenly his heart jumped a little and he thought, Or a slug somewhere in him, by God? A slug Bert Dwyer had snapped off as he fell dying?

Upstairs . . . He finished the rye and went out unhurriedly. There was a parking lot behind the place, and at one side was an outside staircase going up to a small landing and a door painted bright green. There were curtains at the two windows there.

He went quietly up the wooden staircase. The door was locked. He knocked on it gently and then sharply. After an interval he knocked again.

"Who is it?" Cautious voice just inside the door—a man's voice.

"Police!" said Mendoza peremptorily. "I want to see Eric Blaine."

There was a little silence—he could almost feel it to be a panicky silence—and then the voice said breathlessly, "He's—he's not here. He won't be home until—until about eight o'clock. You—'d better come back then."

"Let me in," said Mendoza.

"No. You've got no right—this is his apartment. I'm—just a friend. I can't—— What the hell *police* want with Eric?"

"I can get a search warrant," said Mendoza.

"So go get your search warrant!" The voice was angry and very frightened. "What the *hell*—police——"

"I'll be back in an hour," said Mendoza sharply, and clattered noisily down the stairs. He went back into the tavern. He stopped just inside the door and watched

Charles Blaine behind the bar. He thought, ¡*Adelante—no digo que es verdad,* but if so, God, let me be the one to get him! The one to get him, for Bert.

Within a minute the phone rang behind the bar. Charles Blaine answered it. Mendoza could not see his expression, but he didn't talk long. He hung up the phone, said something to the other bartender, clapped him on the shoulder, and went out to the kitchen through the door behind the bar.

Instantly Mendoza went out of the tavern. There was a narrow alley beside it, on the side where the staircase rose, which gave access to the parking lot behind. On the other side of the alley began another row of shop buildings all joined. The first one was a gift shop. Mendoza stood in front of the window and fixed his eyes on a pink china poodle wearing a silly expression and a straw hat garlanded with daisies. Hands in pockets, he contemplated the poodle and wondered who would consider paying out five ninety-eight (plus tax) for the creature, and out of the corner of his eye he kept a watch on the staircase. He could just see part of the green-painted door at the top.

Dios, had the luck turned? Was there a man up there with a bullet in him? A bullet out of Bert's gun? God, let me get him, he thought.

Next to the poodle was a white china Persian kitten, sitting in a yellow china basket. The basket had blue daisies wound around its handle, and the kitten wore an idiotic simper. Mendoza decided that it was a libel on all felines. Even the poodle was preferable.

Charles Blaine came around the rear corner of the

158

alley and climbed the stairs. He had taken off his bar apron.

A man up there with a bullet in him, and police knocking at the door—for whatever reason—what would they do? If the Blaine brothers were sharing the apartment, Charles Blaine would have to know——

Next to the cat was a rather amusing owl. It was really a sewing kit. Its big eyes were the hollow handles of a pair of scissors, and its body was a pincushion. The owl stared at Mendoza and Mendoza stared back. He began to feel a little conspicuous; this wasn't the kind of shop a man would find so fascinating. Oh, well, he could be shopping for his wife's birthday. He could see his reflection in the glass, and straightened his tie, and reflected absently that at least *he* wasn't bald—nothing so aged a man as losing his hair; but he didn't, in fact, look his age at all. He felt superior. He smoothed his mustache.

The green-painted door opened and three men came out.

Three? thought Mendoza.

Two men, much alike, were supporting the third between them. Those two glanced out anxiously toward the street; Mendoza dodged back. Then they all had their backs turned, going down the stairs, and it was evidently an awkward job for the outside two. The stairs were narrow, and the third man, between them, seemed to be scarcely conscious, hanging limp. They got him down step by step, supporting him by the arms; his feet dragged; they were both panting.

Mendoza watched and timed it. The stairs went

straight down; when they had got the man three steps from the bottom, he abandoned the gift-shop window, quietly walked down the alley, and stood at the foot of the stairs.

He smiled at Eric and Charles Blaine as they lifted the man down the last step. He had his badge in his hand, held out. "Mendoza, Headquarters," he said, smiling gently. "Do please introduce me to your friend, won't you?"

CHAPTER THIRTEEN

The man with the Blaine brothers was one Luther Foote, and he didn't have any kind of record, but he did have a gunshot wound in his lower right shoulder. He was forty-seven, five feet nine, a hundred and sixty, brown-haired, and blue-eyed; he was divorced from his wife; he was a plumber and had his own shop with three employees.

That information, and a welter of more information, came out at once, from the Blaines.

The surgeon told them that the gunshot wound was approximately as old as sometime last Tuesday. There wasn't any slug in the wound—it had gone straight through him; but that was helpful in a way, as showing it had probably been a high-caliber slug; a .22 or something like that probably would have stayed in him. The wound had had some amateur care but was infected; the man wouldn't die, but he wasn't in too good a condition. They could question him tomorrow.

They hardly had to question the Blaines at all. "What the hell d'you think we'd do?" burst out Eric, angry and scared. "This was Joe Sebastian! He's got contacts—everybody says—like with the Syndicate. Big-time gambler like him. Look, neither Luther nor me wanted any repercussions from Sebastian, for God's sake! D'you think Luther'd have looked twice at that dame if he'd known she belonged to Joe Sebastian? Like hell! But she and this redhead came in to the place—our place—alone, and they gave Luther and me the eye, and how should we know who the blonde was? My God." Eric mopped his brow. He hadn't lost his hair, and he looked a vigorous forty instead of the fifty-three he was. Somebody—that customer—had said he was quite a guy for the dames. Mendoza could believe it.

"My God," he said. "So there we were at this apartment, big fancy place right on Hollywood Boulevard, having some drinks, when this guy came in——"

"When was this, Mr. Blaine?"

"Last Tuesday night. And he's a big guy, and he just tells us calmly to get out. I was ready to go, believe me—I didn't like his looks—but Luther gets a little feisty after a few drinks, and he began to argue with him. That's when the guy says that no two-bit punk is going to play around with a girl of Joe Sebastian's, and he hauls out this cannon and takes a shot at Luther. I'd guess the place is soundproofed—nobody seemed to take any notice. I got Luther out O.K., but my God, Lieutenant, am I going to yell 'Cop' and lay a complaint against Sebastian? And get a couple of hoods come gunning for us for real? I'm not that big a fool! I——"

"That's the way it was," said Charles Blaine. "Eric brought Luther home with him, and we've been doing

162

what we could for him. We knew a doctor would report it——" He passed a hand over his face.

"Sebastian?" said Mendoza, and smiled. "Don't believe all you hear. He's not a Syndicate man and he's got no Syndicate contacts. If he had he wouldn't be let inside L. A." This was the only big city in the world where the Syndicate had never got a toe hold. Of course, this last year or so the F. B. I. and other forces had cleaned the Syndicate out of a number of places. Mendoza knew Sebastian's name, vaguely, as that of a reputed big-time gambler who came visiting L.A. occasionally; supposedly he had undercover business interests here, silent partnerships. But he didn't know if he bought this story or not from the Blaines.

"My God, Lieutenant, if you——"

"We'll hear what he has to say. Where were you and Foote last Tuesday between noon and one o'clock?"

Eric Blaine was an intelligent man, if unpredictable. He leaped off the straight chair they'd given him and said wildly, "The *bank* robberies? Oh, my God, you don't think—— *Luther* and me? Oh, my God, how crazy can you get? The papers say it's a man alone—— That's *crazy* . . ."

"We've got evidence that our man winged him," said Mendoza. "Where were you?"

"Dear *God* . . ."

"Sit down, Eric," said his brother. "They were both with me in our apartment eating lunch. I've been thinking of expanding the tavern, and Luther was going to invest a little money in it."

"I see," said Mendoza. "You just chose the right tense,

friend. I suppose you realize you'll lose your liquor license over this and won't be able to get another?"

Charles Blaine nodded tiredly. He looked at his brother and said, "You and your women."

"Well, how the hell was I to know——"

"You and your *women*."

So they went out and picked up Joe Sebastian, who wasn't nearly as big a man as he thought he was, and asked him about that story. Sebastian, a dapper big fellow with a booming voice, heard them out and denied the whole thing. The blonde they'd found with him denied everything too.

"Prove it," said Sebastian coolly.

They tried to. They got a search warrant and went over his apartment. They didn't find any bullet holes anywhere. They heard from the superintendent of the building that a window had been broken in Sebastian's living room last Thursday—an accident. Conceivably it could have been broken by a bullet on Tuesday; the superintendent said no bullet hole, but Sebastian wouldn't have left that there. After the first heat of the moment had passed, he'd start thinking about an attempted-homicide charge. Knock out some more glass with a chair, wait to report it until Thursday. They didn't find a gun on him or anywhere in the apartment.

"You've got nothing on me, gentlemen," said Sebastian. "Those two guys I never heard of in my life. Probably one of 'em shot the other and 's trying to cover up, drag my name into it." He winked. "A lotta people know my name who I don't know."

They didn't find a gun in the Blaines' apartment, in the tavern, or in Luther's apartment. And of course that was all very unsatisfactory indeed, because it left them right up in the air. Anything could be the truth. Maybe Eric and Luther were the pair of X's they wanted and that had been Bert Dwyer's slug that went clean through Luther. Maybe the story Eric told was true blue right down the line. No proof either way.

"Well, what does everybody think?" Mendoza sighed. The two Blaines had been taken over to the new jail—failure to report attempted homicide; they'd be out on bail presently.

"Oh, hell, pay your money and take your choice," said Galeano morosely. "But I guess I think not. Because for one thing, this Luther Foote, by what we hear, built up his own business, started as an apprentice and now owns the place, and that's not the type of guy—steady and hard-working—to suddenly go off the rails. It looks like he just has a weakness for skirts. As per little Eric."

"Well, there's nothing to *say*," said Schenke. And that was late Saturday afternoon. His eye was still faintly discolored; he felt it absently. "I guess I go along with Nick. There sure as hell isn't enough to charge them with the bank jobs."

"Mmh. One thing," said Mendoza. "If they are the boys we want, I think they'll start lying very low. Our boys have been going at it hot and heavy—five in a period of thirty-two days, and the last three not a week apart. I made it that they found out how easy it was and couldn't resist just one more. God, I wish we had the men to stake out every bank downtown they haven't hit. But if it is Luther and Eric, I don't think they'll pull another, after this little scare. Keep an eye on them, anyway."

"The Feds——" said Schenke doubtfully.

The Feds, sitting in on all the Blaine business, had been skeptical from the first. There had just been a kidnapping back East, and fliers sent out to all the western states where it was suspected the kidnappers might have headed, and the Feds had dropped L. A.'s bank robbers back into the lap of Homicide and gone back to their own work. Their, by implication, far more important work. Occasionally the Feds got to acting a little superior and upstage.

Mr. Warbeck had looked at Luther Foote and said, "Oh, dear, I can't really be sure——" And Wolf had looked and said briefly, "No." Well, it had looked too good to be true.

They sat around dispiritedly discussing it for a while. Of course, there were the sketches, in the hands of a lot of bank personnel—in the end that might pay off; and there were men they still hadn't found, whom they wanted to talk to. There was Lester Cullinane, minus an alibi; they were asking around about his pals; they would see them too. There was still a lot of routine to do on it.

After a while Schenke and Galeano went out to snatch some dinner and go looking for one Robert Rhys who had an interesting record and was currently on parole. Landers hadn't been heard from since noon; he was on the track of one Alfred Hardcastle who also had a record of interest. Nobody knew where Higgins was—doubtless after another one like that.

Mendoza sat on in his office, brooding over the Blaines and trying to calculate coincidences, until Sergeant Lake came in and said, "There's a guy out here asking to see you. Says his name's Tommy Canaletti. Ring a bell?"

Mendoza sat up with a jerk. "*¿De veras?* Now what —— O.K., shove him in, Jimmy." Abruptly his mind began to tick over on all cylinders again.

Tommy Canaletti was a sad little man who'd never got very far in life and realized it and minded it. Unlike most Skid Row bums, who lived day to day and had long ceased minding anything but the lack of fifty cents or a buck for another skinful of *vino*, Tommy realized that he was a failure—a weak, ineffectual little man—and that made him all the sadder. He wasn't exactly a wino and he wasn't exactly a bum; sometimes he worked, making deliveries for markets, something like that; more often he just drifted around. And probably one reason why Tommy had turned pigeon was that it made him feel important, helping the cops. He didn't work at that all the time either, just sometimes.

Now what in hell was Tommy doing here? Like all pigeons, he never visited Headquarters—or any precinct house.

He drifted into Mendoza's office and looked around sadly. He was a little man, no more than five-three, very thin and dark, and he had the great mournful dark eyes of all Italian madonnas. "Hello, Lieutenant," he said in his soft voice. He hadn't shaved for a few days, and his Hawaiian sports shirt was dirty, if gay, and his jeans were torn. He had on dirty white tennis shoes. "I was sorry as hell to hear about Sergeant Dwyer," he said sadly. "He was a nice guy."

"Yes, he was," said Mendoza. "Thanks, Tommy. Was that what you came to say?"

"Well, not all of it," said Tommy. "On account, I could do with a sawbuck. Or even two. And I thought this was kind of interesting myself, so maybe you'd think so too. You wouldn't have a cigarette, would you?" Mendoza gave him one. "Thanks. You know the sergeant had been asking all around about this guy got shot over on San Pedro one night? Leigh, his name was."

"Oh." That little thing had more or less died a natural death. "So?"

"Well, like I told him last time I saw him—gee, that's awful, his gettin' shot like that, nice a guy as you'd ever want to meet, wasn't he?—like I told him, the word was this Leigh had gone to see this guy Broadbent—ain't that the hell of a name?—who's a bartender at the Acme Grill, but the word is he's got contacts, you want anything under the counter, you——"

"Yes, Dwyer told me about that."

"Sure. But it seemed kind of funny to me, he was just a cheap bum, what'd he be up to? You know. An' I been askin' around, just casual, you know, like I was just curious, an' I got this word from a guy—another cheap bum—this Leigh shared a bottle with one night. And I think he's nuts, because it don't make no sense, only this particular guy is so far gone on *vino*, Lieutenant, he just couldn't 've made it up, see? So I come to pass it on for what it's worth. Maybe a sawbuck?" he added wistfully.

"Well, what is it?"

"What the guy said was, this Leigh told him he was lookin' for a guy to buy money. Leigh said he was gonna be rich, he could just find a guy to buy the stuff. Like, you know, an agent—a hot-money man."

168

Mendoza sat up abruptly. "¿Y qué es esto? ¡Porvida! Now what the hell—— Is that level, Tommy?"

"I know—it smells. A cheap wino. A bum. But that's what this guy said. I thought it was just funny enough that maybe it'd be worth——"

Wordlessly Mendoza took out his billfold and handed Tommy Canaletti twenty-five bucks.

"Well, gee, thanks, Lieutenant! And I'd like to say again how awful sorry I am about Sergeant Dwyer——"

Walter William Leigh, shot over on San Pedro Street about midnight one night and left dead in an alley. Nobody important. A Skid Row bum.

Trying to locate an agent to buy hot money. The kind of pro crook right at the top of the tree, one of the elite of crookdom.

Why, for God's sake? The bank jobs. My God, the bank jobs.

A hot-money man might take such piddling little sums, if he had a deal going already or expected one, a big fat deal so he could just slip the hot bank bills in with the rest. (That kidnapping?)

Leigh, for God's sake. What the hell was the connection? A third man mixed in? Seven, eight, even ten thousand bucks—so far—wasn't such a hell of a take split three ways, and it'd be watered down considerably if they'd sold it to an agent. Call it between three and four thousand.

So they'd killed Leigh, the other two, to up their take? Or because he was a cheap bum who'd talk too much when he was high? Then why cut him in in the first place? This just didn't make sense, any part of it. But things Tommy Canaletti had come up with in the past had checked out. So . . .

Mendoza went out to the anteroom to talk this over with Sergeant Lake—he had to talk it over with some-body—just as the phone rang. Sergeant Lake picked it up and immediately it started to make loud angry noises at him. Presently Sergeant Lake started to laugh. He laughed helplessly; helplessly he handed the phone to Mendoza.

"—and none of these Goddamned sons of bitches at the new jail knows me, and I thought we had some Goddamned *rules* about prisoners' rights, and can *I* help it if I happen to look like a bum at the moment? All right, all *right,* I'm entitled to one call, you bastard. Now listen, *I* couldn't help it—the son of a bitch started the fight—was I supposed to just stand there and let him maul me?—and he's a big bastard too, I didn't—— Who is this? Jimmy, for the love of Christ, if that's you laughing——"

"Where are you, Tom?" asked Mendoza.

"Lieutenant, thank God, will you for Christ's sake come down here and identify me?" howled Landers. "I'm at the new facility on Alameda, where else? I'm after this Hardcastle character. I get chased around a lot of places he might be. I've been in more dives than—— Well, I catch up to him awhile ago in a joint down on Macy. He's with another guy, and when I go up to him to pick him up, bring him in, he gets all excited and yells Fuzz, and you see this joint isn't exactly the kind where all the customers like cops just so well, and so there's a little Donnybrook, and——"

"I see," said Mendoza. "Very natural."

"*Listen*," said Landers, "there's no law says how *long* I can talk, you stupid bastard! Look, Lieutenant, so he gives me a poke in the eye, and rips my jacket half off, and everybody's yelling and there's quite a crowd in there—it's not a very big place—and I knock him down and get out my gun, and about then a squad car comes up, and what *kind* of Goddamned stupid rookies are we getting these days, anyway?—because, my good Christ, I *tell* them who I am, and I—— But some Goddamned son of a bitch has picked my pocket, and my badge—— And for God's sake, they've got me booked for carrying a concealed weapon and D.-and-D., and I've had exactly two drinks all day and no dinner, and will you for God's sake——"

"Yes, Tom," said Mendoza gently. Sergeant Lake was still speechless, red-faced. "I'll come down, Tom. Right away."

Landers was spluttering. "So all right, it's the newest and biggest damn jail facility in the country—maybe in the world—*which* says something about L. A., for God's sake—and we staff it with a Goddamned bunch of stupid cretins who—— Yes, I mean *you*, you bastard! And take your hands off this Goddamned phone. I've got a right to ——" There was a loud final click at the other end of the wire, and Mendoza handed the phone back to Lake and began to laugh.

"And he's still—technically—on his vacation," gasped Sergeant Lake. Sergeant Thoms came in and stared at them both.

"I'll go down and rescue him," said Mendoza. "Hello, Bill—Jimmy'll tell you all about it. If they don't believe

me, I'll send you an S. O. S. and you can call the chief.
You might call my wife and say I'll be late."

He identified an incoherent, raging Landers, who
looked the complete tough minus a jacket, sleeve torn
out of his shirt, and needing a shave, and calmed down a
dozen suddenly agitated jailers, and sent Landers home.
Hardcastle was safe in the new jail; they'd get to him
tomorrow. He went back to Headquarters to see if
anything new had turned up; also, he wanted to send out
a pickup on that bartender. Sergeant Lake was gone;
Sergeant Thoms was sitting at his desk reading a paperback. Higgins had come in, towing one Robert
Bandhauser who was one of those on the list from
Records, so Mendoza sat in on that questioning. It
wasn't very productive. Bandhauser hadn't any alibi
either.

At ten o'clock he went home, still dinnerless, and was
fussed over and fed. Something, he thought, to be said
for marital domesticities, even if it was productive of
howling twins.

Palliser was now receiving teletypes. Thousands and
thousands of teletypes. Not really that many, but——
Full co-operation soonest, Sheriff, Butte County.
Checking soonest, Sheriff, Alameda County. *Immediate
check,* Chief of Police, San Francisco—Sacramento—
Fresno—Denver—Portland—Spokane—Helena, Montana—Phoenix—Boise—Las Vegas—Santa Fé—Salt
Lake City . . . Sheriffs, hundreds of sheriffs all eager to
help him out, hundreds of police chiefs . . .

Eagerly co-operative Sears' store managers. He was

buried in teletypes. And nothing he could do much personally until all the results of the co-operation came in.

Find the one right gun, in that immense territory? Hopeless.

He went home. His mother's arthritis was better in this heat. It was at least good for something. He felt a little better after he'd had a shower. He called Roberta Silverman at eight o'clock.

"What are you doing?"

"Need you ask? Correcting papers, of course." Roberta taught fourth grade at a South Pasadena school.

"Oh."

"You don't sound your usual bright self. Well, I know, this thing—this sergeant. Did you know him well, John?"

"Yes, I knew him well," said Palliser. "There's nothing to say about that, is there?"

"Except that some of us—who are a little bit involved with any of you—even a *little* bit," she said with a smile in her voice, "sometimes wish you were driving buses or working on assembly lines instead."

"It doesn't really happen so often. Roberta——"

"I said a *little* bit."

But they both knew he'd ask her to marry him when he got his next automatic pay raise. And she liked his mother; they all got along fine.

"I'm supposed to be off Monday, but with all this —— I don't know. I'll call you."

"Yes," she said. "It's all right, John."

Palliser presently went to bed and dreamed that he was drowning. He was drowning, but not in water; it was all yellow; it was a sea of teletypes, long strips of teletypes, more and more being poured on top by a diligent Sergeant Lake, and he was screaming, "Jimmy, don't do this to me——" and Sergeant Lake kept adding more teletypes.

He woke up, sweating—God, it was hot; nights didn't cool off any more—and took an aspirin. He overslept, and he was late into the office; he didn't get there until eight-twenty.

Sergeant Lake, comfortably solid and round-faced and (of course) basking in air conditioning, said, "Morning. I just turned up another one for you. Light-green Anglia. In Pacoima. Sorry."

Pacoima. The very damndest hottest spot of the valley.

Palliser uttered a very rude word.

CHAPTER FOURTEEN

About nine o'clock on Sunday morning the bartender at that dive where Landers had got in trouble showed up and gravely handed in Landers' wallet, complete with badge and I. D., but minus any money. Landers said philosophically there'd only been about four bucks in it anyway.

The other bartender, they were still looking for. Schenke had gone looking for him, but it was his night off and he wasn't home. Schenke lingered until Mendoza came in that morning, to talk about that, and Galeano, Higgins, Landers, and the rest of them heard about that fantastic bit then.

"That Leigh?" said Galeano incredulously. "Tied up to the bank jobs? That's crazy! A cheap bum like that?"

"I know, I know," said Mendoza. "Even Tommy said it was crazy. But there it is. I don't know what it means, but I've thought since the second job that the bank money is being exchanged somehow, and that means a hot-money man, and here's a very funny sort of link to one. Maybe. We treated Walter William a bit casual, because it was such an anonymous kill, there weren't any leads at all, and he wasn't much loss. Right now I'm damn sorry Walter is dead and can't be questioned, and I think we ought to backtrack and find out a little more about him."

"We looked," said Schenke defensively. "There's never much you *can* find out about bums like that. They're—anonymous. That might not even have been his right name. Everything we got's in the files—I seem to remember he lived in a cheap rooming house over on First."

"Yes. I want to see all you got, refresh my memory. His prints weren't in our records, but they could be in somebody's. Let's ask the F. B. I."

"Anonymous!" said Higgins disgustedly. "What the hell could a bum like that have to do with——"

"I haven't the slightest idea, George. But any lead, we ought to——"

"Look, we don't have anything to say this pair *are* selling the loot to an agent."

"I still think so," said Mendoza stubbornly. "I know we haven't, but I think they are. And that being so——" Higgins exchanged a silent glance with Galeano. The boss got funny notions sometimes, and he could be stubborn. If he said follow this up, they hadn't any choice, even though it was reaching way out into space and the rest of them didn't see anything in it at all. On the other hand, sometimes the boss reached out into thin air and came up with something hot. "That being so," said Mendoza, "I'm making up stories about it. Walter William looked like an ordinary Skid Row drifter, but was he conceivably a former pro? In touch with pros?

Once the member of a gang of hoods, fallen to Skid Row? On the other hand, what pro in his right mind, intending to knock over a bank, would trust somebody like Walter in the deal? And you know I said awhile ago, this could just conceivably be a pair of amateurs. All right. Did they know about Walter's possible record and, not having any idea themselves where to find a money agent, figure Walter might know? Or——"

"Oh, for God's sake," said Higgins. "Look. How many amateurs—people on the right side of the fence—know there are such things as hot-money men?"

Mendoza reached behind him for the new County Guide and turned the first page. He contemplated a scale map of the welter of surface streets and freeways that was downtown L. A.—mostly their beat except for a little corner to the left that came under the Newton Street precinct. The tangle of the railroad yards, the Civic Center, the monumental freeway exchange, and all the little narrow old streets everywhere—the oldest part of L. A. He said, "Good and bad in this territory, all mixed together. Rubbing shoulders. Some people just poor, and some pro crooks, and some on the fringes. You think anybody living down here couldn't not know a lot of things—pro talk, pro habits?"

"And what says they live——"

"Nothing," said Mendoza. "But it's in the cards, isn't it? The ones like Walter William rarely leave the area— how would anybody else know him?"

"Well——"

"I want the file on him," said Mendoza. That had been a minor sort of kill; he'd just been cleaning up the Brent business at the time, and he hadn't followed the

Leigh thing very closely—Dwyer and Schenke had been on that. Schenke brought him the file; Higgins and Landers went off to question Hardcastle, and Galeano to hunt for Rhys some more.

The first thing the file told Mendoza shot his eyebrows up. Leigh had been shot by a .45. "¡Qué interesante!" he said to himself, and picked up the inside phone and asked for Ballistics. The man he talked to had nearly forgotten the case, but of course, like the lab boys, the boys up there were very tidy and organized and they never threw away clues, even after years, so they still had the slug taken out of Leigh, all neatly labeled and filed away. "Good," said Mendoza. "Will you do me a little favor and compare it with the slugs from our bank robber's .45?"

"The *bank* robber?" said the Ballistics man. "Aren't you reaching a little, Lieutenant? I understand this Leigh was a Skid Row——"

"You know my hunches," said Mendoza. "It came to me in a prophetic dream. Just have a look, will you?"

"Oh, I'll look if you say so. We're just here to serve you big brains. But I don't see—— Oh, I'll look."

Mendoza read through the file. Leigh had been found by a couple of squad-car men who thought he was a drunk. A lot of people around the area had known him: a drinker, but not as bad as a lot down there. Everybody said amiable, nice fellow, quiet little man, who'd want to shoot him? He'd had a room, a cheap room. He usually had a little money, nobody knew from where. Nobody knew anything about his having an argument with anyone lately, anything like that. It would have looked like the usual Skid Row killing for what was in the victim's pockets, except that he was shot: nobody who had a .45 to pawn would take the trouble to kill a drunk just on speculation. But there hadn't been any leads at all.

Mendoza collected his hat and went out to call on the rooming-house owner.

It was an old, big frame house, probably originally set back farther from the street, before progress had widened that. It badly needed a coat of paint; it had a wide front porch with some old chairs lined across it, and a dingy sign under the second-floor windows said *Rooms.* A very fat and very bald old man was the sole occupant of the porch; he sat and rocked rhythmically back and forth, fanning himself with an old-fashioned palm-leaf fan.

"Good morning," said Mendoza, climbing warped wooden steps. He'd left the Ferrari half a block away, but he had the feeling the man's eyes had observed his whole progress along the block. "I'm looking for Mr. Jason Frick."

"Set," said the fat man. He had on an ancient pair of black trousers held up with suspenders and an old-fashioned silk undershirt. His paunch was tremendous, and he was sweating freely. "I'm Frick. You're fuzz."

"Yes," said Mendoza, thinking again how things overlapped in this kind of neighborhood. Frick probably a perfectly honest man, but using the pro talk. "I want to ask you some more questions about Leigh." He sat down.

"Um. Told you boys about everything I knew before. Not that it wasn't kind of funny, why anybody'd want to cool *him.* I didn't know much about him. Don't figure nobody did. The kind I get renting my rooms, they're the ones alone—nobody to take much notice of 'em—not much money. Nothin' very interesting about 'em. They come 'n' go, and why should I notice, long as they pay me?"

"But you did say Leigh had lived here for some time."

" 'Bout five years. Somebody sent him money ever' week. I'd see the envelope come in the mail. I dunno how much, but it was allus cash and he was allus right there to take it from the mailman."

"But you never saw a return address on the envelope—or noticed the postmark?"

"Maybe I just ain't curious, mister," said Frick, fanning harder. "Jesus God, it is *hot*. I figured somebody, like some of his family, you know, just didn't want him around, paid him to stay away. Well, he liked his booze, sure. But he wasn't a falling-down-drunk drinker. He got awful happy when he was tight—there wasn't any harm in him. He allus got home under his own steam. He allus paid me on the dot, an' that's all I could tell you. Except——" The fat man stopped fanning and scratched his nose. "I didn't think o' that when the other cop was here that time. Not that I s'pose it's got anything to do with his gettin' killed. But about two, three weeks before that he got a phone call here one afternoon. Only time anybody ever phoned him up, all the time he lived here."

"Oh," said Mendoza. "Did you answer the phone?"

"My house, ain't it? Sure."

"Was it a man or a woman calling?"

"A man. Sounded like, anyway. Just asked to talk to Mr. Leigh, so I went and got him."

180

"Did you hear anything Leigh said on the phone?"

Frick shook his head. "Was just on my way out here to set and have a cold beer. But he wasn't on the phone long. About five minutes later he come out, dressed to go out—he hadn't so many clothes, but he allus kept himself pretty neat, know what I mean?—and off he went somewheres. But anyway, he usually went out about then."

Mr. Frick was a very incurious man. Mendoza sat in the Ferrari, ruminating and baking gently in the really remarkable heat, and finally drove down to Second Street to the Hi-de-Ho Bar, which was one of Tommy Canaletti's favorites. He left the Ferrari in a lot and went into the bar. Tommy was there. Mendoza waited patiently until Tommy turned and saw him and lifted a quiet finger. Three minutes later Tommy joined him on the sidewalk.

"You maybe decided it wasn't worth the quarter century?"

"No, not at all," said Mendoza, "What I'd like now is the name of this bum who told you the funny story."

"You wanta get it from him straight? That's sad, Lieutenant," said Tommy. "I'm real sorry. For you, not him. I told you he was real far gone. They carted him off to the General last night and I unnastand he's dead. You could see. His name was Buddy Pargeter."

"Hell and damnation!" said Mendoza.

They picked up Alfred Broadbent, the bartender who reputedly had contacts, at four o'clock that afternoon. Broadbent was a real tough, even if he hadn't a record. He looked as if he'd been everywhere and done everything, and it looked as if he'd had experience with cops before, because all he did was sit stolid and unmoved at the battery of questions they threw at him and continue to repeat, "I don't know nothing about it."

He didn't know Leigh; Leigh had never come to ask him anything; he didn't know nothing about nothing.

They had to let him go, and they all agreed it would be no use at all to put a tail on him. He was a wise one and he was going to be keeping very clean while he thought the cops were interested. And they couldn't keep a tail on him forever.

But about five o'clock the man from Ballistics called, sounding incredulous. "How do you do it, Lieutenant? With the gypsy fortunetelling cards?"

"By God, it checked?" exclaimed Mendoza. "Don't tell me——"

"It's a match. The slug from Leigh is out of the same gun that shot the guard and the teller and Sergeant Dwyer. That S. and W. 1955 target revolver."

"¡Como!" said Mendoza softly. "¡Aquí está! Now just fancy that. Thanks so much." He put down the phone and looked at Higgins and Landers. "So I'm reaching," he said. "So we've got nothing to link Walter William with the bank jobs and I'm just peering into my crystal ball again and being obstinate about a hunch. They're not all duds, you know. So now we know that the same gun which got the guard and the teller and Bert also fired the slug into Leigh."

They stared at him. "I will be Goddamned," said Higgins. "I'll be—— What the *hell* could be the link?"

"I don't know. I just can't imagine." said Mendoza.

"But there it is. Let's keep working and find out, boys. If it's humanly possible."

Before that, when he'd got back from his abortive talk with Tommy, Mendoza had been cornered by Piggott, who argued that they ought to get Verne Coffey to take a lie-detector test. Mendoza had thought about that himself. "But there are a couple of factors to consider," he pointed out. "It's not absolutely infallible, you know. Usually, yes—but there are factors that can—mmh—nullify it. And if Verne is already very nervous of cops, and authority in general, he could tell nothing but the gospel truth and still his heart would go jumping around and his blood pressure shooting up, to give us the wrong picture."

"I see that, but those fellows are pretty smart about interpreting reactions. I still think we ought to."

"And I think I agree with you. They're not," said Mendoza, "going to like it. But it does seem indicated. I'd better go with you."

But at the Coffey house they got an unexpected reaction. They found all the Coffeys home and for the first time met the married daughter June and her husband Frank Best. Mendoza did the talking, as tactfully as possible, and whatever he had expected the Coffeys and Verne to say, it wasn't what he heard.

They were incredulous at first and then they got mad. Even Sam Coffey. Mrs. Coffey faced them like a brown avenging Valkyrie.

"You mean to say you got it in your heads my Verne murdered his own sister? *Verne?* I never heard anything

183

so crazy in my life! I thought policemen are supposed to be halfway bright these days, but when you come saying *such* a thing——"

"My boy never done such a thing, crazy's right, all right—where d'you suppose he'd get a gun, anyways? How d'you suppose——"

Verne just stared, openmouthed. Obviously it came as a complete surprise to him. "You think *I*—what for 'd I want to hurt *Carol?*"

"Well, it seems to *me,*" said June Best, her eyes flashing dangerously, "you can't be looking very hard for whoever *did* do it, when you can get such an idiotic, downright foolish idea—Verne! Why, he——"

"Now, Mrs. Coffey," said Mendoza, "we're not saying he did—we just want to be sure, you——"

"Sure!" she cried. "Well, I should most certainly say you're going to be sure, Lieutenant! Verne'll take your old lie-detector test any time you say—I never *heard* such nonsense, respectable people like—— And he'll tell you the truth like he's been taught, and your machine'll tell you he's told the truth! He'll go along with you right now and take your silly test. Verne——"

"Why, sure," said the boy, looking a little scared but more bewildered. "You think *I*—why, I never figured you'd—I never wanted to hurt Carol! Why'd I—— I take your test whenever you say——"

"You take him *now!*" stormed Mrs. Coffey. "We'll get this foolishness cleared up right away! Maybe you'd like *me* to take the test, see whether I killed my own daughter! Maybe you'd like *Sam* to take it! You——"

"Now, Mrs. Coffey——"

"You go 'long right now, give Verne the test——"

But a lie-detector test was a delicate sort of thing, and the victim had to prepare for it twenty-four hours in advance. They gave the Coffeys instructions—no stimulants, eight hours' rest, and so on. Verne would take the test Monday afternoon; they set it up with the lab.

Verne took the test. The lab men said he was a good subject. And they fiddled around with their graphs and figures, and they told Homicide something which put the Carol Coffey case into the realm of the impossible.

They said Verne Coffey was telling the absolute truth. He didn't know anything at all about how his sister came to be shot.

Carol Coffey had been shot, in her own home, while people were round about to watch all four sides of the house. Nobody had approached the house; no car had passed, and the only person inside the house with her at the time really didn't know anything about it.

On those facts Carol Coffey shouldn't be dead at all.

But she was.

And just where else were the Homicide boys to go looking?

And then everything died on them, in all the cases they were working. They didn't have much of anywhere else to look, and yesterday the high had reached a hundred and one at the Civic Center, and today it was going to reach a hundred and two, and the morning *Times* said no relief in sight.

And it was Tuesday, and a week ago Bert Dwyer had been alive, walking down a street thinking about the birthday present he was going to buy his wife, and now he was dead and cold and rotting in the ground, and they wanted the bastard who had fired that gun. They weren't finding him or any lead to him.

Palliser wanted to get him, too, but he'd been assigned to the Walsh case and he would also like to find out who had beaten and shot nineteen-year-old Jimmy Walsh. The best lead he had, of course, was the light-green Anglia.

At four-thirty on Tuesday afternoon he found it.

The D.M.V. had found one hundred and four 1963 and 1964 models of the Anglia De Luxe with plate numbers starting out HAH, registered in L. A. County. Sixteen of those were green. None was the right one. So then they found forty-seven Anglias registered in Orange County, and four of those were green, but none of those was the one either. So then they found thirty-one Anglias registered in Ventura County, and only two of those were light green, one registered to an owner in the town of Ventura and the other to an owner in Oxnard.

So on Tuesday afternoon Palliser drove up the coast highway, enjoying the brilliant sparkle of sunlight on the calm Pacific to his left, to check those out. He came to Oxnard first, of course, so he looked up the address and found it with a little difficulty. It wasn't a town address: it turned out to be an old ranch house on the outskirts of town, a handsome old house in the middle of a lot of landscaped land, with an impressive line of poplars behind it as a windbreak.

The Anglia De Luxe sat in the driveway. There was a three-car garage behind the house, and in it, in lone grandeur, sat a brand-new Mercedes-Benz sports car.

It was the right Anglia. It had ski carriers on its roof.

"Police?" said Mr. Richard Brock. "Well, what on earth——" He stared at Palliser's badge. "Well, anything I can do—— My God, it isn't Johnny, is it? My brother—not an accident?"

"No, sir, I just want to ask you a few questions. I'm from Los Angeles, not local."

"Oh," said Brock. He was a tall, good-looking man about thirty, dressed in very snappy sports clothes. Palliser wondered if this was the same green shirt Rosario del Valle had noticed. He was beginning to have the dispirited feeling that this hot lead—and God, the work the D.M.V. had done on it!—was going to peter out before his eyes. This man, this house, said Money. This man, holding up a gas station for forty bucks? Beating and shooting a kid?

"Well, what can I do for you? Sit down—did you say Sergeant? Can I offer you a drink?"

Palliser could have stood a drink. God, after the routine they'd done on this—— "No, thank you, sir. I'd like to ask you—a week ago last Friday, were you in L. A.? On Figueroa Street, at about nine in the morning? With two other men, in that Anglia De Luxe out there in the drive?"

"Why, yes, I was," said Brock. "Why on earth? We didn't get a ticket, or——"

"No, sir. You stopped at a Shell station, at a few minutes after nine. But not, evidently, to buy gas. Why?"

"Oh," said Brock. He looked still more bewildered. "I guess it was a Shell—I didn't notice. Yes?"

"Why did you stop there? What were you doing in L. A., and who was with you?"

"For God's sake," said Brock, "what is this? I don't ——Well, I suppose you've got a reason to ask, come all the way up here! Sure, it seems—— But anything you want to know. I was with Johnny and Bob, my brothers. We live here together, none of us married. Bob had been up north looking at a parcel of land we're thinking of buying. He has a thing about planes—he never flies—so he'd come down on the Owl and Johnny and I drove in to meet him, there was another business deal we had cooking with a man in L. A. So we met him at the Union Station when the train got in and we started uptown to check in at a hotel—we were staying over the weekend. What the *hell* this is all about——"

"The Shell station on Figueroa."

"For God's sake!" said Brock. "I needed a rest room. Sudden attack of diarrhea. I told Johnny, pull into the first one he came to. He did. I went in and used the rest room. Matter of fact, the damn thing kept up all day, it was damned annoying—don't know what started it. I was O.K. the next day. Now what's all this about, Sergeant?"

"Did you see any attendant there at all?"

"Don't recall that I did. I wasn't looking for one—I was in a hurry."

Palliser stared at the floor. He wondered why he'd ever thought of joining the force. Land deals. A Mercedes-Benz. Money. Man perfectly open and frank.

"Do you own a gun, Mr. Brock?"

"A—— Now what? Yes, I own a couple of guns. I own a rifle I use for deer hunting, and somewhere around here is a .32 automatic we keep in case of prowlers. What——"

188

Palliser sighed. The one nice hot lead they had, petering out to nothing. All Rosario del Valle had given them was a lot of practice at the routine. The deadly routine.

All they had now, on the Walsh thing, was the gun. The gun—somewhere—with a broken trigger guard.

CHAPTER FIFTEEN

"But that sounds just impossible!" said Alison. "What possible connection could there be—— Don't you know anything more about this Leigh?"

"Let's hope we will. Nick found a fellow this morning who used to pal around with him a little. One time, says this fellow, something came up about Fort Worth, Texas, and Leigh mentioned that he'd been in jail there once. So we wired back to Fort Worth, but they'd never heard of him—under that name, anyway. And they don't keep records on vags, it could have been just that." It was nine o'clock on Wednesday night; the twins were asleep, blessedly. Three cats were spread out decoratively on the credenza, and El Señor was asleep on Mendoza's stomach. "We've sent his prints to Washington. If he ever accumulated a record anywhere, we'll hear about it sooner or later. But right now it all looks like a very peculiar setup indeed." His tone was absent.

Alison eyed him. "But you're brooding about something. Have you had an insp——"

"*¿Por qué no? ¡Válgame Dios!*" said Mendoza violently. "Yes, I am brooding over something. God." He lifted El Señor to the sectional beside him, sat up, and felt for cigarettes. El Señor complained bitterly about being moved and ostentatiously retreated to the farthest end of the sectional from Mendoza. "That morning," said Mendoza. "We had those sketches to get to the banks. I told Jimmy to make up lists, and what other way would he do it? He looked them up under their individual names, of course. Eleven branch banks, Security-First National. Eight branch banks, Bank of America. Four branch banks, Bank of California. And two Federal Savings, and a Coast Federal Savings. And what the hell else would I do? I cut up the list to roughly eight or nine apiece and handed them out at random. I thought at random. So it was Bert who got the one at Seventh and Grand, the Security-First. Why didn't Higgins get it, or Galeano? Both bachelors."

Alison was silent and then said, "Destiny. Who knows? It's nobody's fault, Luis. It just happened."

"No, but what made me hand *that* list to Bert? I don't remember if he was nearest or what. I don't know, *querida*—it all seems so damned at random, that's all." Mendoza passed a hand over his eyes. "And either we're not being very bright these days or the luck's running dead against us, or both. Damn it, unless Washington can give us something on Leigh, where do we go from here?"

"Can't you do anything about tracing the gun—the one from the bank jobs, I mean?"

"And just how? He—whoever—could have got it under the counter years ago, or two months ago, just anywhere. These damn scaremongers," said Mendoza, "talking about stricter laws on possession. Senseless. New York thought they were being smart with the Sullivan law, but anybody can still get a gun there any day, under the counter." He sounded savage; he felt savage. The whole machinery of routine had ground almost to a standstill on this. They were still looking at those men out of Records, the ones without alibis, and tracking down all their pals; but they'd nearly run out of them, and they hadn't found any more gunshot wounds or anything suspicious at all. Palliser's case looked very dead, too, and as for the Coffey thing—! And for one matter, this kind of fumbling delay, however hard they were working, didn't make them look so good to the public reading the headlines, NO CLUE YET FOUND. Mendoza swore and ground out his half-smoked cigarette.

"*Amante*," said Alison, "you'll get him. You'll get them all."

"When? A year from Christmas?"

She came and sat beside him. "Suppose you stop bringing cases home with you and start remembering you're a husband."

"Mmh," said Mendoza. "Are you by any chance propositioning me—or complaining?"

"You figure it out."

"Well, it might take my mind off other things, true."

"What a compliment," said Alison. "I *am* flattered. Of course, you've been a husband for some time. Maybe it's starting to pall."

"Well, I wouldn't exactly say——"

"Well, what would you exactly say?"

"Well, what do you think?" said Mendoza, and reached for her.

On Tuesday they had set up a lie-detector test for the Blaine brothers. Foote was still in the hospital. The Blaines took the test on Wednesday, and on Thursday they got the results from the lab and all uttered some rude words about it.

Neither of the Blaines was lying. The artistic little tale about Joe Sebastian was gospel truth.

Among other things, it was annoying because lie-detector tests were not admissible evidence and they still couldn't charge Sebastian with attempted homicide.

The heat wave still held, and the weather forecast each morning still said no relief in sight. But at least Scarne was back, another man to help with the routine.

The routine had taken them just about as far as it could.

"So I'm thinking now," said Mendoza to Hackett that afternoon, "that I may just have rung a bell with the little idea that it's a pair of amateurs. Hell. If either of them was in Records we'd have turned him up by now, surely to God."

"I don't see that at all," said Hackett. "We know one of them at least is in the fifties. How many times does somebody that age suddenly go on the bent? On bank robberies yet, for God's sake! And no hesitation about using a gun. It could be a pair from somebody else's records. We've got no way of knowing until we get them." They hadn't, of course, any prints or much of anything else to ask Washington about. "And what in the name of God this Leigh is doing involved in *that*—

it's wild! So all right, you said if it's amateurs maybe they knew he had a record—and we don't even know that— and got him to find the hot-money man. You said they might know about that possibility because of living down there, rubbing shoulders with pros. Then why for God's sake—when they've been so cute otherwise—let a bumbling old guy like Leigh in on it? Why not just go out looking for one themselves?"

"Which is a point," said Mendoza. "All this—it's like walking in quicksand. Slipping and sliding around. No landmarks. Nothing to get hold of. I hope to God Washington can——"

"You know how it goes," said Hackett. "We both know. Objective view, Luis. Remember all the times something's been tough going, not one single lead, but you go on worrying at it and all of a sudden it comes unstuck and there's X staring you in the face."

"Playing Pollyanna."

"No, but it does." Hackett readjusted his pillow. "In the long run we don't muff many of them, boy. And it's funny, too," he added thoughtfully, "lots of times when we do uncover X, he's so damned obvious you want to kick yourself for not seeing it before. There was that funny business about that Greek coin collection—hell, it was all such a tangle, not one thing to it made any sense, what with that ex-con and that idiotic French woman and the Greek and all. And then when we pulled the right string, why, it was all simple and obvious as—as broad daylight."

"So you advise us to sit it out patiently and wait for the right string to come along for pulling?"

"It'll come," said Hackett. He added seriously, "I

don't think whatever arranges things will let Bert's killer get clean away, Luis."

Palliser was still getting teletypes. All those sheriffs and police chiefs so eager and willing to help out the L. A. boys with their holdup killing had gone out to check recently sold Hi-Standard .22 revolvers. They had among them (in that wide area) looked at a lot of guns, but none of them had so far seen one with a broken trigger guard.

Palliser was looking at guns too. In Los Angeles County, he was informed late Wednesday by the giant Sears central warehouse, six of those revolvers had been sold in the last four weeks. They had, of course, been sold through the catalogue, and each order had been duly accompanied by the voucher clipped from page 739 of the catalogue, filled out and signed. This voucher read:

"I certify to the best of my knowledge that ———— who resides at ———— and who desires to purchase a .22 caliber pistol or revolver from Sears, Roebuck and Co., is a citizen of the United States, over 21 years old and of sound mind; is not under indictment, nor a drug addict, nor a fugitive from justice, and has never been convicted of a crime of violence." Under this was an indicated line for "signature of officer of law" and for "official position or title" and "official address" and the date.

For which reason Palliser was more or less certain that none of the six people who had purchased one of those guns was the X who had beaten and shot Jimmy Walsh. But of course you had to do the routine on it.

All those vouchers were enclosed with the other

information, names, and addresses. So on Thursday Palliser went out and about looking at guns himself. The new owners were wildly scattered all over the county; some of them weren't home, and he ran into one suspicious housewife who refused to let him see the gun. But by four o'clock he had managed to see four of them, and they were all quite intact.

Piggott had quite frankly given up on the Carol Coffey case; he said in his opinion the thing would never be solved and they might as well write it off. Maybe, he said, God had struck her dead from heaven; he couldn't figure out who else could have remained invisible. He had gone down to that Shell station on Figueroa to ask more questions all around. He said you never knew what might turn up.

Palliser, at four o'clock, was in Highland Park, having just seen his fourth gun. On the other two, he had his choice of La Crescenta or Arcadia, and he chose La Crescenta as the lesser evil. He got on the Pasadena freeway and drove back to Glendale, found La Crescenta Avenue, and started up the hill.

The house was on Altura Avenue, and it was a shabby sprawling old ranch-style in need of paint, with a wide front yard in need of watering. A man and a woman were standing at the front steps talking. Neither was young; the man was nudging fifty, the woman perhaps the same age. Palliser got out of the Rambler wearily— of course it was hotter up here, too—and went up the front walk.

"Mrs. Adler?" he asked.

They both stared at him. "Why, no," said the woman. "I'm Mrs. Page. Mrs. Jane Page."

"Oh," said Palliser. "But a Frederick Adler does live here?"

"Well, not now," said Mrs. Page. "Why?"

Palliser nearly said, "Oh, hell." He introduced himself, showed his badge. The man looked interested. "Sergeant, hah? Well, I'm Don Kimball, Detective second-grade, Glendale force." He held out his hand.

"Then you signed this voucher," said Palliser, and produced it.

Kimball peered at it and said sure. "What about it?"

"Well, we've got the hell of a job on our hands," said Palliser, "tracking down all these .22's sold the last couple of months. I needn't go into details, but I'd like to see this Adler's .22. He's moved, you say?"

"That's right," said the woman. "He decided to go home. He's only a boy really, Freddy. I mean, he's twenty-two, but he don't look it, and this was the first time he'd been away from home. He's a nice boy, but he was lonely, didn't make friends out here."

"Where," asked Palliser, "is his home?"

"Oh, Plainville, Kansas."

"Do you know his address there?" Of course she didn't. He looked at Kimball. "You hadn't any hesitation in signing that voucher for him?"

"Why, no, I didn't, Sergeant. See, I live right next door. I'd seen a good bit of Freddy when he roomed here. He was here nearly a year, wasn't he, Janie? I wouldn't say he's a big brain, he didn't finish high school —he was a box boy down at the Thriftimart on Glendale Avenue all the while he lived here—but he's a nice enough kid. I felt kind of sorry for him, the way he couldn't seem to make friends. Reason he wanted the

197

gun, he said, he used to work late some nights, and a couple of times he'd been roughed up a little by some big kids hanging around the street corner where he got the bus. He said he figured if he just showed them the gun, they'd leave him alone. No, I thought he was O.K. to have it."

"When did he leave to go back to Kansas?"

They consulted. "It was a week ago last Monday," said Mrs. Page. "He seemed to get fed up with California— he said so—he didn't like the job too well, and then he was lonely. He left that morning, along about nine o'clock. I think he was going back on the bus."

"Well," said Palliser, "thanks very much, anyway. Nice to have met you," and he nodded at Kimball.

Routine, routine. Try gun number six this evening?

It was ten to six when he got back to Headquarters. He sent off a teletype to the chief of police of Plainville, Kansas, requesting co-operation. Would somebody please locate Frederick Adler and have a look at his Hi-Standard .22, see if it had a broken trigger guard? Thank you very much. He started out of the office, and Sergeant Lake beckoned to him. He was on the phone; he handed it over to Palliser.

"I got something!" said Piggott excitedly. "This you'll never believe, but I think we got a break at last! I found this woman—Mrs. Ruth Watts, Lebanon Street—and she saw a kid go into that station that morning just before nine. She even knows the kid's name—she——"

"How come she didn't say so before? There's been enough publicity about it."

"Yeah, but that's it. She was leaving on her vacation that morning—her boss let her take off Friday because these two girl friends she was going with don't work and they'd gone and got reservations over on Catalina for that night, without consulting her, see, so he let her go. She works at a restaurant over on Hill. So she was waiting for them to come and pick her up, about eight-thirty, when she remembers she's forgotten to get some of this special tea she likes to take with her——"

"Look, have you got a point to make?"

"I'm getting there," said Piggott. "So she figures she's got time to walk down to this little grocery on Figueroa that carries it, and she hurries off, and the grocery is a block down from that station and two blocks from where she lives, and she says as she came past the station she saw this boy just going into the garage. He's a neighborhood kid, she knows his name—Alvin Cooper—and she never thought anything of it at the time, just thought maybe he knew the boy who worked there."

"Be damned," said Palliser. It could be a lead. After the letdown over the Anglia and Richard Brock. He'd worked it out that the Brocks must have stopped at the station after the holdup, if only just after. Jimmy Walsh had been beaten and shot at the rear of the garage, and his body had been partly concealed by a Ford sedan the mechanic was working on. The public rest rooms opened off the front of the garage, just inside the door. Brock could easily, in the dimness after bright sunlight, never have noticed the body.

"And she just got back to her place in time to meet the girl friends—what am I saying? They're all well into the forties—and she says you know how it is on vacation, she never looked at a paper, didn't hear about Jimmy getting shot until she got back yesterday, and she was figuring maybe she ought to tell us, except that a nice boy like Alvin wouldn't do anything like——" Piggott's silence was eloquent.

"She's definitely sure it was this boy?"

"Says so."

"Well, so where do we find him? He go to school?"

"Widney High on Twenty-first, but——"

"But he wouldn't be there now—damn, I'm too tired to think straight." Palliser yawned. "Got an address for him?"

"St. Paul Court, other side of the Harbor Freeway." Piggott added the address.

Palliser said, "I'll meet you there in twenty minutes." This could be a hot lead.

It was an unpretentious neighborhood of old houses. Next to it was another old house with an enormous sign in front, *Chinese Herb Doctor, Len Fen Yu, Best Remedies*.

The Cooper family was having dinner. There were, it seemed, a number of Coopers—parents, six kids, one set of grandparents, and an uncle. They were all seemingly very surprised and bewildered to be invaded by police officers. *"Alvin?"* exclaimed Mrs. Cooper. "Has Alvin *done* something? Why, he'd never——"

"We'd just like to talk to him," said Palliser. "Please." But all the Coopers were so concerned that they followed Alvin en masse from the dining room to the living room.

"I never done anything, sir," said Alvin. "Why'd you think I'd done something?"

Palliser looked at him. Certainly anybody who knew Alvin Cooper should recognize him even at a glance.

Alvin was about five feet eight, perhaps eighteen, and too fat. He had a round moonface, a slight case of acne, and he was a good forty pounds overweight. Glandular, thought Palliser; somebody should have taken Alvin to a doctor long ago, but that wasn't any of his business.

He said, "We have somebody who says you were going into that Shell station garage—you know the one, where Jimmy Walsh was shot—between eight forty-five and nine o'clock that morning. How about it, Alvin?" He and Piggott stared at Alvin hard: the first moment of surprise sometimes revealed something.

"*Me?*" said Alvin. His voice shot up to a squeak. "Me, in that—you mean, that same *day?* Why, I never was there—I never went into that place in my life! I didn't know the Walsh kid. That's a lie—who said I was there?"

"Where were you at that time that day?"

"Gee, I don't remember what day——"

"Two weeks ago tomorrow." It seemed, thought Palliser, like two years. God, and Carol Coffey shot that same afternoon (who the hell *had* done that and how the hell had it been done?) and then the next Tuesday, Bert. God. Dead ends, nothing but dead ends. But here, maybe another lead.

"Oh," said Alvin. "Oh." He looked at his mother; there was sudden great relief in the expressions of all the Coopers. "Oh, then you just got the wrong guy, 's all. It must be, maybe, somebody looks like me? Because if that was the day, mister, I wasn't here. Father Whitley or anybody else'll say."

"That was the day you left," said his mother. "Friday. Sure. See, mister, the father—the church, it sponsors these weekend camp trips for city kids. Just up in the Angeles forest, you know—Friday to Sunday. Alvin went that weekend. The father picked up all the kids about maybe seven o'clock that morning, in his jeep. He'd say —it's St. Luke's over on——"

"Musta been somebody just looks like ole fatty Alvin," piped up one of the younger kids. Alvin flushed darkly.

Palliser nearly said, "Oh, hell," again. He looked at Piggott, who just shut his eyes. Even Piggott, reflected Palliser, probably wouldn't feel like trying to grill a respectable Catholic priest.

They said all the indicated things and bowed out. "Well, it *looked*——" said Piggott.

"Sure," said Palliser. "Hell. So it *was* somebody who looks like Alvin? Possibly the Watts woman needs glasses and won't wear them? So, maybe somebody too fat?"

"*I* don't know," said Piggott gloomily. "I'm fresh out of ideas. Seems like every time we turn up a new lead on one of these things, it peters out right away."

"Yes," said Palliser. "Oh, yes, indeed." He sighed.

At eleven o'clock on Friday morning the inevitable happened. Mendoza had foreseen it, but there was an old saying about omelets and eggs.

An excited bank guard at the Security-First branch at Sixth and Spring called in incoherently to say he had the bank robber. He'd spotted him from the artist's sketch and collared him, and he was now all safely tied up in the president's office and they could come and collect him.

Mendoza, Higgins, Galeano, and Landers, and two

squad cars, hared over to the bank, to confront an incoherent red-faced man under the grim surveillance of a dozen tellers, vice-presidents, and assorted executives.

"An *outrage*—I have never experienced such—— Just what you think you are doing—— And I assure you, I shall remove *all* my business affairs from this bank at once—— I have *never* considered," spluttered the portly man amateurishly bound to the desk chair with hastily commandeered neckties and belts, "I have *never* considered doing business with the Bank of America—America indeed, it was the Bank of Italy and that Democratic scoundrel Giannini—but I *assure* you, after this *outrageous*—— I am Henry Reinholt Snyder, Junior, and I demand——"

He was, of course, Henry Reinholt Snyder, Junior. As ample evidence in his billfold confirmed. Unfortunately he bore a superficial resemblance to the sketch.

Mendoza apologized profusely; the bank personnel apologized. Mr. Snyder was not appeased.

It all took up some time, and it was another dead end.

"But the sketches may pay off in the end," said Mendoza. "Sometime. You never know. Art said, wait for it. For—whatever arranges things—to show us the right string to pull."

He wished he could believe it would show up.

It was being a tough one.

But they'd never stop hunting and looking. Not when X had got one of their own.

CHAPTER SIXTEEN

There had been a suicide at a hotel on Grand yesterday. On Thursday some people named Brent had reported their eighteen-year-old daughter missing, and on Friday she'd turned up dead of an overdose of heroin at another hotel, so there was that to go into. The situation at Headquarters Homicide was very seldom static.

When Mendoza came in on Saturday morning, Galeano was waiting for him. "How do you like Lester Cullinane for the bank jobs?" he asked flatly. "I like him fine, since about seven o'clock last night."

"¿Por qué?"

"I didn't like him the first time we had him in. And that time he was fairly cool. But since this Warbeck character tells us for pretty sure Bert winged one of them, and we've been taking a look at all the pairs as well as the single possibles, I wanted to talk to Cullinane again. I did, on Wednesday. And that time he was very damn nervous. And I also find out just yesterday that a guy he went around with some, drinking and womanizing, hasn't been seen around at all for the last week or ten days. And so I figure he could be the one with the slug in him, because he lived at the same place as Cullinane, and it could be Cullinane's got him tucked away at a cheap hotel some place, trying to nurse him. At their own place somebody might have got curious."

"Now you don't tell me," said Mendoza. "That could be, all right."

"And it could also be," said Galeano grimly, "that some maid is going to get a little shock finding the pal's body—his name is Knuth, by the way, Pete Knuth— because now Cullinane has blown town. Apparently. Last night, I find when I went to see him, he paid off the landlady and, pffft."

"You *don't* say," said Mendoza. "That's very interesting, Nick." All the possible suspects had been told not to leave town, of course.

"He left some stuff from his room, the landlady says, asked her to keep it for him. I want to go through it and ask her some questions, but she raised a little fuss and said I'd have to get a warrant." Galeano's broad dark face broke into a humorless smile. "I asked for it overnight. Here it is. Want to come?"

Mendoza held open the door and they went out. "It's suggestive, you know," said Galeano. "Very suggestive. And just the way you said, too—you notice we haven't had a bank knocked over since Bert got it. X wouldn't have known who he was, even when Bert hauled out a gun—it would have been a little shock to find out they'd shot a cop. They'd know how we feel about that."

"If it was Cullinane and Knuth," said Mendoza, "they can't run fast enough or far enough to get away clear. But how the hell would that Leigh tie up to them? What's the address?"

It was a very old and very large sagging frame building, looking almost derelict, on a queer little old narrow street not far from the old Plaza. This was the very oldest part of L. A. down here, and this place might, on looks, almost have dated from the founding date of 1781, except that it wasn't Spanish architecture.

The woman who opened the door to them told them about the building. "Oh," she said, seeing Galeano, "you're back. You got that warrant?"

"I've got it, Mrs. Buckley."

"Well, come on in, then. It's just I like things to be legal—no offense meant." She was about fifty, a strapping, tall woman with a lot of grayish hair, which had once been blond, in a large careless bun on the nape of her neck. She was wearing a crumpled cotton dress and dirty rubber thong sandals on bare feet. "Who's this one?"

"Lieutenant Mendoza, Mrs. Buckley."

"Hum," she said. "Mexican and Eytalian. Force sure is broad-minded these days. No offense. You interested in my place?" Mendoza was looking around the surprisingly large room—or lobby?—they had come into. "It's a real interesting old place. I was lucky to get hold of it, picked it up for a song, fifteen years back. D'you know it's over a hunnerd years old? Believe it or not, this was one o' the first hotels built here—by Americans, I mean —after we got California from Mexico. It was for the old stagecoaches, you know. Built in eighteen fifty-eight. Ain't that something? There's thirty rooms here, besides this one." There wasn't much furniture in the room; a large old desk in one corner evidently served as a counter for registering guests. Oblong strips on two walls showed bare plaster where some built-in had been knocked out. "D'you know it's even got a basement?—kind of a scary place. I guess they used to keep the liquor there—it was a saloon, too, you know—this room and that one there. I had the bar knocked out—that's where it was."

"Very interesting," said Mendoza. "Now, about Mr. Cullinane and Mr. Knuth——"

She answered questions, incurious. In fact, here was another rooming-house keeper who seemed singularly lacking in curiosity. Cullinane had lived here about two years, she said, and Knuth only about a year; she guessed they'd made friends because their rooms were side by side. She didn't know what kind of jobs either of them had or if they had jobs. Knuth had gone—she thought and made it a week ago last Wednesday. (Mendoza glanced at Galeano.) "Did he give you any reason for leaving? You saw him, I suppose, when he——"

"Well, no, I didn't," she said. "It was Mr. Cullinane told me he'd gone. He had to go home, see a sick mother or something. Mr. Cullinane asked me what he—Mr. Knuth, I mean—owed me, and I told him, and he said Mr. Knuth'd asked him to pay me, and he did. You see, he left in a hurry."

"So he seems to have," said Mendoza. "When was the last time you saw Mr. Knuth?"

"Well, that did make it seem a little funny," said the woman. "Because that was when him and Mr. Cullinane was having a fight. Going at each other hammer and tongs when I knocked on the door. That was the Tuesday night. As a matter of fact, I'd come up to ask him for the rent—he was nearly a week behind."

"This was in Mr. Knuth's room?"

"Well, sure. You could hear 'em alla way down the hall. No, not really fighting, just cussing each other, you know. It was over some girl, I think—they kept talking about some Helen, Mr. Cullinane saying what he'd do to Mr. Knuth, he didn't keep away from her."

Mendoza raised his eyebrows at Galeano. This was off the track. "Did you see Mr. Knuth? Did he look all right?"

"All right? Whaddaya mean, all right? Sure he was all right, except he was mad and kind of red in the face. They'd been arguing, see? Mr. Cullinane looked awful mad, too, but they shut up when I come in, and I—— What you asking all this for, anyways? I asked about the rent and he said tomorrow for sure. He'd allus paid up before, so I said O.K. So then the next day about one o'clock Mr. Cullinane come down and I was just takin' in the mail, and it was then he said Mr. Knuth had left, and paid me. So I figured they musta made up their argument."

"Oh." Mendoza was a little puzzled. Another something that had looked interesting and might still look a little interesting. "Look, Mrs. Buckley. I'll be frank with you. We think Mr. Knuth might have had a gunshot wound on him somewhere. Did you see him, oh, favoring one arm, or—did he look pale, or anything like that?"

She stared at him, brushing back wisps of straggly hair. "A gunshot—— Why, for the lord's sake, why ever should you think such a thing? Quiet sort he was, come home high once in a while, but—— Well, of *course* he never had no such thing! You mean, when I saw him then, a week ago Tuesday?" She laughed, shrill and high. "It was a hot night, mister. He'd taken his shirt off, he come to the door in nothin' but his skin and a pair o' shorts. Not that he had such a big chest to show off—he looked kinda weedy, especially next to Mr. Cullinane. If he'd had a bullet hole in him I'd've seen, and he didn't. Only, like I say, as I went back down the hall I hear 'em goin' at it again, swearin' at each other something fierce, so I did think it was just a little funny about Mr. Cullinane, when he come next day and paid up Mr. Knuth's rent. But men," she added philosophically, "do all sorts o' funny things. I don't pay no mind. I run this place myself since Buckley died, got three-four strong Mex girls do the cleaning, and ever' one o' my roomers knows I don't stand no funny business, chippies brought in or like that. Otherwise I don't pay much attention to 'em. Not such a fancy place maybe, but there's gotta be cheap, nice, clean rooms for men like my roomers, don't have a lotta money."

"Yes," said Mendoza. Galeano had stopped smiling.

"He did go off in an awful hurry—Mr. Knuth," she said. "Somebody sick, I think Mr. Cullinane said. Left everything in his room, guess he just went off with what he had on. I went up there the next day, see if it needed cleaning bad, and there was Mr. Cullinane packin' up all Mr. Knuth's clothes. Mr. Cullinane said he'd asked him —Mr. Cullinane, I mean—to do that and send them on. Even left his transistor radio. No, I dunno where he went. Mr. Cullinane didn't say."

"Oh," said Galeano suddenly. He looked at Mendoza. "Are you thinking what I'm thinking?" He looked incredulous.

"Mrs. Buckley," said Mendoza, "you told Detective Galeano that when Mr. Cullinane left last night he left some of his things with you? What are they and where are they?"

Again she stared. "Why, I don't know—odds and ends. When he come, he had this old-fashioned steamer trunk, he asked could he put it in the basement, and it's been there ever since. He just said he was leaving a couple things. I s'pose whatever he didn't want to take with him he put down there. What's a little space down in the basement to me? I don't use it for nothing, don't keep nothing down there myself—— No, I didn't see him go down there before he left, but——"

"And I don't suppose," said Mendoza, "this place is centrally heated? No furnace in the basement?"

"Well, no. I got a couple gas heaters put in——"

Galeano was looking faintly horrified.

"Mrs. Buckley," said Mendoza gently, "I wonder if we could see your basement?"

"Why, what *in* the world——"

"We do have a search warrant, you know."

"Well, for the lord's sake! You're about the queerest pair of cops I ever meet! Sure you can see the basement." She led them through old, dark, musty-smelling passages (the place must be ridden with termites, thought Mendoza, and he only hoped it wouldn't fall down while they were in it) to an enormous dark kitchen which still had its original cavernous hearth on one wall. She pointed out a narrow closed door. "It's prob'ly locked, but the key's in it."

The lock, interestingly, had recently been oiled. They

went down breakneck rotting steps to the great dark cave of the basement. Mrs. Buckley had rummaged and found a fading flashlight.

He was there, of course—Pete Knuth, not a very big man, who fitted quite neatly into the old steamer trunk. There wasn't, as far as they could tell, any bullet wound in him; it looked as if he'd been bludgeoned to death. But of course it was damned hot weather and he'd been dead about ten days.

"For God's *sake!*" said Galeano. They didn't say much; they got out of there in a hurry and called up reinforcements.

Mrs. Buckley was openly fascinated. A murder in her house—reporters flocking around—envisioning headlines and personal interviews, she beamed steadily.

"So now we know why Mr. Cullinane was nervous the second time you picked him up," said Mendoza.

"And also why he has run. I will be damned."

"So, some more routine." Mendoza sighed. "Senseless little argument over a girl—probably some cheap chippy at that—but it makes a little work for us. Get fliers out on Cullinane. Find out who Helen is. And so forth. Why the hell do you have to be such a smart detective, Nick? Probably nobody's going to miss this fellow any, he could have quietly rotted away here until Judgment Day. Whereas now we've just made more work for ourselves by finding him. Oh, I know, I know—just as well to get hold of Cullinane and stash him away before he loses his temper with somebody else."

Dr. Bainbridge arrived, looked at the corpse, and asked acidly why they couldn't just once find him a nice whole clean one, who'd died quietly in bed and been found ten minutes later. "In this *weather*," he said testily. "One like this."

They set up the routine on it. They got the Prints boys going over both rooms, the steamer trunk, and so on. They got up a flier on Cullinane, to be copied and sent out in all directions, at once. They got a formal statement from Mrs. Buckley. They issued a formal statement to the press boys. They notified the Feds, who might have a new vacancy on their Ten Most Wanted list: Cullinane was a prime candidate.

"With everything else we've got to worry about," said Palliser disgustedly, coming in about two o'clock to hear about their trunk murder. "Any teletypes for me?" There weren't. "Hell," he said. "I'm getting nowhere fast on this Walsh thing." He stared glumly at Galeano. "So you're the smart boy around here, making deductions. Maybe we ought to turn you loose on the Carol Coffey thing. Nearly everybody else has had a whirl at it. Maybe——"

But, as it happened, they weren't destined to have the Carol Coffey thing on their hands much longer.

At a quarter to three that Friday afternoon, just two weeks nearly to the hour since pretty, respectable, ambitious Carol Coffey had been shot to death in her own living room, Sergeant Lake put his head in at the door of Mendoza's office and said, "Somebody to see you. I think maybe could be something important. On Coffey."

"Oh?" Mendoza put down the report he was reading. "O.K."

Two people came slowly into the office. He stood up.

The woman was black—no question of that. She was a small woman, deep brown, about forty. She had been crying and still clutched a crumpled handkerchief in one hand. She was very neatly dressed in a crisply starched blue cotton dress, and a little blue straw hat with flowers on it, and Cuban-heeled black oxfords. Mendoza thought, her best clothes.

The boy had been crying too. She was holding him by the hand. He was a boy about twelve, and he was deep brown too. He was a nice-looking boy, and he was also very obviously dressed in his best clothes, a blue wool suit, very neat, with a white shirt and a tie.

They came in drearily and looked at Mendoza.

"Mrs. Catesby," said Sergeant Lake.

"Mrs. Catesby?" said Mendoza. "You wanted to see me? Won't you sit down?" He smiled at the boy.

"Yes, sir, thank you, sir." Her voice was still a little thick from weeping. "This is my boy Norman, sir. I didn't catch your name, I'm sorry."

"Lieutenant Mendoza."

"Yes, sir. I——" She looked at him imploringly. "I—it's about this terrible thing that happened to Miss Coffey, sir. I—we got to tell you. I've always been a law-abiding person. I was brought up that way, you've got to be honest. We had to come, I said that—as soon as I *knew*—what had happened. But I want to say, sir, it's part my fault—it's not all Norman's blame, sir. Because I ought to have thought, about how boys are about guns. They can't help it, I guess—something built into them." She stopped, her eyes filled, and she gave a deep dry sob. "I'm sorry, I'll try—tell it better."

"Please, Mom," muttered the boy, "I could——"

"I better tell it, Norman. I guess they'll want to—ask you questions and all, but——" She lifted sorrowful dark eyes to Mendoza. "You see, sir, I—I lost my husband last May. Joe worked for the city, he drove a truck and so on like that for the Parks Department, you know, keeping all the parks nice all over town. And he g-got killed last May, when his brakes went out on the freeway. So Norman and I, we was left alone, and it's been hard——" She swallowed convulsively; her hands clasped each other tightly on the cheap plastic bag in her lap. "I'm sorry, I don't mean go into that, it's our own trouble. Well, you see, sir, people were nice and there's a little pension but not much, and I've got to work. And Norman's twelve, old enough I can leave him days. I graduated from high school, but it's hard to get a job like clerking in a store, and I've got a domestic job for a lady in Pasadena, I take the bus. I don't want take up your time, sir, but I got to explain how—how it come about."

"Yes. That's all right, Mrs. Catesby. Take your time."

She took a deep breath. "We live on Ceres Street, sir. We were paying on the house before Joe—and I'm trying keep up, finally get to own it. It's a nice block there, lots of nice quiet neighbors, but I guess I don't have to tell you, sir, there's streets and people around there that aren't so good. I never worried about prowlers and such when Joe was—— But after, last July, we had a couple like that, and a man tried to break in one night. You know, it gets around, about a place where there isn't—isn't a man." Her hands clutched tighter. "There's some folk down there, and coming from further off, too —like these drug addicts—they'd do anything. And I—

214

and I—got a little nervous about that—I mean, I know your police are awful good, they come quick as could be when I called that time, and they were nice and polite—but I figured maybe best I'd have a—a—a gun in the house, ready." She stuck again.

"I never *meant*——" gulped the boy.

"Yes, Mrs. Catesby. That was very natural," said Mendoza. "You got a gun?"

"I don't—I didn't know anything about guns. I asked Mr. Clay. He lives next door. I told him—I asked—— And he said he thought it was a good idea, a woman alone and just Norman—— He went with me—to this Leiter's pawnshop—it's on Main Street. Mr. Clay has a grocery store down our way, and he always keeps a gun in case of holdups, you know? So he knows something about them. And I found out all about the regulations," said Mrs. Catesby anxiously. "They said I didn't need a permit for it unless I was going to be carrying it around, but I thought how sometimes the lady I work for has late parties, and I'm coming home after dark, and maybe sometimes I'd want to—— So I got a permit. I've got it right here. Right in this building, downstairs, they gave it to me—there wasn't any trouble about it." She bowed her head. "I should have *thought*—how boys are about guns. Just something in them."

"I never *meant*——" said the boy. He began to cry.

"I know you didn't, honey, but we got to tell the truth. No matter what they do to you for it. He never *meant*—but I should have known——"

The boy raised anguished wet eyes to Mendoza. "I—I never saw a gun close up before, and I thought how it'd be to really fire it off, how it'd sound and all—— Mom

215

always said, don't meddle with it, it was always in the drawer of the table in the hall, but I kept wondering how it'd——"

"I knew something was wrong," said the woman pitifully. "With Norman. He was acting funny, picking at his food like—and I thought, maybe something at school. But when he stayed out so late, scare me half to death—he's always good about coming home on time—and I could see he was worrying at something, and I finally got it out of him and I knew we had to come tell you the truth whatever you do to him for it, and please, sir, he never *meant* anything bad, and oh, dear Lord, those poor people—that nice young girl—we never even *knew* the Coffeys, next street over, but——" Suddenly Mrs. Catesby began to cry.

The boy burst out, "I never meant to *aim* at nothing! I just kept wondering how it *felt*, fire off a gun, and it was in the table drawer and Mom was gone all day, and I was with her when she bought it and Mr. Clay and Mr. Leiter showed her all about loading it and all, and there was a box of extra cartridges—— And I thought—I thought I could just shoot it off once and see how it felt and put another cartridge back in so Mom'd never know, and I—and I—and I—*I never meant shoot anybody!* I didn't *aim* at nothing but a—but a—but a ole tin can I put on top of our back fence! And I didn't hit it—but—but—it said in the paper, the same kind o' gun—I heard Mr. Leiter say what ours was—and—and——"

"The Coffey place," said Mrs. Catesby with difficulty. "It—their property—it's right back of ours, on the next street. Please, sir, Norman never *meant*—— But we knew we had to——"

216

Mendoza said softly, "*¡Pares o nones!*" And who or what decided the throw of the dice? A one-in-a-million chance. Young Norman, curious to know how it felt to fire a gun. Firing a gun, at a tin can on a fence.

Sam Coffey taking off the screens to repaint the frames. Just then.

Carol Coffey, who got A's in English and wanted to be a teacher, dusting the living room. Standing in that doorway, facing it and the rear bedroom window—just the few moments when her mother was in the side yard . . .

The moment young Norman fired the gun. A nice well-brought-up boy, who never meant to hurt anybody.

The millionth chance. The wild bullet, wide of the innocent target, going across the narrow back yard there, into the open bedroom window, into Carol's heart.

At random. Death was so random.

You could ask, Why? That list of banks—why Bert Dwyer? And Carol. Ambitious Carol, a nice girl, with her A's in English. Who would probably have been a good teacher.

You could ask. You could wonder. And also about the bank guard and the teller.

Besides Bert.

Death was wanton. There was no sense at all to where or when or how death came.

"I—I brought the gun," said Mrs. Catesby falteringly. "I know there's tests you make and all." She reached into her purse and laid the gun on Mendoza's desk. It was of course, a Colt Official Police .22. "Please, sir, I know Norman's got to be—to be—punished. But when he never *meant*—when it was really a kind of *accident*—please, sir——"

Mendoza stared at the gun. There really seemed to be, he thought, no sensible order to life. To life or death. As a man with a very strong sense of order himself, it confused him. He felt angry about it. It was all wrong that someone like Bert Dwyer, someone like Carol Coffey, should die for such trivial reasons. In such trivial circumstances. Because they had been at a certain place at a certain time.

Death was so very damned at random.

It would be nice to be able to believe that—whatever arranged things—had some valid reasons.

CHAPTER SEVENTEEN

"Oh, my God," said Alison, looking sick. "The answer as
simple as that. As—as appalling as that. Just random
chance. That poor woman—and the Coffeys. What will
happen to the boy, Luis?"

Mendoza shrugged. He was drinking black coffee and
staring absently at Alison's own portrait of El Señor,
sitting beside a witch crystal, which hung above the
credenza. The house was very still; apparently the twins
were asleep. "What can we do? The boy's only twelve,
and there was no intention. It was an accident, pure and
simple. And don't make with the psychological double
talk and tell me there's no such thing. Accidents happen
all the time—this was just one more. It's a little as if
Carol Coffey had been knocked down by a bus as she
crossed the street . . . Norman. Poor Norman. There'll
be a hearing in juvenile court, thrash out the whole sad
story, and very probably the judge will remand him in
his mother's custody, put him on probation until he's
eighteen, something like that. Which won't make the
Coffeys feel any less bitter."

"No. What an awful thing. It makes you wonder—why was she standing there, just that second? And——" Alison broke off and uttered a little scream as Sheba landed on her shoulder from behind her chair. "Don't *do* that, you little monster!" Sheba unconcernedly walked down her to her lap and settled down to manicure her claws.

"Ifs," said Mendoza. "No profit, *chica. ¿Para qué?* And what is the answer to the answer? If Norman was a wild kid, had been in trouble before, was a potential troublemaker, would it make any more sense? If Mrs. Catesby didn't live in a district like that, where she had cause to want a gun handy—— If the normal twelve-year-old boy wasn't fascinated by a real-life gun—— What's the profit in saying if? It's just a senseless, meaningless accident that's brought tragedy to two families. It's no good asking why."

"I don't," said Alison, "*like* the idea of destiny. I don't like to feel that every last little thing that's ever happened to me or is going to happen is all—all blueprinted out already, and nothing I can do about it at all. It's not fair."

Mendoza laughed. "What is fair about life, anyway? No rules say anything's got to be fair. You like the idea any better that things happen because you were born under a certain star? What *I* don't like is the—the untidiness of it all." He sounded angry. "All I can say is, if there is something making all these arrangements, it's being done in a very damned disorderly way."

Alison laughed and sobered. "Nothing. Only you sounded as if you were complaining about a careless maid sweeping dust under the rug."

Mendoza got up and wandered around the room, hands in pockets. "And it is rather like that. Careless planning. When there must be hundreds of, for instance, senile old people nobody would miss—idiot children—psychopaths——"

"High-pressure door-to-door salesmen," said Alison.

"And unrealistic judges, and all those silly people who want to set up a Police Board of civilians to watch over us——"

"Art critics," said Alison dreamily.

"Instead of Bert. And Carol Coffey. Nobody can know the answer . . . That poor damned woman. Yes, of course we had to hold the boy. He's at Juvenile Hall, which is ridiculous because it's crowded as hell and he wouldn't run, but technicalities—— This fine new jail they build us, and do you know what it cost? Seventeen million bucks. And the nice new women's jail over in east L. A., at ten million. But do they consider a new Juvenile Hall? *Porvida*, no, have to think of the tax-payers' money! So the kids are sleeping on mattresses in the halls. I wonder why the Fire Department hasn't got after the council . . . Yes, I saw the Coffeys."

"I suppose I don't have to ask how they felt. I know how I'd feel."

"Why did this have to happen to us? Yes. But why does anything have to happen to anybody? Why to Bert? Why to Mary Dwyer? I don't like the only answer either."

"I ought to go to see her," said Alison somberly. There was a silence, and she added with an effort at lightness, "At least a few people are—getting something out of all this. You said that Mrs. Buckley was thrilled at

221

the idea of a murder in her house. What another sense-less thing, but louts like that—— And Mr. Warbeck stopped by today to ask if you'd found the man yet. He was quite proud of himself, giving important evidence to the police."

Mendoza smiled. "Important all right, but it doesn't seem to be taking us anywhere, damn it. And Art could be right, that they're in somebody else's records and not ours. Which is a cheerful thought."

"I still can't see how on earth that Leigh comes into it."

"You are not alone, my love," said Mendoza sardonically. "Of course, if we could count out all the vague talk about Leigh wanting to find a hot-money man and so on, we could explain him away very easily. The X who carries the gun doesn't seem hesitant about using it. So we could say either that Leigh was just somebody who got into an argument with him at a bar somewhere, or we could say that Leigh had——" He stopped with his mouth open. "Oh," he said. He started on and tripped over El Señor who had suddenly decided to abandon the green chair and make a beeline for Alison's lap. "Hell," said Mendoza, stumbling against the sectional and feeling his thigh. "That cat——"

"Inspiration has just visited you, *amador*? No, Señor, now Sheba got here first. There isn't room for both of you——"

"Well, I was going to say, maybe Leigh stumbled on the fact that X was the bank robber—or one of them—and was blackmailing him. And then it just suddenly occurred to me that we've blithely passed up one way of maybe getting some more information about Leigh.

That money he had sent to him every week . . ." Mendoza went out to the hall, to the telephone table. He looked up the number and dialed.

"Hey?" said an indistinct voice.

"Mr. Frick?"

"Yep."

"This is Lieutenant Mendoza. I was asking you some questions the other day about Walter Leigh."

"Oh, yeah."

"Well, you said that every Monday he got some cash through the mail, but you'd never noticed a return address or the postmark. Have you noticed since?"

"How d'you mean, have I——"

"Well, let's see, he was killed on a Saturday night. If the cash was mailed locally, it'd have to be mailed on Saturday some time to be delivered on Monday, and if it was mailed from outside the county, it'd have to be mailed on Friday at least, and from anywhere farther away, probably on Thursday. So at least one more envelope had to reach your house that next Monday, before whoever sent it knew he was dead. What did——"

"Nope," said Frick. "Didn't ever another one come after he was killed . . . Sure I'm sure. I thought o' that myself, and I watched out for the mailman and looked all through the mail, that Monday after. Wasn't nothing there for Leigh."

"I see. Thanks very much," said Mendoza. He put the phone down slowly. That might say several things. Frick dishonest, holding onto the nice anonymous cash? He didn't think so; the man hadn't impressed him that way. If the cash sender was local, that said one very funny thing: it said that the cash sender knew Leigh was going to be killed on Saturday night, so he or she hadn't troubled to mail the usual cash on Saturday. Did it, could it say that the cash sender was his killer *and* one of the bank robbers? That sounded utterly ridiculous. Didn't it say that the cash sender had to be local or at the very least somewhere in southern California, because Leigh's death wouldn't have been reported in any other papers and the cash sender wouldn't have known he was dead? But that didn't matter, because the cash hadn't been mailed to reach Leigh on Monday. The cash sender knew he wouldn't be needing it by then.

Which in turn said, thought Mendoza (because the cash would have had to be mailed locally by Saturday afternoon, for Monday delivery), that whether the cash sender had been his killer or had just learned about it from the killer—Leigh's murder had been premeditated.

One more wild and impossible element—now whoever had, for a long time, been generously sending Leigh money suddenly turned out to be involved in his death. Why?

There didn't seem to be any answers to anything anywhere.

"Teletypes!" said Palliser with a groan. "I've started dreaming about them." He looked at the sheaf waiting on his desk and groaned again.

"I looked through this latest batch," said Mendoza. "All negative. You're getting a lot of nice co-operation from all these upright officers of the law. I hope you're thanking them properly."

"My mother always impressed on me never to forget please and thank you," said Palliser. "Right now I don't feel so damn much like adding the thank you to Chief Roland Cunningham of Plainville, Kansas."

"What's he done to you?"

"Handed me another deadly piece of routine to do. I told you about this Frederick Adler? The box boy at the Thriftimart? Who bought one of these Hi-Standard revolvers only about a month ago? And then decided to go back home to Kansas?"

"Yes. What about him?"

"Well, it means damn all, you know. I don't see whoever killed Jimmy Walsh, for no reason at all probably, after holding up that station, as being anybody who applies all legal to carry a gun. This Kimball on the Glendale force, who signed that voucher for Adler, told him he'd need a permit to carry the gun and helped him get one. Then all of a sudden, couple of weeks later, Adler decides he's fed up with California and heads home for Kansas. And I doubt very much that he's our boy, but he did have one of those new models, so I have to check it out. So I ask Chief Cunningham back in Plainville to find Adler and take a look at his gun." Palliser sighed. "And what do I get back? Yesterday morning? A nice teletype from Chief Cunningham saying he's found Adler, who's back home with his parents at such-and-such an address, and asked him about the gun, and Adler hasn't got it any more."

"How frustrating," said Mendoza. "What did he do with it?"

"He tells the chief he figured since he was coming home he'd have no further use for a gun, and he sold it to a fellow he knew, the day he left. A fellow named Max King, who used to work at the same Thriftimart."

"So now you're chasing Max King, all in the sacred name of routine. Any luck yet?"

"No, and what's so damn frustrating about it, of course, is that when I do eventually find him, he'll haul out the gun all innocent and it'll have its trigger guard just as intact as it was when the factory shipped it out."

Higgins came in and said, "Morning. You got any suggestion for action?"

"There's a little more routine on our trunk murder," said Mendoza. "Somebody from the F.B.I. is coming over to copy down Cullinane's record and get extra mug shots of him."

Higgins sat down at his desk here in the sergeants' office and drummed on its top restlessly. "Haven't we *anywhere* else to——" And then suddenly he got up again and looked beyond Mendoza and Palliser, who turned around.

Mary Dwyer had come in and hesitated just inside the door. She gave them all a faint smile. "I just—I wanted to come and thank you all, for all your letters and so on. You've all been so good and helpful."

"Won't you sit down, Mrs. Dwyer?" Mendoza laid a hand on the nearest chair, but she shook her head.

"I won't stay. I just wanted to stop and say thank you." She was a very pretty woman indeed, and she must, Mendoza thought, have been somewhat younger than Bert—in which he erred, but then he'd been married awhile and had maybe lost a little of his old sure touch with females. She wasn't very tall, and she had a very nice figure even in the sober brown linen sheath she wore. She had a creamy complexion and the true black hair so seldom seen, and big gray eyes and a short straight little nose. "I'm—going away," she said. "I'm getting the eleven-o'clock train for Portland, so I thought I'd just come over here from the station a minute to say thank you, Lieutenant."

"We haven't done much," said Mendoza. "How did you expect to find us all here on Sunday, Mrs. Dwyer?"

She smiled faintly again. "Lieutenant, I was married to a cop for twelve years. I knew you'd all be here."

"You know we'll get him, don't you?" asked Mendoza abruptly.

"Yes. I know that. You almost always do."

"Are you—moving away for good, Mrs. Dwyer?" asked Higgins.

Her eyes moved to him. "Oh, no. My mother wanted me to come and live with her, but I don't like Portland much, and the children are settled in school here, and we like the house. And then my mother doesn't like dogs, and there's Brucie—— No, I'm just going up to stay with Mother a week or so, while my sister stays with the children. Then I'll come back and start looking for a job. I'll have to. The pension will help, of course, but——"

"Yes," said Mendoza. "If you need any help there—a recommendation or——"

"Yes, thank you, I'll remember. But I don't think I'll have too much trouble there, Lieutenant. I worked for a while after—after Bert and I were married. I'm a pretty good photographic retoucher, and there's nearly always a job open in that line." She sighed, touched the little tan pillbox hat she wore, with its nose veil, and said, "The children are pretty responsible and old enough to leave alone during the day. Laura's only eight, but she's—

mature. Well, just—just thanks for everything, all of you." She turned.

"Now look," said Higgins. "Don't you—don't hesitate to call in now, anything we can do. Me. Look, I know how it is for a woman alone, and that's not a very new house, Mrs. Dwyer." His tone was earnest; he took a step toward her. "Faucets needing washers, plumbing going wrong, electricity—— Look, I'm pretty handy at things like that. You need any help with anything like that, don't you hesitate to call me, see? I mean, I know—Bert did most of the work like that himself—and electricians and plumbers, they come damn high these days. I'd be happy to——"

She looked a little surprised. "Well, that's awfully good of you, Sergeant."

"You remember, now."

"Yes, I will. Thank you again, and good-by."

Mendoza and Palliser swung to stare at Higgins. "Well, she's a nice girl," said Higgins. He sounded defiant. Higgins, supposedly the confirmed bachelor at thirty-seven, was not a handsome man. He had started out with craggy, irregular features, and a twice-broken nose—once in a melee in high-school football and once at the hands of an ex-heavyweight turned junkie— hadn't improved his appearance. No girls turned to look at him in the street, or if they did it was for his impressive shoulders and seventy-five inches. Now he flushed a dark red under the stares of his colleagues. He said, "So what *about* it? We ought to do what we can for her."

"*Pues sí*," said Mendoza.

"Besides——" said Higgins. "Oh, well, hell." He

passed one of his massive hands across his face. "What have we got to do today, anyway? Let's get started."

"God knows," said Palliser, "I've got enough to do." He eyed the mass of teletypes gloomily and went out without reading them.

And Mendoza, eying Higgins where he sat hunched over his desk reading a report, wondered a little amusedly if Higgins had been captured at last, too. He also wondered just what kind of a chance George Higgins would stand with a girl like Mary Dwyer. A girl who had been married to one cop for twelve years and knew a lot about cops. About their work. About their lives. About the statistics, and how any city is jam-packed with potential victims of violent death, but how any cop runs just a little better chance of getting involved with violence.

With the random death.

Higgins looked up and stared at the wall opposite him. "My God," he said, "anyway, she could take her pick. Couldn't she? And why the hell should she ever want to—get involved—with a cop again? Another cop?"

According to the teletype, young Adler hadn't known Max King's address. Palliser had gone, yesterday, to that Thriftimart where, said Adler, King had once worked as a box boy. The manager there gave him, after search, an address in Montrose. So Palliser had gone there, and it was a private house belonging to a widow who took in roomers, and found that Max King had moved away six months ago.

So Palliser had gone to the Montrose post office, which of course had been closed on Saturday afternoon, but he'd got in by knocking on the door and holding up his badge. He asked about change-of-address cards, and after a long search they had turned up an address for him in La Crescenta. So Palliser had, late yesterday, gone there, and it had been another private house belonging to an elderly couple who took a roomer, and they had told him that Max King had left about a month ago to go back to Montana where his brother lived and had a ranch. Actually, said Mrs. Keller helpfully, it was a half brother —no, she never recollected hearing Max say his name and couldn't say what town——

A couple of four-letter words formed soundlessly in Palliser's mind.

"Wait a minute, Mother," said Mr. Keller suddenly. "Now don't you recall me telling you, just the other day it was, he's back. Max is. Nice young feller. You recall, I ran into Frank Foster down in Montrose—he runs a restaurant there, Sergeant—though what in time the *police* want of Max I can't think, nice a young feller as you'd want to meet—and he was telling me Max came back. Didn't like the ranch work. I know he always said —Max, I mean—as how he'd like to get to learn T.V. repair work. He's good with his hands, a real smart boy."

"Well, thanks very much," said Palliser. The deadly dreary routine. It had to be done. Somebody had to do it.

And that had been at nine o'clock last night, and when he got to the restaurant Frank Foster ran, it had been closed, and so he'd looked up Foster's home number and called and got no answer. So then he had gone home.

So this morning he drove back up to Montrose and found the restaurant open, and found Frank Foster, and asked about Max King. Sure, Foster said, Max was back, he'd been in just the other day, and no, he didn't know where Max was living, but he had a job at a lumberyard down in Glendale and was going to school nights, to learn electronics. Going to Glendale College nights, Max had told him.

And the only lumberyard in Glendale was, of course, Lounsberry and Harris, so Palliser went there, and of course it was closed on Sunday, but there was an emergency number posted on the door, so he called that and eventually got the superintendent's name and routed him out.

"Really," said the superintendent. "Really, for such a trivial—— I was planning to take the children to the zoo——"

"Well, this could be important," said Palliser wearily. He didn't think. The damn routine.

So the superintendent looked for Max King's address, and so Palliser—in ninety-nine-degree heat—drove back up to Montrose, to Briggs Avenue, to the house where Max rented a room.

He found, at long last, Max King.

A pleasant-faced middle-aged woman let him in, not without surprise at the sight of his badge. Max King was watching a golf match on T.V. in the living room. He was a husky blond fellow about twenty-two, ruggedly good-looking.

"Police?" he said, looking astonished. "What the hell? *Me?* What've I done? Oh-oh. The car. Is that it? But I didn't think I had to re-register it until January, even if it has got Montana plates. I bought it from my brother, been over there awhile, but those open empty spaces I

231

can't stand. Brother, give me the big city any time! Is it the car? I didn't——"

"No," said Palliser. "You used to work at the Thriftimart, and you knew a fellow named Frederick Adler, and——" He explained about the gun. "I'd just like to see the gun," he said. This deadly routine.

King stared at him. He said flatly, "Mister, you fell for a real snow job. That smells. I never bought a gun from Fred Adler. Nor from anybody. I don't have a gun. I never have and I never will. I had a kid brother shot all accidental by a gun that couldn't be loaded. I don't like guns, mister. Somebody told you a fairy tale."

CHAPTER EIGHTEEN

Palliser stared at him. Quite suddenly the routine stopped being so very routine. "Is that a fact?" he said. "You could be lying to me, Mr. King."

"Oh, for God's sake. Anybody who knows me knows *that* about me. Could tell you. It's Adler who—say, what is this anyway? Has that lout pulled something and tried to put it on me?"

"Mr. King," said Palliser, "I haven't got a search warrant, but would you allow me to look through your room, please?"

"Still think you're going to find it?" King was half angry and half puzzled. "Sergeant—did you say Palliser? —you can look anywhere you want to. All over the house—I don't think Mrs. Wechsler would mind, because none of us has anything to hide. Sam Wechsler agrees with me about guns. And I just moved in here ten days back, and Mrs. Wechsler was in and out of the room while I was unpacking, and she could say——" He turned and led the way to a good-sized room furnished as a den with a studio couch and desk.

Palliser looked, and there wasn't any gun.

"What *is* this, anyway?" asked King. He stood smoking, watching Palliser go through the chest of drawers. "That Adler—trying to push something onto *me*? I didn't know him hardly at all, just to know his name, you know. I don't figure anybody did."

Palliser looked up. "Why not? What was wrong with him?"

King shrugged. "Oh, hell, I suppose it's not his fault. Glands or something, but he's a funny one. Not anybody a real guy 'd want to pal around with. Slow, for one thing, no brain you know, and then he's so fat and sloppy. A slob. I was surprised he even got that job, and I think they were going to fire him at that. This was maybe a month back, when I quit and went to Montana. But why the hell he picks *me* to—— What did he do?"

"We don't know that he's done anything," said Palliser, "but this all looks interesting. You say he's fat?"

"A real fat boy." King nodded. "Why, don't you know him? I thought you'd picked him up, you said——"

"He's in Kansas." Unfortunately. "Go on. Fat?"

"Fat," said King. "Unhealthy-looking, know what I mean? You know how some peoples' glands go wrong, and they get fat. I knew a girl like that once, only she kept a real nice figure, taking these thyroid pills. I wondered why this Adler lout didn't see a doctor. Because he must be fifty pounds overweight—— Listen, and I wish I had him here right now, telling you a fake story like——"

"Mr. King," said Palliser, "you're not planning to leave town, are you?"

"I am not. You'll find me right here any time you

want me. Or at my job. Or three nights a week in room three-fourteen at Glendale College. What the hell———"

"That's just fine," said Palliser. "Thanks very much. Now if you'll just give me your brother's name and address, that'll be it for now . . ." He got back into the Rambler and started downtown, thinking how suddenly the routine could sometimes turn up a big surprise.

He also thought about Mrs. Ruth Watts, who said she had seen a boy named Alvin Cooper going into the garage of that Shell station the morning Walsh had been shot, at about the right time. And the boy hadn't been Alvin Cooper, but Alvin Cooper was a big fat boy whose glands had gone wrong, and here was another big fat boy . . .

He came into the office and found Mendoza grumbling to Piggott about the slowness of the Feds back in Washington: they hadn't heard yet from the F.B.I. about anything they might have on Leigh. "Listen, Lieutenant," said Piggott soothingly, "they got requests coming in every hour from all over the place, and there's only twenty-four hours in a day. If they've got anything, we'll hear about it sooner or later."

"Well, it's aggravating. I try to make up stories about how he could be tied up to a pair of bank heisters, and there's just no plausible way—— You look a little excited about something, John. Something hot?"

"Could be," said Palliser, not stopping. He went straight on to the communications room and sent off a long teletype to Chief Cunningham in Plainville. Up to now, of course, all these co-operative law-enforcement officers had been working blind; now Palliser gave Cunningham a detailed account of the gas-station

235

holdup and the connection with the gun. Frederick Adler claimed he had sold the gun to King; King denied it; King didn't have the gun and looked clean. (There was, of course, the chance—the very small chance—that King had not actually been at his brother's ranch in Montana on the day Jimmy Walsh had been killed, that he was that particular X and had since ditched the gun somewhere. Palliser would check that out.) Now he would like Chief Cunningham to question young Adler again, and he'd also like to know something about young Adler. Had he ever been in trouble, and so on.

"And damn it," he said to Mendoza, after bringing him up to date, "*I* don't know what sort of cop this Cunningham is, whether he's competent or a hick-town fool. He——"

"Plainville doesn't look so small on a map. And some of those hick-town cops are as smart as they come," said Mendoza, thinking of John Lockhart. "It all looks suggestive, anyway. What about King?"

"He smells all right—he acts all right. But of course I'll check him too." Palliser looked at his watch; it was ten minutes to one. "Don't suppose I can expect anything back from Cunningham until tonight or tomorrow. I headed it urgent, but he might be off on a picnic or something, on Sunday, or if he isn't the Adlers might be. I think I'll get that other teletype off and then go get some lunch."

"All right, I'll wait and go with you. I wonder," said Mendoza, "if those Washington boys are pawing through their records by hand."

Palliser sent off a teletype to the sheriff of Lewis and Clark County in Montana, requesting co-operation. Mr.

Max King claimed to have been at the ranch of his half brother, Mr. Alexander Ross, in that county, on such and such a date. Would the sheriff please verify?

Then he and Mendoza went up to Federico's and had lunch.

Nothing showed up from Washington on Leigh on Monday. But this break in the Walsh case continued to look good.

At eleven o'clock Palliser had a teletype from the sheriff of Lewis and Clark County, Montana. About a dozen people could swear that Max King had been just where he said he'd been on the relevant date. Palliser teletyped back brief thanks and thought about Frederick Adler. But what sense was there in Adler for it? Such a damn fool way to—— Well, he thought, were they ever very bright, the smalltime pros? But on the other hand, Don Kimball, a plain-clothes man on the Glendale force, had thought Adler looked sufficiently O.K. that he'd helped him get a gun, and the Glendale boys weren't bad as a rule. What added up?

When he got back from lunch he found a teletype waiting from Chief Cunningham—a long one. Cunningham didn't sound like a backwoods hick cop; he seemed to be on the ball. He sketched backgrounds: Frederick Adler was twenty-two, the only son of a local Civil Service clerk and his wife. Modest circumstances. He had dropped out of high school in his second year, had held a few lowly jobs but never for long. School authorities had recommended medical treatment for his obesity when he was fourteen, but the parents belonged to some obscure religious sect which didn't believe in all this newfangled doctoring (Palliser read between lines) and nothing had been done. The boy didn't have the education or evidently the brain to hold much of a job. He'd been picked up once, with a couple of other boys, for a little street scuffle, and once again on a D.-and-D., only last year. He'd left town after his father had paid his fine on that and just returned about a week ago.

And he was still insisting that he had sold the gun to King.

Palliser sent back a brief message to Cunningham: *King absolutely clean. Press Adler on gun.*

He hadn't really anything to do but wait for answers to come in. He sat at his desk and thought. He thought about Roberta Silverman and decided they could get along nicely, really, on what he was making now, and anyway, she might want to go on working a year or two so they could make a down payment on a house.

After a while Higgins came in, looking tired and hot, with a dumb unshaven lout who was a drinking pal of one of the possibles from Records, and it was always better technique for two or three men to sit in on a questioning, so Palliser and Landers, who had been arguing with Sergeant Lake about baseball teams, had the chance to do a little work.

Nothing came in from Cunningham by six o'clock, so Palliser went out for dinner. The hospital Art Hackett was in wasn't too far from the Civic Center, so afterward he dropped up there and brought Art up to date.

"*Nothing* else on the bank jobs at all?"

"We've run it into the ground," said Palliser morosely. "And you notice they're lying low—no more jobs. Bert scared them. I'm beginning to think the lieutenant's right—it's a pair of amateurs. For one thing, isn't it usually the amateurs who start spraying bullets all around? Your typical pro heist man plays it cool, he isn't asking for a homicide rap."

"Well, I don't know," said Hackett. He was lying here counting the hours; on Thursday he was going home, to be cosseted and fed by his Angel. "There's the other heist job, where it looks like a senseless kill. How's that?"

"Hot," said Palliser, and told him about that. "I want to get back and see if anything more's in from Cunningham."

"You'd better also start thinking about extradition proceedings," said Hackett. "That's clear as glass."

"Well, I don't see it's quite as certain as——"

"It's obvious," said Hackett impatiently. He shifted his bulk restlessly in the high bed. "You said King didn't know Adler well, or vice versa. But King quit his job and went to Montana while Adler was still here. It could very well be—maybe in overhearing talk between King and some others at the market—that Adler knew King was going to a ranch—his half brother's ranch—in the wide open spaces—and even that it was a different name. He could figure that King might be almost impossible to track down, to find if he *had* that gun or not. Adler might figure that even if we did eventually track down King, it would be so long after Walsh was shot, memories would be confused, we'd think King was just lying to us, had dumped the gun. One thing sure Adler didn't know was that King was going to get fed up with wide open spaces and come back so soon."

Palliser stared at him. "Maybe we ought to establish you permanently as an armchair consultant. How right you are. I hadn't got that far. Of course, you are sitting here in refrigerated air conditioning all day. Maybe once you're at home, sweltering like the rest of us, you won't be quite so bright."

Hackett laughed. "I tell you, for four different walls to look at and a few of Angel's meals, I wouldn't mind the anteroom of hell!"

"That's what you think now," said Palliser wisely.

At eight o'clock that night there arrived a teletype from Chief Cunningham. Adler had changed his story. He now said that he'd told the tale about King because he hadn't thought they'd ever find King, and what he'd really done with the gun—the reason he'd told the lie—was, he had sold it to a fellow he knew in L. A., and he was a nice enough fellow, but he'd been in trouble once and had a little record, so he wouldn't be allowed to have a gun, and Adler couldn't remember his last name but his first name was Joe.

Palliser could almost read the sardonic tone of Cunningham's voice as he'd dictated that. The story, of course, smelled very rank indeed.

He teletyped back: *Oh, yes? Do you use lie detector? If so try.* He sat and thought a little. Adler was looking very hot indeed.

Palliser had often enough heard Mendoza's maxims about detective work. He tried to use one of them now. The one that said, What detective work comes down to in the end is the story about the idiot boy and the lost horse. If you were a horse, where would you go?

All right, said Palliser to himself. I am Fred Adler, the fat boy nobody wants to make friends with. I have just committed the very serious crime of murdering somebody. My first serious crime, apparently, because Plainville didn't have anything much on me and there's no gap between then and when I showed up in California. I am not a very bright young man, and I am probably scared and confused. (Why, by the way, downtown L. A.? I have been living in La Crescenta and working in Glendale.) I know the gun can tie me in, because (for God's sake) I bought it openly, and the serial number is recorded on my permit and the bill of sale. Also the gun has a piece broken off the trigger guard. I want to get rid of the gun. Permanently. What would I do with it?

Some fifteen minutes later Schenke came in and said, "What the hell are you doing, Sergeant, daydreaming about your best girl? Or is it just indigestion?"

Palliser, who had jumped nervously and opened his eyes, said, "Hello, Bob. That was quite a large yard, and a lot of trees at the end of it, and it didn't look as if she took much care of it. Not a gardener." His tone was absent.

"Is that so?" said Schenke.

"Kimball's place, and most places along that block, are kept up," said Palliser to himself. "Grass kept watered, and bushes trimmed. But that place—it wasn't. Lawn needed cutting too. Looked as if she doesn't pay much attention to the yard."

"Naughty naughty," said Schenke. "Everybody ought to keep up their yards. What're you talking about?"

"Mrs. Jane Page," said Palliser, and he got up and went out to where Sergeant Thoms was monitoring the phone with his feet up, reading a paperback, and he said,

"Bill, I want a search warrant. For tomorrow. I'll give you the name——"

Mrs. Page was upset and concerned and bewildered. "Freddy *Adler*?" she said. "You think Freddy *Adler* did something wrong? Why, he's a nice boy, he wouldn't do anything—— Why, he never even went with girls, he's not——"

Palliser reflected a little sadly that, if this was so, that was probably one reason. If this was so. Not that he went along with all the psychiatric jargon, but anybody with common sense could see that the physical handicap of any sort, maybe call it a social handicap, too, in this case, would set up frustrations which might somehow lead to violence.

And it was the hell of a big yard to hunt through, a grove of trees at the end of it, a disused garage, and another outbuilding—but they had brought along a metal detector. All very scientific these days.

It was an old house and a lot of things had got buried on the property over the years. They turned up broken rusty tools, a tire rim, a shoe with metal cleats, and assorted nails, nuts, bolts, screws, a dog collar with a metal plate and license tag, half of an old brass watering can, a broken toy pistol, a rusty alarm clock with the works missing, and a lot of stuff like that. Piggott and Galeano, who were manning the shovels, got very sarcastic with Palliser; it was another hot day, and one of the reasons they'd both studied to make rank was to get out of so much physical labor.

"I'd rather be back riding a squad car," said Piggott mournfully. He mopped his face.

"Hold it, here's another spot," said Palliser. "Here, I'll take a hand awhile." He took Piggott's shovel.

"Well, well, he's actually forgetting he's a sergeant," said Piggott.

"All very democratic," said Galeano.

"Lay off it," said Palliser, and drove his foot against the shovel. They had worked their way down from the rear of the house, past the garage, and were now—searching in horizontal strips across the property—just coming up to the disused outbuilding. Palliser dug and turned up a tarnished broken-apart picture frame made of aluminum.

"Hah!" said Galeano. "Big deal." Mrs. Page was standing on her back porch watching them.

"All *right*," said Palliser. "We've got to cover it." He took back the metal detector. He considered the terrain. They were standing a couple of feet from the little ramshackle building. He thought probably it had been built for a chicken coop, before the town grew and outlawed the keeping of livestock within city limits. He walked over to the fence at the left side of the yard and came back slowly, holding the detector out before him. He brushed against the front of the building as he passed, to the fence at the other side. Nothing.

"Getting hunches just like our Luis himself," said Piggott, "yet."

"Well——" said Palliser. He looked at the little building and then ducked his six feet two to enter it. Part of the roof was gone, so he could see.

The detector said strongly, Metal. Here.

"Hand me a shovel," said Palliser.

"I will say you're a stayer," said Galeano.

243

.Palliser dug. He didn't have to dig far. The shovel clinked metallically with its third mouthful, and something fell from it to the hard-packed earth.

Palliser squatted and looked at it. He sighed. He said, "Hunch be damned."

It was a J. C. Higgins Hi-Standard .22 nine-shot revolver, and its trigger guard had a tiny piece broken off it.

A lot of times the slogging routine paid off.

He went back to Headquarters and gave the gun to Ballistics. There were a good many prints on it, it turned out. They didn't have Adler's, but they would. It would turn out that the prints were Adler's.

He sent off a teletype to Cunningham asking about extradition procedures.

As it happened, they didn't have to go through all that rigmarole. Cunningham had already given Adler the lie-detector test and proved he was lying six ways from Sunday, and after some persuasive talk Adler agreed to waive extradition.

Chief Cunningham flew out with him on Tuesday night and they listened to him on Wednesday morning, at an interrogation room at Headquarters.

Neither of his parents had accompanied him, which said a little something.

"I didn't think you'd ever find the gun," said Adler. "I guess maybe you're smarter than I figured." He blinked nervously.

"I guess maybe we are, Freddy," said Mendoza.

Palliser, Piggott, Galeano, Landers stood around. Cunningham, a big good-looking man with a shock of gray hair, was in on it, too; he was looking around surreptitiously, taking in this immense, very modern Police Facilities building. Probably quite a contrast to his own headquarters.

"What were you doing in downtown L. A. that day, Freddy?" asked Palliser.

"I—I tell you how it was," said Adler. "I see you got me for it, I didn't think—but—but—you see, how it was, I'd just got fired. Off that lousy job." His eyes filled with tears. Frederick Adler certainly wasn't a very prepossessing character. He was about five-seven, and he weighed around two-fifty, and it was soft, unhealthy fat; under his blue cotton shirt you could see the flabby suggestion of feminine breasts, and his hips wobbled as he walked, and he had a sallow moonface with tiny eyes and a wet mouth. "I—never keep a job," he said resentfully. "The way I look. People don't like me. It's no wonder. I don't like *myself* so good. It's all my *dad's* fault! It's all *his* fault! I—I—that teacher at school said a doctor could do something, and I asked Dad, and he said —he said—about against God's will, I'm just meant be fat, and——— It's not *my* fault!"

"We'd like to hear about Jimmy Walsh," said Mendoza.

Adler blinked up at him. "Who's he?"

And it came to them then, he hadn't even known the name of the man he'd killed.

"The gas-station attendant," said Palliser. "That Shell station."

"Oh," said Adler. "I——I tell you how it was, I guess I ain't got no choice. I'd got fired, see. I didn't know what to do. I didn't tell Mrs. Page where I roomed. I just went off usual time like I was going to work, I——"

"Did you buy the gun because you were planning a holdup, Freddy?"

"No, no, I wasn't, I——not then. It was because these guys, they went and roughed me up, where I hadda wait for the bus, see, they made jokes and they said I was—was—was—you know, like no good with girls, and—— It's not *my* fault! No, I never—— But then I thought I'd go home. That day. My dad said about washing his hands of me, that time I went and got tight and the cops —— But at least I knew *some* people back there, and maybe—— I'd got fired and I didn't know where to go to get another job—some kind—and I didn't have any money. I'd spent all I saved up on the—the gun. And I didn't sleep very good that night, and so I got up early and I thought I'd go down to the railroad station and find out how much it'd cost to go back to Plainville. And I took the bus downtown, and that was about eight o'clock when I got there, and the man at the station said by chair car it was forty-nine fifty, and I didn't have that much. All I had was six dollars. So then I thought—I thought the Greyhound bus would be cheaper, but I didn't know where a ticket office was to ask, so I was just walking along then thinking and there was this gas station and a phone booth right on the sidewalk and I went in to look up the—the address. Of the Greyhound, see? And while I was in there I thought all of a sudden maybe I could hold up the station—there was just this

246

one guy there that I could see—and maybe there'd be forty-nine bucks in the register. It was just a—just a sudden *idea* came to me, see?"

"Yes. So you did?"

"I—I—that guy, he wasn't in the little office, so I went into the garage part. I——"

"You had got into the habit of carrying the gun?" asked Palliser.

Adler licked his wet lips. "I had it, sure. I—it always made feel sort of *better*, feel it there. You know. I mean, people could laugh, but *I* knew I had the gun there on me. *They* didn't know—*they* didn't know—what I could do if I wanted. There was this kid there. In the garage. I showed him the gun. I thought it was easy. Listen, if I'd been like any other guy I'd never *be* into all this! If a doctor—— *I never meant* get into all this!" Tears started running down his fat cheeks. "I—I—the kid didn't put up a fight. We went to the office and he give me the money. Out of the register. Then I—then——"

"Why did you kill him, Freddy?" asked Mendoza hardly. "He gave you the money. You didn't have to kill him for it!" Nineteen-year-old Jimmy Walsh, who had wanted to be a lawyer.

"I—don't—know," said Adler dully. "Yes, I know. He laughed at me. He didn't put up a fight, but he laughed at me. He said—he said—I sure didn't need the dough because—I was starvin' to death—— And I made him go back to the garage and I—and I—— It's not *my* fault!" And that was a half-hysterical scream.

Mendoza straightened up slowly. He looked at

Palliser. And they both wondered whether Jimmy Walsh might be alive today if Frederick Adler's father hadn't belonged to a funny religious sect which taught that all this newfangled doctoring was sinful.

Random chance. Just chance—a combination of circumstances.

CHAPTER NINETEEN

"Now you are not saying," said Mrs. MacTaggart, "that you're not going to catch that pair of robbers?"

"You must have *some*——" said Alison.

"Tell me," said Mendoza savagely. He sipped rye. "Tell me how and where! Especially if they're a pair of amateurs, no records. We've checked out nearly seventy possibles out of our own records and the Feds', and it's no dice. *Absolutamente nada.* So sure, sure, some of those—a lot of those—haven't got an alibi. There's no positive evidence to say yes or no."

"But, Luis——"

"It doesna seem *right*," said Mrs. MacTaggart, picking up Master John.

"Sure, sure," said Mendoza, "so if we've guessed right on the M. O., and if they pull another job, we might have a better chance. We think one man, the one who actually pulls the job, stays in the building. So the next time a bank gets knocked off, we shoot a lot of men over there *pronto* to go through that building, screen everybody there. But that's just *if* they pull another one. We haven't had one since Bert was killed, and it could be that finding out he was a cop scared them off. But good. Damn it, they could have left town—they could be in New York. They could have——" He uttered a startled grunt as Sheba landed on his shoulder from behind. The glass toppled from his hand; rye splashed over the coffee table. El Señor appeared as if by magic, leaped onto the table, and began to lap rye. "You little devil!" said Mendoza to Sheba.

"I can't imagine," said Alison, "where she picked up such an obnoxious trick. She's doing it more and more. She even did it to the meter reader today, scared the poor man out of his wits. If she'd give some *warning,* but —— It's really that tough, *amante?*"

Mendoza passed a hand over his eyes. "Nothing in yet from the F.B.I. on Leigh. Maybe they haven't got anything, but then why the hell don't they say so? And if they haven't, that's our last lead gone dead. Nobody here knew much about Leigh, we don't even know where he came from or if he was a native son. Nothing but dead ends, damn it. And there's this new one come up to work —that high-school girl dead of heroin. Not much there either, damn it."

"But if some of those men you've checked *could* be, if you got them in and really grilled them—searched wherever they live for the gun and so on——"

"*Cara,* haven't you been married to a cop long enough to know we've done all that? We haven't just been sitting around making wild guesses, you know. It's going dead on us. Dead as—as Caesar."

Mrs. MacTaggart came back to fetch Miss Teresa, who was lying on her back on the floor, dreamily sucking one big toe. "And there's a word about rendering unto Caesar," she said severely. "And rendering unto God. Maybe if you was to be making a few sincere prayers about it, you'd be given help. And you needn't be sneering at that, you heathen man. I'll drop into St. Mary's first thing tomorrow and put up a prayer or two to St. Joseph, he being the one to find lost things, which to all intents and purposes is what you are all trying to do. I'll not believe that God would not let you find these villains, shooting a policeman and all."

Mendoza laughed as she went out, and she frowned at him over her shoulder. "Just what Piggott said. Lay it on the Lord's lap and have faith. Well, with both the Catholics and the Methodists working on it—— I don't know. The routine usually gets us there in the end—as per that Walsh thing I was telling you about—but on this, right now——" He shook his head. Sheba had walked down him onto his lap and was making bread on his knee steadily, doing no good to his trousers with her long claws. "It may sound funny, but I'm hoping to God they will try another one—with what we know, or think we know, it could give us a chance to pick up one of them at least, and knowing one, we'd probably lay hands on his pal without much trouble."

"But if one of them was wounded I should think you could——"

"So it looks now, over two weeks later, that it can't have been a very serious wound. If he'd died of it, the body would have turned up. The chances are now it was superficial. Oh, sure, when and if we pick him up there'd be evidence of that, but——"

Alison eyed him and said, "You really needed that

drink you didn't finish. I'll get you another, and then dinner'll be ready." She picked up the glass and went out.

And Mendoza, who hadn't set foot in a church for twenty-five years, wondered fleetingly and tiredly if maybe Mrs. MacTaggart and Piggott might be just a little help, at that.

In a situation like this you needed help *wherever* it came from.

Whether God had anything to do with it or not, the very next day he got his wish.

The call came in from a squad car at seven minutes to one. Bank robbery at the Security-First at Pico and Alvarado. The guard had called in as soon as the man was out the door—the chief teller had run over to him as soon as the man left his window—and the squad-car man thought they couldn't be less than five minutes behind him, because the car had been just past the corner of Twelfth on Alvarado when they got the call, only a block away.

Before Sergeant Lake had finished telling him, Mendoza was on the inside phone. "Get me Traffic, *¡inmediatamente!* Jimmy, chase everybody here straight over there—I'll be right behind them . . . Mendoza, Homicide. I want at least twenty men in the nearest cars shot over to Pico and Alvarado, *pronto!*—it's the bank heisters. Send all you can get over there. I want that building searched—a cordon around it five minutes from now! Step on it! A man at all doors to the building, and everybody——"

When he had set that up, he snatched up his hat and

fled. Higgins, Palliser, Galeano, and Piggott were three minutes ahead of him. When he got to the bank, traffic was snarled and drivers cursing, six squad cars double-parked in both narrow streets and one uniformed man at the intersection trying to keep traffic moving.

Mendoza ran to the nearest door, leaving the Ferrari double-parked; the door was the door to the lobby of the building, and a uniformed man was there, talking to a stocky elderly man in the first derby hat Mendoza had seen in years.

"I'm sorry, sir, you can't leave the building. There's been a little——" The uniformed man turned to Mendoza. "I'm afraid you can't come in, sir. There's—— Oh." He looked at the badge. "Excuse me, sir, could I ask you—uh?—"

"Lieutenant Mendoza."

"Yes, sir. We had orders to stop everybody going out, sir, but this—uh—gentleman——"

"What in the name of God *is* all this?" demanded the elderly man. "I happen to have an important lunch engagement, and I must say if the police think they can act so highhanded as to—— After all, it is lunch time and there are quite a few people working in this building who eat lunch. Outside the building, Officer." He was only a little angry; he looked curious and annoyed.

Mendoza hesitated. That was indeed going to pose a little problem. This was a ten-story building and God knew how many offices it had: doctors, dentists, lawyers, tax consultants, all the usual tenants. Right now there'd be people coming back from lunch, people wanting to go out to lunch, and if they tried to hold them all at the doors, they'd have crowds milling around to impede them—crowds through which one man might more easily slip through.

He said, "Yes, I see that. All right—what's your name?"

"Slocum, sir. Patrolman."

"Anybody who wants to go out, Slocum, get the full name and address and occupation—office number here where he or she belongs. O.K.?" He wheeled to cover the other doors.

He heard the elderly man giving information imperturbably. "I am Henry J. Barker. General practitioner, office six-oh-six. You want my home address? It's——"

At the other four doors of the bank he found there had already accumulated several people wanting to leave or enter. He issued the same orders and went into the bank.

It was in a kind of orderly confusion. Higgins and Galeano were talking to two men in front of one of the counters; whispering knots of tellers stood about inside the counters; patrons, sensing something unusual going on, stared. Palliser and Piggott were talking to a couple of men at another counter, and evidently Jimmy had called the Feds, because Dale was just coming in at a side door. Higgins turned, saw Mendoza, and beckoned him urgently.

"Something, George?" One of the men with Higgins and Galeano was the uniformed bank guard; the other was a tall, good-looking youngish man, who was looking excited.

"Mr. Lamarr, the chief teller," said Higgins. "Lieutenant Mendoza."

"How do you do, sir. I can only tell you," said Lamarr, "that I am sure. I've got a very good eye for details, always have had. And as soon as he showed me the gun, I said to myself, you're going to inventory every last little thing you can about this fellow, for the c—the police. I don't lose my head very easy, Lieutenant."

"Mr. Lamarr gives us something new," said Higgins. "Something funny."

"Let's hear it."

Lamarr was appraising Mendoza's beautifully cut gray silk suit. "That set you back something," he observed. "I'm interested in clothes myself, Lieutenant. We're expected to dress pretty well, you know. One reason I spotted this. That bird wasn't wearing a suit, he had on a corduroy jacket and slacks, almost matching. Gray. But the jacket was a reversible one."

"A rev——"

"Sure. They're kind of the latest sports craze—two jackets in one. Solid color one side, plaid or stripe on the other. All finished, seams and pockets and so on, both sides. I'm sure of that because I was looking at one myself just the other day, and you see, in order to get an ordinary-sized inside breast pocket—a fairly deep one, you know—on both sides, the breast pocket you can see on the outside is about twice as deep as usual. You can see the stitching. And I can tell you something else, sir. When I handed over the money in the paper bag, I'm pretty sure he put the bag in his right-hand outside pocket——"

Which Wolf, their smartest witness, had also said.

"And when he did that, he"—Lamarr gestured—"pulled the jacket down and a bit to the side—see what I mean?—and I just caught a fast glimpse of the inside pattern of it."

"Jacket unbuttoned? Yes." Dale had drifted up and was listening intently. Mendoza slid a hand into his jacket pocket, looking down, and saw that as pressure pulled the jacket down on that side, the same side of the unbuttoned front turned back very slightly. "So what was it?"

"It was a dark-green plaid," said Lamarr, without hesitation. "Something like the Black Watch but not exactly. More like—oh, the Douglas tartan, or the Forbes . . . Yes, sir, I know tartans. My mother was Scottish."

Mendoza reflected resignedly, so now they'd have to get Máiri MacTaggart to help, tell them all about the Douglas and Forbes tartans.

"I didn't notice a thing, not a *thing*," said the guard excitedly. "I was standing over there next to New Accounts, and Mr. Lamarr came running across and told me—the man was just going out the door then, I only saw his back—and *then* I noticed that the curtains on that door were pulled down, and I couldn't imagine——"

"*¡Abran paso!*" said Mendoza. "By God, we're right behind him, George, keep your fingers crossed! We've spotted the M. O.—he doesn't leave the building—he pulled down those curtains again so nobody could see which way he turned. *Por Dios,* he's got to be here yet—handed the loot and the gun over, and X number two sailed out, but the first one is here somewhere, I swear it, and by God——"

The whole building was jumping now. More squad

cars had arrived. Palliser and Piggott, and presently Higgins, were organizing the search. They weren't going to leave so much as a private office lavatory unlooked at. It was quite a job, but they had about thirty uniformed patrolmen and it was being done systematically, floor by floor.

People coming in from lunch, mostly girl secretaries and stenographers and receptionists, stared curiously and lingered to ask questions. "You work here, miss? I'll just ask you to go straight to your office, then, please. This is just a routine——"

It took them over four hours, until long after the bank had officially locked its doors for the day. After a while Traffic got a little irate at all those patrolmen off regular duty, but the Feds filled in with a few more men. They covered it. Very thoroughly they covered it. By five-thirty one or more cops had poked his nose into every office, lavatory, public rest room, coat closet, and broom closet in the entire building.

Approximately sixty people, in that period of time, had left the building by one exit or another. People coming away from dental appointments, doctors' appointments, lawyers' appointments, salesmen from calling on prospective clients, people like that. Every solitary last one of them left a name, address, and occupation with one of the uniformed men manning the exits.

And they didn't turn up one damned thing.

Mendoza swore. He went on swearing.

"We *couldn't* have missed him!" said Palliser violently. "We're pretty damn sure he stays in the building awhile—that's the object of the whole exercise, let his unseen side-kick get away—we said, my God, probably he stays until all the excitement's over and the cops have all gone! And this time we couldn't have been five minutes——"

"Longer," said Mendoza. "The first squad car got there within minutes, but we didn't really get the exits guarded for at least ten to fifteen. He *could* have—— If he saw that squad car pull up so soon—— Hell. I'm beginning to think we're jinxed on this one, boys. Or he could have slipped by, giving a false name and address, of course. That was a risk, but—*¡por Dios!*—our best chance was a quick search right then, and if we'd kept all that mob milling around—— Here's these lists of people who left the building. We'll have to check it out anyway." God, and how long would that take?

"And if he left a fake name, what help is that going to be? Tell us how he got out, is all! And I'll tell you something else, Goddamn the luck," said Higgins ferociously. "Now, after he saw how we reacted to this caper, and being such a cute boy, he knows *we* know their M. O., and he'll know if they try another one that way, we'll get the place covered even faster and the chances are we'd nab him. So they're going to lay low and keep quiet. They're not going to be pulling another one. So it's another dead end, damn it!"

And that was at eight-fifteen on Friday morning.

The uniformed men who had covered the building's exits had all been told to leave their notes at Homicide. Mendoza had picked them up from Sergeant Lake when he came in ten minutes ago and was just now settling down to glance over them: the lists of the people who had left the building while the search was going on.

"And damnation," said Palliser, "this reversible-jacket bit—I had a thought there, could it be that as soon as he actually gets out of the bank he—— I mean, if Lamarr was right and it *was*——"

"*¡Santa María!*" exclaimed Mondoza loudly. "*¡Diez millón demonios desde infierno!* For the love of Christ, what cretinous imbecilic son of——" He reversed the sheet he was looking at and grabbed at the phone. "Get me Traffic, *pronto! . . .* Mendoza, Homicide. You've got a"—he swallowed convulsively—"*patrolman* down there named Harvey Schultz. I want him. In my office in ten minutes, or even sooner! He has—some information I need. Right now . . . All right." He slammed the phone down. "*¡Vaya por Dios!* What kind of God-damned stupid rookies——"

"What's up?" asked Palliser. "You've found——"

Mendoza shoved the sheet at him. Piggott got up and glanced over Palliser's shoulder. He looked puzzled. "So what's wrong? Just a lot of names."

"For the *love* of—— What year were you born, Matt?"

Piggott looked even more puzzled. "Nineteen thirty-five, why?"

Mendoza laughed sharply. There was no humor in his eyes at all. Higgins took the sheet from Piggott and looked at it. Suddenly he said, "For God's sake! What idiot couldn't spot——"

"Apparently Patrolman Harvey Schultz," said Mendoza in a hard tone.

Patrolman Harvey Schultz, peacefully cruising down Wilshire Boulevard in his squad car, was yanked back to Headquarters in a hurry. Fifteen minutes later, panting slightly and wondering what the hell this was all about, he stood in front of Mendoza's desk, cap in hand, and said, "Yes, sir?" He'd heard a little about Mendoza's reputation, and he felt slightly awed and ill at ease with Mendoza and all these other big Homicide detectives staring at him, but he tried to sound efficient.

"Yesterday afternoon," said Mendoza, "you were on duty at the Pico Boulevard entrance of that bank, among other things taking down the names and addresses of everybody who left the building."

"Why, yes, sir. I'm sure nobody slipped through," said Schultz earnestly. "We all knew how important it was, a cop killer——"

"How long have you been on the force?" asked Mendoza.

"T-two years, sir. I——"

"All right. All right," said Mendoza. "Christ. We are sure as hell jinxed on this one. I needn't lose my temper about it. How old are you, Schultz?"

"I'm—twenty-three, sir. I—did I do something wrong? I thought I——"

"Oh, God. Not exactly," said Mendoza. "It's just the damn luck put you at that door. It's not your fault. Look, here's your list of everybody who left the building by your door."

"Y-yes, sir? Did I——"

"Didn't," asked Mendoza gently, "the name of Nelson Eddy ring a tiny little bell, Schultz?"

"N-no, sir, why? It was just another name. I mean, I don't recall the particular guy but a little bit, but I do remember him sort of because his job was a little unusual. He said he was a singing teacher——"

260

"God," said Higgins. "It had to be a rookie not dry behind the ears!"

"Blame the luck," said Mendoza wearily. "For your information, Schultz, Nelson Eddy is a singer. Back in the thirties he was a very popular movie star. I am reasonably certain that he was not in that building yesterday afternoon. But I shouldn't really have expected a man who hadn't been born when Mr. Eddy was at the height of his popularity to have recognized the obviously fake name."

"Oh, gee," said Schultz in dismay. "Oh, Jesus, Lieutenant, is that—? Well, my God, I sure never recognized——That guy was *him?* The robber? My God——"

"What do you remember about him, anything at all?"

"Jesus, let me try to think—I passed about eighteen or twenty altogether, I couldn't—— He had on a plaid jacket," said Schultz suddenly. "Corduroy. I thought it was funny, in all this heat."

"Oh, my good Christ, I'll cut my throat," said Higgins passionately as everybody else groaned. "You *had* him— you had him right there, you could have—— God, if you'd been ten years older——"

"Well, Jesus, I'm sorry—how should I—— But, Lieutenant," said Schultz. "Look, Lieutenant." He swallowed nervously. "I mean, you know, how it got out in the papers, some of what you've got on this guy, and it seems he's bald. So how could it be that guy I saw? Because one thing I *do* remember definitely about this Nelson Eddy, he's got hair. Quite a lot of hair. He didn't have a hat on."

They all stared at him. And then Mendoza said, "*Caray.* Now I do wonder——"

And maybe God, urgently reminded by both Mrs. MacTaggart and Piggott—or St. Joseph—had a little something to do with it after all. Because at three-ten that afternoon Sergeant Lake came in and laid a long yellow teletype on Mendoza's desk. "The Feds at last," he said. "What they dug up from their records on Walter Leigh."

"*¡Por fin!*" said Mendoza, and started to read rapidly. Palliser and Higgins drifted in from the sergeants' office.

Walter William Leigh was his right name. He'd last been picked up in New Orleans in 1957, on a petty theft charge. He had formerly served a year's term in a county jail in Pennsylvania for extortion. Before that he had done time in New York for petty theft, extortion, and bookmaking. A very smalltime pro, and a drifter; he had little records in New Jersey and Massachusetts and in Michigan and New Mexico. A drifter. Not quite a bum. His record, in fact, went all the way back to 1920. And that charge——

In May 1920 Leigh charged with corrupting morals minor probation no sentence. At that time age 16 was residing with——

Mendoza looked at it. He didn't believe it. Then he did believe it, and he was filled with a cold, incredulous fury, and he snatched up the outside phone and dialed and said, "I want Wolf! Be damned if he's on a tail or what, I want him! He's there? *Bueno.* Tell him to make tracks—we'll give it a try—over to Seventh and Grand." God, God, the very place where Bert—— "Tell him to snap into it, fifteen minutes!"

"What is it?" asked Palliser. "You've got——"

"Come on," said Mendoza. He got up. "We don't

262

know whether he's got his gun on him, and one cop is one too many to lose." He was getting out his own gun. "Yes, we've got him. I don't believe it, but we've got him. We'd have had him last week if the Feds hadn't been so damned slow about looking up records." He picked up his hat.

"But what the hell——"

"Who——"

"Come on!" said Mendoza savagely.

"You got a lead?" asked Wolf eagerly. He had been waiting for them in the lobby—the lobby where Bert Dwyer had died, gun in hand.

"We've got X, period," said Mendoza. They were in the elevator; he had pressed the button for eight.

"Something in the F. B. I. report on Leigh, he won't say," said Palliser.

They got out of the elevator and walked down the hall. Mendoza turned at the door whose frosted-glass panel said 812. It was unlocked. They went in.

A man and a woman were in the room, bent over an old scarred desk. They both looked up. Higgins said in naked astonishment, "But that's——"

"Why, Lieutenant. Is there something I can do for you?"

Mendoza went to the man and took hold of him, not tenderly. He pulled him violently around so that he stood in profile to Wolf, and he looked at Wolf and asked, "What about it?"

"Oh, my God. Yes. Yes, that's him. That's the one. *But*——"

"Lieutenant——"

"What the *hell*," said Palliser. "You don't mean——"

The woman said breathlessly, "What's the meaning of —— Who are these men? You can't——"

And Mendoza let go of the man and reached to the man's untidy shock of dark hair and tugged at it, and it came away in his hands, and the man had a shiny domed bald head.

"And that," said Mendoza in a grim remote tone, "was what Bert started to say. Tried to say. A *toupee*. Not two men. A toupee. He saw you putting it on. *Didn't he, Mr. Warbeck?*"

Eugene Warbeck shrank back from him, but his expression didn't change for a moment.

"Who are these——"

"It's—it's all right, Miss Corsa," said Mr. Warbeck in his gentle voice. "At least, it's not, but—— Yes. Yes, that's so. But it was for the children, you see." He looked unhappy. He said softly, "I'm sorry about the police officer. I didn't know who he was, of course, and he'd have stopped me getting the money—for the children."

—was residing with mother and younger step brother Mrs. May and Eugene Warbeck 1312 Walbrook St., Auburn, N. Y.

CHAPTER TWENTY

And they had been savage to get this one, for vengeance on the one who had killed one of their own, and secretly all of them had been hoping that when they caught up, perhaps he'd run, or fight—so they needn't bring him in all docile, like the gentlemanly cops they were. But now, they still couldn't quite believe they'd got him, and of all of them standing around him there in an interrogation room, nobody had any impulse to raise a hand to soft-spoken Eugene Warbeck.

Because Eugene Warbeck probably wouldn't see the inside of the gas chamber. He wasn't realizing the enormity of what he had done at all. He was explaining —sadly he was explaining. Now that he'd been stopped, all he wanted was the chance to explain.

"It was the children, you see—so many poor, deprived children needing so much! The appeals we send out never seem to bring in much. People give to the big, organized charities, not small groups like ours—but we think we really accomplish more, at the—the personal level, as it were. Things like the Holderby girl's teeth—I was feeling quite desperate about that, we simply didn't have the money, and it's *so* important—— The poor helpless children . . . Yes, sir? Oh, Walter. Poor Walter. Yes, sir, I'll tell you. I'd always looked after Walter, because I promised Mother on her deathbed I would. He was—weak. He never meant any harm, but there's no denying he was *weak*. Yes. But he knew he could always count on me, the little I could afford to send him—because of Mother, you see—and so I usually knew where he *was*. I think it was Marion Holderby's teeth that really decided me, you know." Mr. Warbeck looked up at Mendoza and Higgins standing closest over him and uttered a pleased little giggle. "I've always been quite a detective-novel fan, and I'd often thought *I* could devise quite good plots, and I was right, wasn't I? Wasn't I?"

"You certainly did, Mr. Warbeck. Where did——"

"Banks—all those banks full of money—not like taking it from a—a *person*. *People*. My goodness, my wife would have been surprised—I was a little surprised myself, to find I had the—the courage and boldness to do such a thing. But once I had made up my mind, I meant to *do* it. Do it *right*. Because then I could help the children." He looked earnestly at Mendoza; he said, "Grownups aren't helpless, they can—can change things for themselves, if they really want to. But children—— And you see, I—I lied a little, before, when I said I had enough money to get along. It's only just enough, with what I had to send Walter. When they fired me from the department store—really, I always did resent that. It was most unfair!

"But when I *did* decide to do it, I worked out a plan

266

very carefully. Of course I thought of my toupee at once, because I look quite different without it." He flushed a little. "*I'd* never have bothered with such a thing, but in my job—my job as it was then, floorwalker, you know, you have to—to keep up appearances, and Emily said I should, it made me look so much younger, and I've got into the habit of wearing it. And I thought, and I read about a lot of real-life bank robberies, and it seemed to me that the basic mistake all those men made was in running away, at once I mean. They'd have elaborate plans for changing their—er—getaway cars and so on, but they were always caught. It seemed to me that if I should just quietly go upstairs in the same building and wait awhile in a—a public lavatory, you know, and with my toupee back on, too, nobody would look twice at me coming out——"

"It was just a dandy plan, Mr. Warbeck," said Higgins grimly. "Now, where'd you get the gun? And where is it now?"

"Oh, it's at home. In the room I rent, sir. With everything else," said Mr. Warbeck sadly. "I was especially pleased to find that reversible jacket. I thought that should really make it work. The only little difficulty might be if there should be anyone in the lobbies when I came in from the bank, but that only happened to me once, and I simply walked quietly past and up the stairs and stopped on the landing to put on my toupee and reverse the jacket. You see, what I'd *do*," and he was quite proud, explaining his cleverness, "I'd put the bag of money in my *outside* pocket and then just a few moments later, when I'd reversed the jacket, the money would be *inside* and I'd be taking my toupee out of the outside pocket that was inside before. It really worked very well. And I was surprised at myself, how I didn't hesitate about firing the gun at all. I was quite cool. Those people would have stopped me and taken the money away, and the money was for the children. That's —that's what Walter didn't understand." He suddenly looked very unhappy indeed.

"So you had to—put him out of the way?" asked Mendoza. He was curiously fascinated by Mr. Warbeck; glancing at Higgins, Palliser, Galeano, he saw the same expressions mirrored in their faces.

"Well, you see—I told you I read a lot of detective stories, and I knew the banks would likely have records of the money, and I'd read about these men who—who buy—ah—hot money, it's called, and I thought—it would be so much safer if—— And of course I hadn't the slightest notion of where to find such a man, but I thought Walter might. He—he wasn't a real *criminal*, you know, but he—well, he was rather on the fringes, you might say. I never had much personal contact with him of late years—he—he followed me out here, you know, it was an easy life for *him*, with me sending him money like that—but of course I'd promised Mother—— But when I had the plan all made I did telephone him and met him—down in Pershing Square actually— and asked if he could find such a man. Well, naturally he was curious, and I had to tell him a bit about it before he'd promise to look. And then it turned out no use after all," said Mr. Warbeck dejectedly.

"He didn't find one?" asked Palliser.

"Oh, yes, he did. Somebody he knew—I think he said a bartender—told him a name. I had thought, you see,

Walter could exchange the money, so I'd never be——
But it seems men like that don't—don't deal in the sums
I had to sell. Only really big money. I've got nearly nine
thousand dollars," said Mr. Warbeck, sounding awed,
"which seems like a great deal of money to me—just
think what I can do for all these poor children with so
much money! And so then I didn't see how I *could* use
the money and not—not be caught, you know. And then
Walter got difficult. He was such a weak, selfish fellow—
exactly like his father, Mother used to say. He wanted to
use the money for *ourselves!* It was wicked—that was
what he couldn't see—it was money exactly like the
money we might have in our little Good Samaritan
treasury, it was for the *children,* it didn't belong to me!
Really, you know, Lieutenant, I'd never have dreamed
of stealing for *myself!* But Walter got very difficult, and
he said there might be a reward for telling, and then,
too, he—he sometimes drank too much, and I knew he
was apt to say anything when he was—like that. So I
decided it was really the only way—— You know, I was
really—er—getting quite a kick out of it all, as they say,
by then. Did you know, Lieutenant—I'd never known
that before myself—that having a gun in your hand
makes you feel very, very important? Because of what
you can *do*—if you want to. Just if you want to."

"I have heard that, Mr. Warbeck," said Mendoza very
gently, and even to himself his tone sounded sad.

"I'd thought about that very carefully, too, you see. It
seemed to me that the first object was to make people
realize you were *serious,* and I thought, the bigger and
more dangerous-looking the gun was, the better. So that
was the kind of gun I wanted——"

"You got it," said Higgins. "Where?"

"Oh, Walter helped me with that too. He said he knew a pawnshop where I could buy one with no questions asked, so we went there, but all the man had were quite small guns and I didn't want any of them, so I went to a real gunshop where they sell new guns, but they were all too expensive, and besides, the man said I'd have to wait three days and then get a policeman to sign something for me or show them a permit, and—— So a few days later I went back to the pawnshop, and then he had a really big gun in, and I bought that. And really, the first time it all went off so beautifully, without any hitch at all—and there I was with all that lovely money —Marion Holderby's teeth, and the operation Jamie needed, and—— But that was when I had the trouble with Walter. He was the second one I shot," said Mr. Warbeck thoughtfully, "and you know, it was really quite exciting in a way. You have no idea of the surge of power—just like an electric current through you. That bank guard, the first one—I'd never owned a gun before, but with a big gun like that, at practically point-blank range, I could hardly miss. It was exhilarating, in a funny kind of way. *Adults* have a *choice*. Those people *needn't* have tried to stop me—then I wouldn't have shot them. It's the poor children who are so helpless, at the mercy of society—cultural patterns—ignorant or cruel or negligent parents—you don't *understand* what a great need there is——" Mr. Warbeck brought his clenched fists to his temples. " 'And whosoever shall offend one of these little ones that believe in Me, it is better for him that a millstone were hanged about his neck, and he were cast into the sea!' They *needn't* have come

after me—it was their own choice, their own choice!"
Suddenly he looked up, a little wildly. "How—how did
you guess I stayed in the buildings? Yesterday when I
came out of the lavatory up on the third floor and saw all
those policemen——"

"We are sometimes pretty good guessers," said
Mendoza. "Why Nelson Eddy, Mr. Warbeck?"

"Oh, did you guess about that?" He was suddenly
docile again; he smiled. "That was really very funny. I
was startled, I don't deny it. But I had been noticed, you
see—coming out—and in any case I could see they were
searching the building. I just quietly walked down the
stairs and then when I saw there was a policeman taking
down names, why, my mind went quite blank. I only saw
that I mustn't give my own, because I hadn't any real
reason to be in that building. And it was queer—the
very first thing that came into my head was Emily—my
late wife—and how she was always saying that I wasn't
resourceful, hadn't any imagination at all. My, Emily
would be surprised! And then I remembered for some
reason how she'd enjoyed all those old pictures—we used
to go quite often, before her arthritis came on—all those
old Jeannette MacDonald pictures with Nelson Eddy—
Sweethearts and so on. So did I—they were very nice
pictures. And so——"

"Yes," said Mendoza. "Will you tell us why you picked
banks downtown, Mr. Warbeck? In the most crowded
section?"

"And the only address I could remember offhand was
the place my landlady takes her cat for doctoring—I
helped her once—so I gave that. Oh, about that? I had
thought that out very carefully too. For one thing, I had

a legitimate reason to be downtown several days a week —our little group, you know—and then, more important, I thought where the streets *are* usually very crowded it would seem natural that the bank robber had just mingled with the crowd and vanished. And you did think that, didn't you?"

"For a while," said Mendoza. "And then—you shot a third man, and you found he'd been a cop."

"Fourth—he was the fourth," said Warbeck almost petulantly. "You forgot Walter. That was a really most peculiar thing, you know, and it almost makes me believe in the doctrine of predestination. As I told you, Lieutenant, I'd never owned a gun before. Those other people, they were quite close to me—the guard had his hand on my left arm, and the teller was right up against me—all I had to do was pull the trigger. It was a—a most unusual feeling of—of *power*, but I wasn't *surprised* at having shot them. I couldn't have helped hitting them. But that police officer—I wonder now if it *is* so, that each of us has just a certain allotted time here? Because he would have been familiar with guns, wouldn't he? And he must have been twenty feet away from me. When I came out of that bank, you see, there was no one in the lobby at all, and so I went up to the foot of the stairs where there's a little shadow, and very quickly I turned my jacket inside out and I was just fitting on my toupee —I'd got very quick at putting it on, I'd practiced at home—when he—er—challenged me, and when I turned around he had his gun already out. He fired before I did, when I took *my* gun out, but he missed me —and I just fired blindly, aiming as best I could, but I didn't really know how. I *was* surprised when he fell down. But he *needn't* have got out his gun! It was *his* choice! In another thirty seconds I'd have been on the second floor and taking the elevator up to our little office —I really was expecting Miss Corsa, as I told you——"

"And when you heard it was a police sergeant you'd shot, you got a little nervous, and you thought you'd play very clever by telling me a pretty little fairy tale," said Mendoza.

"Well, I knew, of course—from all my reading—that you'd be all the more anxious to—er—*get* someone who had—— Yes, I'm afraid so, Lieutenant. I thought if you were convinced that the bank robber was injured, it would——"

"Send us off in the wrong direction. So it did. You made some nice plans, Mr. Warbeck," said Mendoza.

"Well, I thought so," said Mr. Warbeck simply, pleased. "Except when it came to the actual money, that was being difficult." Piggott and Scarne were up at the Laurel Canyon house where Mr. Warbeck rented a room, going through that. "Your men will have found it by now, I expect," and on that he sounded depressed again. "Such a *waste*—all I could have done with it! But I knew at least some of the bills would be recognized eventually. Actually I was going to start spending some of it next week. The first payment on Marion Holderby's braces is due, and I thought I would give some of the money to Dr. Gold, the dentist. By the time it was identified, he couldn't possibly say who had given it to him, and he's a busy man with a large practice. I'd hoped ——" He sighed. He looked from one to the other of them, standing there staring at him. "You *do* understand? It was for the *children*——"

They didn't talk much about Mr. Warbeck. They got all of that down in a formal statement, and he signed it quite meekly. Piggott and Scarne came in, looking incredulous and bulging with money—the whole sum of the loot, which had been neatly stacked in paper bags in Mr. Warbeck's closet. They also had the gun and a box of shells.

"I doubt very much," said Mendoza, after they'd got Mr. Warbeck formally charged and booked into the new jail, "that he'll ever see the inside of San Quentin. I think they'll find he's legally insane."

Palliser agreed. "God, what a thing. A regular obsession?"

Higgins said, "What he said about his wife—and I gathered the mother was another strong character. Maybe a whole big bunch of aggression piling up in him all his life, until something had to give."

"*Caray*, you going all psychological, George? That could be. I think the head doctors are going to be interested in him. And at least we've got him locked in tight, boys, and he isn't going to be shooting any more cops—or anybody else—and also without much doubt something new will come along very shortly to plague us all over again, so let's for God's sake go home now." Mendoza yawned. They were standing on the steps of the new jail. Hopefully tonight's ten o'clock temperature felt just slightly cooler than last night's.

Higgins yawned in sympathy. "That high-school kid. Karen Flagg, with all the H in her. I got a vague sort of lead on that today. I guess you're right. See you in the morning." He strode off toward his car.

Mendoza lit a cigarette. "You ever wish you'd decided to go in for plumbing or journalism or something, John?"

Palliser hesitated and laughed. "Not really, I guess. At least it's what you might call varied work—you see a lot of types and run into a lot of different things."

"Now there's the understatement of the month," said Mendoza dryly. "*¡Solo Dios sabe qué pasará*, how true, how true! Go home. I'll see you tomorrow."

"It's my day off."

"So it is. Monday then. I have every faith," said Mendoza, "that something else will come up to keep our noses to the grindstone by then. It nearly always does. See you." He walked away toward the Ferrari.

Alison kept interrupting him with little shocked exclamations, but Mrs. MacTaggart listened in grave silence, her lips compressed.

"—so without much doubt they'll tuck him away at Atascadero, and that's that."

Mrs. MacTaggart said slowly, "I wouldna have believed it. I wouldna have *believed* it. It just doesna seem possible. And all for nought, when you come down to it —all for just nought. Four people deid. It does seem, times, God isna just so very orderly. A body's just got to have faith it's all arranged for some good reason we'll maybe understand in good time."

She went out quietly. They had heard the single pronouncement Máiri would make on Mr. Warbeck.

"Such an awful—— I can hardly believe it either, he seemed like such a mild little man!"

"That's how that kind looks, a lot of times. I wonder if it's too late to call Art. He'll be interested." Mendoza looked at his watch. "Probably not. If I know Art, after all that hospital regime where they firmly turn out the lights about eight-thirty, he's sitting up watching the Late Show." He went out to the phone and dialed. Alison trailed after him.

"No, I was still up," said Hackett. "What——"

"Still feeling better?"

"Well, the only thing, damn it," said Hackett, sounding indignant, "after all that damned bland hospital food, *now* Angel feeds me her nice exotic French gourmet stuff and I get indigestion!"

Mendoza laughed. "This is not a perfect world, *compadre*. Very possibly it never will be. I thought you'd be interested—we've got him . . ." He told Hackett the story, and Hackett asked excited questions and said several times he'd be damned.

"One like that. God, so they won't even——"

"No, they won't even."

"*¡Cuidado!*" said Alison, and Mendoza braced himself; Sheba landed midway up his back and clawed up to sit on his shoulder.

"*Where* she learned such a——" said Alison.

"Just one of the cats," said Mendoza. "You'd better go to bed. I'll drop over soon, unless something else urgent comes up." He put down the phone, lifted Sheba to the floor, and said, "At least, the main thing, we got him. I ought to write to Mary Dwyer."

"Mmh," said Alison. She smoothed his mustache. "So, can you stay home awhile for a change? Most of the night?"

276

"*Tal vez.* It's to be seen." He put his arms around her lightly and then harder. He laughed. "I wonder now. I do just wonder."

"*¿Como?*"

"About George. Higgins. Well, she's a damn good-looking woman. Bert's wife. When she came in that day, he did look—smitten."

"Oh, really," said Alison. "Sergeant Higgins? He's quite the confirmed bachelor, isn't he?"

Mendoza absently rolled a lock of her red hair round his forefinger. "Mmh. Ask me, preconceived idea that no respectable pretty female'd look twice at him. Well, he's no movie star. But when you get to know him, George is quite a guy. Only—would she? Even after a while?"

"You mean because——"

"Mmh. Suppose I got shot up tomorrow——"

"Knock on wood, fingers crossed."

"*¡Supersticioso!* Would you be thinking seriously about marrying another cop, a year from now?"

"I would not," said Alison. "You need a shave. I didn't marry a cop. I married Luis Rodolfo Vicente Mendoza."

"Lady," said Mendoza sadly, "sometimes I think there's no separating the two. Why would any sensible woman want to marry a cop, anyway?"

"Well, there are cops," said Alison, "and then there are cops . . . There go the twins. Isn't it *heavenly* to have somebody *else* to look after them? Didn't you know, I married you for your money, *naturalmente*."

"*¡Naturalmente!*" said Mendoza. "So come and earn your bank account and your charge accounts."

"You know I don't believe in charge acc——"

But cops are technically on duty twenty-four hours a day.

At three minutes after one Mendoza was just drifting off to sleep, drowsily and comfortably aware of the familiar carnation scent that said *Alison* snuggled close, when the phone rang.

He stirred. Alison murmured something.

The phone rang again, insistently. Mendoza sat up. He said into the darkness, "Damn." He groped for the bedside lamp on his side of the bed. The phone rang again.

Alison said sleepily, "Well, at least——"

"Mendoza here."

"I'm sorry as hell to disturb you, Lieutenant," said Sergeant Thoms, "but we've got this thing. Might be quite a thing. See, the squad-car men called in about five minutes ago. Disturbance at a bar down on Flower. What it is, this guy apparently went berserk. In the bar. He shot up a lot of people—three ambulances on the way, by what the squad-car boys say, four-five people hurt, maybe bad. And he was talking wild about shooting his wife and kids, and he ran out before the squad car got there, and the bartender says he knows him, a regular customer, but he doesn't know his name or where he lives, and—— Well, it could turn into quite a thing, you can see. I thought I'd better—— I sent two other cars over, and Schenke's on his way, but——"

"Yes. O.K. See what you mean. I'm on my way too." Mendoza got out of bed.

"A *cop*," said Alison indistinctly.

"*Desafortunado*," said Mendoza. He dressed rapidly. He checked his pockets—billfold, badge, keys, cigarettes.

He went quietly out the back door to the garage and backed out the Ferrari.

The situation at Headquarters Homicide was very seldom static.

And always it had to do with death. Random death, stalking the streets of the city at random.